N‿

DEADLY

MEDICINE

Trudey Martin

ISBN: 9781702721646

Excerpt from The Hippocratic oath

"I will prescribe regimens for the good of my patients according to my ability and judgement and never do harm to anyone.

I will give no deadly medicine to any one if asked, nor suggest any such counsel."

MONDAY

1

Looking back I probably shouldn't have picked it up. I should have left the notebook lying on the ground where the elderly gentleman had dropped it and walked on to my rendezvous with Collette.

I was already ten minutes late and I knew she'd be anxious. She was one of my oldest friends; I mean oldest as in 'known the longest time' rather than in terms of her age. She was a good five years younger than me. She had been an absolute rock since John, my husband, had died about twelve weeks before, very suddenly in a car crash. He'd been on his way to a meeting in Hull, driving the Volkswagen Golf that we'd shared. He hadn't been far from Hull, a few miles away, when he'd been hit head-on by a lorry that had just disembarked from a ferry. The driver was from Norway, or Denmark or somewhere Scandinavian and had been tired, had lost concentration and had been driving on the wrong side of the road. Sometimes I hated this man I had never met for being so careless. Sometimes I felt sorry for him, having to live with the consequences of what he had done.

John, I was assured by the police, had died instantly. Not that that was much of a consolation; he had only been 45 years old, way too young to die, and I had been struggling to find my balance ever since then.

John had, thankfully, paid into a company pension, which meant that I'd received a sizeable lump sum and a reasonable portion of his pension. It meant that I had a choice. I could give up work if I wanted. I wouldn't have as much money as I was used to but it meant I could think about what I really wanted. I could use my time off to see whether I wanted to return to my job at the local college, teaching the drivel dished out by the government to uninterested students who had little motivation to learn. I seriously doubted that I did.

My life with John had all seemed to come to a shattering, shuddering halt with his death and, although it had been a few weeks now since I'd had a day where all I wanted to do was lay in bed and cry, I knew Collette would be worried that I was late.

I was rushing from our home, my home, on a little road called Steeple Lane just beyond the top of Steep Hill in Lincoln. It was a bright and crisp autumn morning and the city looked beautiful tumbling down the hill ahead of me. I didn't always look to my left as I passed the cathedral, having passed it almost every day for over twenty years, but I did that day. It was bathed in an autumnal glow, the sun low in the sky causing a rosy hue to be cast over the stone towers. No doubt about it, it was an impressive building inside and out.

I had just reached the bottom of the hill, where the street widens out and the shops become a bit more mainstream than the quirky individual ones that line the hill. I had arranged to meet Collette in our favourite little independent coffee shop and was walking purposefully towards it when I saw the man drop the notebook as he walked in the opposite direction towards the start of Steep Hill. He was a tall, slim, elderly gentleman with a full head of grey hair and a matching grey moustache. He was wearing a heavy camel coloured wool coat and he carried a walking stick, although he didn't really look as if he needed it. The notebook he'd dropped was a small pocket size beige coloured Moleskin. Without really thinking I picked it up and shouted after him.

"Excuse me." I took a few steps back up the hill towards him and tried again. "Excuse me! Sir!" But he didn't hear me, the wind carrying my voice away towards the High Street. He carried on striding up the start of the hill. I flipped the notebook open and on the first page glimpsed an address. I'd pass it on my way home. I thought about running after him, but then I thought of Collette waiting for me and decided that it wasn't that important, I'd drop it in on my way home.

I pushed open the door to the coffee shop and immediately spotted Collette sitting at our favourite table near the back, the one with the comfortable chairs. She'd grabbed a newspaper and was reading that whilst she waited, with a half-drunk cup of coffee in front of her. I was almost next to her when she looked up and saw me.

"Vee," she said. "How are you doing? Are you okay? I was bit worried when you were late."

"I'm fine," I answered. "Just got a bit delayed. I did think about texting but then thought I'd be even later, so I just ran out of the door. Do you want more coffee?"

"No thanks. I'll finish this one. I'll have a scone though." She grinned. Having a scone, or a cake, with our coffee was our weekly treat.

I went up to the counter, ordered a coffee and two scones and then went and joined Collette on the comfy chairs. She looked at the notebook and raised an eyebrow in query.

"An old man dropped it. Almost outside here, actually, just up the road." I gestured vaguely in the direction the man had been walking. "I picked it up and shouted after him but he didn't hear me. It's got an address though; it's on my way home so I'll pop it through his door on my way back."

A young waitress came over with my coffee and the two scones, which we ate whilst we chatted. Collette picked up the notebook. It was a slim book and it had an elastic band incorporated in the back cover, wrapped around to mark a page. Collette flicked through it. There wasn't a lot in it. She put it back down on the table.

"I'd be tempted to just throw it in the bin. It doesn't look as if there's anything important in it."

"Well, it's right on my route home. It isn't any trouble. I'll just poke it through the letterbox. I'm sure the old guy will be pleased someone took the time to return it."

"Softie."

We spent almost an hour catching up on what was happening with Collette's two children, Charlotte and Sophie - seven and five respectively.

"I'm so frustrated with the school," Collette vented as we started on our second cups of coffee. Charlotte was having a few problems at school with bullying. She was a bright girl but was a little awkward and something of a bookworm. Her bottle-bottom glasses didn't help and the other children exploited it a bit. Collette got exasperated with the school for not handling things as well as they could. She was a very protective mother. Charlotte would be ok; she'd grow up to be some kind of intellectual, a scientist maybe or a novelist, and everyone would marvel at her uniqueness. Sophie was the polar opposite, outgoing, lively and cute as a button with long, curly blonde hair and eyelashes that made me very jealous. She had settled into school without a problem and although she was nowhere near as clever as Charlotte she enjoyed school a lot more.

"I've organised another meeting with the head teacher," Collette announced. "I need to keep an eye on the time. Don't want to be late." She paused. "They have to do something, I'm seriously considering moving the children to another school."

I told her I thought it was a bad idea; Sophie had settled really well and had loads of friends, and Charlotte, well, I thought she would still have problems in another school but I didn't voice that opinion out loud. Collette rolled up her sleeve and looked at her watch.

"Look at the time," she exclaimed as she stood up and put on her coat. "I'd better be heading off. I'm in town on Thursday again if you fancy meeting up?"

"Great. I'll be here. Same time?"

"Yeah, see you then," she said before rushing off out of the door for another meeting with the long-suffering head teacher.

2

I left the coffee shop feeling brighter than I had done in quite a while. It was good to be able to talk about someone else's problems and really take an interest, rather than feeling that I didn't care about what was happening to other people. Getting over John's death was a hard and slow process, but I was gradually becoming less self-absorbed. I adored Collette's children, I was godmother to them both, they were so different and each had a vibrant and interesting personality. I loved watching them grow and develop and become their own little people. Thinking about them, and the difficulties they were encountering as they grew, had taken my mind in a different direction, and I smiled at that as I drew in the crisp autumn air, setting off back towards home.

    I double checked the address in the notebook. It was written in a very neat script that could only belong to an elderly gentleman and had been written with a proper ink pen.

Dr Michael Neasden
3, Prosper Lane
Lincoln

I knew the road well; it was just off Steep Hill to the right about halfway up. I walked fairly slowly up the hill – it is not called Steep Hill for no reason - and looked in a couple of shop windows on my way up. There were lots of people going both up and down the hill, brought out by the sunny Monday morning perhaps, or being extremely well prepared and starting Christmas preparations early. Christmas; my heart lurched. I hadn't even thought of having a Christmas without John. For the last however many years we had gone away for Christmas, since my parents had both died and his mother, a widow for years, had been admitted to a nursing home through advancing dementia. We would spend ages picking a country hotel together somewhere cosy and suited to a winter stay. Generally, we picked somewhere different each year, ranging from mid-Scotland to Devon, although we had found a couple of hotels that we'd returned to once in a while. We'd pack up the car with the presents and head off on Christmas Eve then return on the day after Boxing Day. Being in a hotel with other people had made the whole holiday feel a bit more festive. We had no children, John had no siblings and my only brother lived in Australia, so staying at home on our own would have been too like every other day of the year. I had loved going away; I hadn't a clue what I would do this year. The thought filled me with dread.

I was brought back to the real world when I was almost knocked over by what I assumed to be someone out for a run pushing past me and running down the hill. He was dressed in a scruffy tracksuit, and he sped off down the hill. Easier going down than up I thought to myself as I realised I'd almost missed the road, and turned into Prosper Lane.

Dr Neasden's house was the third one along the lane, the numbers going up in sequence as there are only houses on one side of the street. There was a little garden at the front and a passageway leading around the back of the house, where I assumed the door had to be. The garden was well kept and tidy with a few shrubs planted in tubs. The windows could have done with a lick of paint, but the outside of the house seemed in reasonably good condition. I followed the path round the side of the house and saw the dark red door towards the rear. The path opened out onto a paved yard, which had a few planters with the last remains of summer flowers in them. Dr Neasden was obviously preparing for winter colour as there were a couple of packs of baby pansies and chrysanthemums ready for planting when he felt the petunias had had their day. The back of the yard was walled off and the area was a lovely sun trap. In the corner, just beyond the door, there was a small table and chairs, which looked as if they had been recently used; an empty mug stood on top of a daily newspaper as if the doctor had been sitting outside but had just nipped inside for something.

The door was ajar so I knocked cautiously but got no answer. I knocked a little louder, thinking perhaps Dr Neasden had left the table to go to the bathroom and was upstairs, but there was still no response.

I pushed at the door. It opened into the kitchen. I was going to shout out Dr Neasden's name but I was taken aback by the state of the kitchen. Drawers were open, cupboard doors were gaping and all of the contents had been pulled out. Cutlery and crockery were scattered across the floor, saucepans and frying pans pulled out of cupboards, and a toaster was turned on its side on the work top. The bin was lying on the floor with the rubbish pulled out across the vinyl. Letters and papers were piled on the kitchen table and some had spilled onto the floor. I could sense that this was not the usual state of affairs, the place was too well kept to belong to someone so untidy and there was no dirt, no washing up left in the sink or on the drainer. This was not the mess left by someone who normally lived like this.

I walked into the kitchen and called out.

"Dr Neasden."

There was no reply.

I was beginning to feel very uneasy, my heart pumping increasingly fast. I tried again.

"Dr Neasden! My name is Verity Spencer. I picked up your notebook earlier. I was just calling round to return it."

I heard something. I stopped and held my breath, listening intently. I heard it again. A muffled *hmmmph*.

I took a step into the kitchen. A window over the sink looked out over the courtyard, and a door on the other side of the kitchen led through to the hall. I walked slowly over to that, pushed it open and went into the hall; this presented a similar picture. All the coats had been pulled off the coat rack and thrown onto the floor. The hall table had its drawer open with all the contents spilled out. An old-fashioned telephone lay on the carpet, its handle and curly cable off to one side. On the floor there was a smashed vase and fresh flowers in a pool of water.

At the far end of the hall was a stairway. Between the kitchen and the stairs there were two doors on the left of the hall. The first was a small dining room. It was furnished with old dark wood furniture – an oval table and four chairs and a sideboard. The room was a vision of chaos. The doors of the sideboard had been left open and all the posh crockery that had been stored in there for smart dinner occasions had been emptied out. A canteen of cutlery had been pulled from the drawers and tipped onto the floor. Papers and bills were everywhere. A4 files had been opened and everything ripped out and thrown onto the floor. I called out again and heard the same faint *hmmmph* in return.

I returned to the hall, this time moving faster. My mind racing. On the floor, by the far door, was Dr Neasden's walking stick, discarded and lying across the doorway. *This is not right. This is not right.* I ran the few feet down the hall, past the upturned vase, to the front room and stopped in my tracks. The room had a plain but old-fashioned three-piece suite which had all the cushions pulled off and piled into the middle of the floor. An overturned coffee table was surrounded by broken ornaments littering the carpet. A smashed mirror hung at an angle above the fireplace and the pictures were all broken or pulled off the wall. Instinctively, I put my hand over my mouth. I could not understand what had gone on here. Then I saw a leg sticking out from behind the sofa and the soft moaning could be heard coming from that direction.

I hurried around the back of the sofa, clambering over the pulled-off cushions, and saw him lying there. Dr Neasden was covered in blood and had clearly been beaten up. His face was swollen and red and he had blood trickling down his face from a cut on his forehead. His tweed jacket was torn in several places. His left arm lay across his body at an angle that I couldn't quite figure out but the neat hole in his midriff, surrounded by an expanding pool of blood, left me in no doubt that he had been shot in his stomach.

3

I had no time to think. I gathered up one of the net curtains that had been pulled off its wire and made it into a ball, pressing it into the wound in Dr Neasden's stomach. Blood was coming out of his back and soaking into the carpet.

"Don't worry," I said, trying to hide my mounting anxiety. "I'll call an ambulance and the police, they'll patch you up in no time." I looked at the gathering pool of blood beneath him and hoped that it wasn't as bad as it looked. I pulled my iPhone out of my pocket to call the emergency services. The notebook fell out of my pocket at the same time. Dr Neasden clutched at the air with his good arm, raising his eyebrows and struggling to drag words from the back of his throat.

"No, no," he whispered, pointing at the book.

I pressed onto the wound with my left hand and concentrated on getting my call through to the emergency services and giving clear instructions to the woman on the other end of the phone. I turned my gaze from the doctor, still trying to get my attention and pointing at the notebook.

"You have to go to the top of the hill," I continued. "And then turn left to come back down to this point. There's no way in or out at the other end of the road." I disconnected, thinking that it was going to be at least ten or fifteen minutes before the ambulance arrived and hoping that I could keep the doctor hanging on that long. I put my phone and the notebook back in my pocket before returning my full attention to the man lying on the floor in front of me.

"The book," he whispered, struggling to speak. "Hide it."

I stared blankly.

"Hide it," he forced the words out. Then with the arm that wasn't all twisted he fumbled for something in his pocket. His wallet. He was giving me his wallet. What on earth? I didn't understand.

"Give...give...that," he said, trying to lift his head off the ground.

I didn't want him exerting any energy or using his strength on anything other than staying alive, so I took the wallet and put it in my pocket. I found a cushion and put it under his head. He was struggling to breathe and I was struggling to keep pressing the net curtain into his wound. It was soaked with blood and he was becoming weaker. His eyelids were drooping, blood and mucous were bubbling at the corner of his mouth, and his complexion was taking on the grey tone of approaching death. My arms were beginning to ache and I willed the ambulance to arrive. I didn't think he could last much longer – looking at the growing pool surrounding my knees, I didn't think he could have much blood left.

"Who did this?" I asked. "Was it a burglary?"

He didn't answer. His eyes started sliding upwards and his breath became more laboured.

"Dr Neasden," I shouted, trying to keep him awake. Trying to remember desperately anything at all from my first-aid course at the college, and then I had the sinking realisation that what Dr Neasden needed was way beyond first aid.

"Stfnmm," he mumbled.

"What? Sorry…what did you say?"

"Stfmm. Stefum."

I tried hard to decipher what he was saying but I really wished he would just concentrate on staying alive. "Stephen?"

He nodded. "Talk to Stephen," he whispered. "Prmiss. Tk t Stfmm."

"Talk to Stephen? What?" I had no idea what the doctor was talking about, but the thought kept circulating in my head that he ought to be conserving his energy and not trying to talk at all, so I left it at that. He tried lifting his head again; he was finding it harder to summon up the strength but he wanted to tell me something.

"Nt buk."

"Notebook?"

He nodded again.

"You want me to talk to Stephen about the notebook? Stephen who? Where is Stephen?"

The doctor's eyes began to slide again and glaze over. "Prmiss."

At last the distant sound of sirens filtered into the room and I hoped that the ambulance was here first. I pressed the curtain tighter into the wound and prayed to anyone who cared to listen to get the paramedics in here quick.

And then I heard them screech to a halt outside. I heard the doors opening and closing and the footsteps of the ambulance men clattering down the passageway. Dr Neasden gripped my hand. He had shown no strength at all until that point but he clung on tightly, pressing his hand hard over the hand I had pushing down on the bullet wound in his stomach. He breathed in sharply and tried to say something. Nothing. Each time he breathed in it sounded like a whistle. He tried again. A whisper. And then, as the ambulance men came crashing through the back door and into the kitchen, and the wails of police sirens could be heard heading down the road, he pulled me to him.

"Trust no one"

I was dragged aside, and I stepped back to let the paramedics take over. They put an oxygen mask over the doctor's face and checked his wound. They rushed around calling to the doctor to stay awake, telling him he would be at the hospital in no time and that everything was going to be okay. They were lying. Everything was not going to be okay.

A young police constable had arrived and stood looking dangerously out of his depth in the middle of the chaos that was Dr Neasden's sitting room. I hadn't noticed him come in with all the activity going on by the window. He asked me what I was doing here. How had I come to find this, he struggled for the right word, situation.

"I came to return something that Dr Neasden had dropped," I said.

"What was that then?" said the policeman. I know it's a cliché but he really did look young enough to be in school.

I glanced over at the doctor, and he caught my eye. Caught me looking at him. He tipped his head slightly as if trying to nod. And then I understood. He turned away and closed his eyes.

"His wallet," I said, holding out the wallet that the doctor had given to me. "He dropped his wallet in town earlier."

"He's gone," the paramedic said and stood up.

4

An hour or so later I was sitting at the table in Dr
Neasden's yard talking to Detective Sergeant Mike
Nash and drinking a takeaway coffee that had appeared
from somewhere. I didn't remember asking for it, but it
was exactly how I liked it, so I guessed I must have told
someone what I wanted at some point. I was cupping
my hands around the takeaway cup to keep myself
warm. Suddenly I started to shake and shiver. It was
shock, the policeman told me. He had listened to what
I'd said, nodding and taking notes and he seemed okay
although he'd occasionally sounded a bit sceptical. Or
maybe that was just my imagination. I had used the
sink in Dr Neasden's kitchen to rinse the blood off my
hands and arms. I couldn't believe how much of it
there was. No matter how much I had washed, there
had seemed to be more. There was a mirror near the
sink, to the side, on the wall and I had looked in that

and removed the blood that had splashed onto my face. Then I had gone outside with Detective Sergeant Nash to answer his questions. A lady police constable hovered in the background. I assumed it was she who had fetched the coffee.

It turned out that Dr Neasden was a retired GP and he'd lived here, in this house for a long time; that was fairly obvious from the décor, it felt like the home of an elderly couple. Well, what I could see of it under all the mess. I wondered if he had been married; I guessed that he had, the house was full of feminine touches. Then I wondered how long he had been a widower, on his own like me, adjusting to a different kind of life. I thought about John and wondered what he would have made of all this. I wondered if he would have done anything differently. According to Nash, Dr Neasden was 72 years old and spent some of his spare time doing voluntary work for an organisation that worked with people who had no recourse to public funds. He'd told me this because he had been trying to establish if I knew the doctor, but I had never met him before to my knowledge and had never heard his name mentioned. When he had worked, it had been at a surgery just on the edge of the city; the opposite end of the city to my current GP's. I imagined that I could easily have walked past him at some point, but in a city of over eighty thousand people he would have gone unnoticed. I had a vivid memory of him striding up the hill with the stick he didn't seem to need, but if our paths had passed before then I couldn't remember.

"So run it past me again," said Detective Sergeant Mike Nash. "You are?"

"Verity Spencer, aged 42, live in Lincoln…"

I sighed. I'd been through it several times now. Every detail, every feeling, every impression. It was all one hundred per cent exactly as it had happened save for one element – I had told him I'd picked up Dr Neasden's wallet and not his notebook. I hoped I was convincing. I was generally hopeless at lying. John, on the odd occasion I had tried to spin him some story or other, could always tell. I was no good either at keeping secrets and surprises because my face always gave me away. Once, I had tried to organise a surprise long weekend away for John but it had all gone horribly wrong as I had struggled not to reveal all. I'd ended up telling him what I was planning. I looked at the policeman, expecting that he might be able to read my thoughts and I concentrated hard. It was perfectly believable that I could have picked up a wallet and wanted to return it. *Stick to the story, Verity.*

"So you went to have coffee with your friend, err…"

"Collette."

"Collette Smith."

"Yes."

"And you talked about her children?"

"Mostly, yes."

"You mentioned the wallet."

"I mentioned it, yes, I said I would post it through the doctor's door on my way home."

"How did you know the doctor's address?" The first time they had asked me that I had panicked. I hadn't looked in the wallet. I didn't even know if there was an address in there. Luckily the young constable had been holding the wallet open at the time to assess the contents. I thought I'd seen a pink card in one of the credit card slots. I had taken a gamble.

"I looked in the wallet and his driver's licence was in there. It had his address on it."

"But when you got here you didn't just post it through the door. Why was that?"

I sighed again. "As I said earlier, I noticed that the door was open and the kitchen was in disarray. The newspaper and mug were still outside so it seemed odd. When I called out to see if there was anyone here, I heard a muffled sound. So I followed it."

"And you found the doctor lying in the front room?"

"Yes. I could see he had been injured. He had a bullet wound in his stomach."

"You are familiar with bullet wounds?"

"No," I said wearily, "I am not familiar with bullet wounds. In fact, apart from on TV programmes, I have never seen anyone with a bullet wound."

"But you assessed it as such?" He sounded so like a stereotypical policeman.

"Well, the gaping hole in his abdomen and the blood pouring out his back led me to that conclusion. But I am willing to be proved wrong if the pathologist thinks otherwise." I didn't know why I was feeling like this. Probably trying to save someone's life took it out of you. Then having to answer the same endless questions over and over again didn't help. And there was no reason for him to be facetious in the first place.

"And you didn't see or hear anything suspicious?"

"No."

He paused and reviewed his notes. He looked up, and I thought he was going to ask me something else. I closed my eyes and sighed, feeling weary.

"Okay, thanks, Mrs Spencer. I think that should do it for now. Would you like someone to walk you home?"

"No, that's fine. I only live ten minutes' walk away. I'm fine thanks." I paused. "What happens now?"

"If we need anything else we'll be in touch. You may need to give evidence if we ever find out who did this." He gestured generally towards the house. He handed me a card. "If you think of anything else, let me know."

"What like? I've been over and over."

"You'd be surprised how often people come back later with details they remember that didn't seem significant at the time. Or that they'd forgotten until something prompted their memory."

"Okay, I'll bear that in mind." I put the card in my pocket. The same pocket that guarded the doctor's notebook. I looked up at the detective thinking he would be able to tell what I'd felt in my pocket. I'd lied to the policeman. I had never done that before. I felt guilty, I had always been such a conformist; John used to laugh at me when I would run back into supermarkets to pay for items I had inadvertently hidden in the trolley. But this was nothing to feel guilty about, it was nothing major; it was only one small detail. Or that's what I was telling myself anyway. The doctor had been so sure. '*Promise me.*' I brushed the thought away. My involvement had been adequately explained. The notebook was a sideline. It probably had nothing to do with this. This was most likely a burglary that had been disturbed. I smiled at Detective Sergeant Mike Nash.

He held out his hand. "Thanks for everything. Medics said you did a great job keeping the doc going until they arrived."

I smiled a weak smile. "Not good enough, clearly." I glanced towards the house, from where the doctor's body had been recently removed.

He shook his head. "I don't think the best doctor in town would have been able to save him. You did good, Mrs Spencer, you did very good."

I thanked him and, about four hours later than planned, headed up the hill to my house on Steeple Lane.

5

I walked into the house that, for almost twenty years, I had shared with my husband. A photo of our wedding day greeted me as I entered. We looked so happy. I struggled to keep my emotions in check after all that I had just been through, and I glanced around at the house beyond attempting to delay the tears. But it just served to remind me that I was now alone here, just me and the wedding photo, with a version of me who had thought we had so much life ahead of us. We'd bought the house not long after our marriage. It was bigger than we needed for the two of us, but we'd always anticipated that we would have at least two, if not more, children. Despite our best efforts, that hadn't happened and, after a few years of trying, we'd become resigned to a childless marriage. We'd considered going for tests, thought about trying IVF, talked about adoption but had decided that we would let fate take its hand. We'd never used contraception, apart from the first year we'd been married when we'd thought it was best to 'settle down' first before starting a family. I smiled at the recollection of the conversation, as if we had been in control and that, as soon as I stopped taking the pill, a baby would appear as if by magic. I'd been crushingly disappointed when it had become clear it wasn't going to go according to plan but I wasn't going to let becoming a mother dominate my life. I'd had friends, who had had difficulties conceiving, putting themselves through agonies every month trying to get pregnant, miscarrying, failing. They had become obsessed, their whole lives revolving around their monthly cycle, pregnancy tests, injections and hormones. They couldn't think of, let alone talk about, anything else. Getting pregnant became their entire reason for living and each month that reason was horribly denied them when they sat on the loo and saw that their period had, once again, arrived. I hadn't been prepared to put myself through that.

Now, returning to an empty house, I thought that maybe if I'd had a child, a piece of John, to come home to it would have felt better. Perhaps I would have felt his death less keenly if a reminder of him, in the form of a child, remained. I somehow doubted it though. It might have been harder. Depending on the age of the child I would have had to explain their father's death, explain how he was never going to return. And, anyway, I had friends' children to dote on. And I especially liked being able to relinquish responsibility when things got difficult. People used to constantly be asking when we were going to have children, as if it was something they had a say in. I just used to smile and say that children weren't on our agenda, but it made me angry that people felt they had the right to interfere.

Secretly, I think I might not have made a great mum. I wonder if, secretly, John felt that he might not have made a great dad too. We'd easily slipped into a childless existence, doing whatever had suited us and not having to fit things in around a never-ending schedule of ballet and tennis and gym, which was what Collette's life seemed to consist of. Although I occasionally felt sad that the choice of having children had been taken out of my hands, in another way I was pleased. Our life as a couple had suited me well. We'd had a good social life and hosted, or attended, dinner parties regularly with various combinations of our group of friends. I didn't think that I had missed out.

I headed upstairs and got undressed; my skirt was covered in blood. As I took my black tights off they left smears of dark, dried blood on my legs. There was blood on my bra and pants too; it must have soaked through my clothes. There was blood all over me; I didn't know why I hadn't noticed how much there had been before. I wondered what people must have thought as I'd walked through the streets. I put my clothes in a bag, deciding to throw them away despite the skirt being one of my favourite recent purchases. I got in the shower and stood there for what felt like ages, letting the hot water run off my head and shoulders and trying to wash all the memories away. I kept looking down, thinking I still had blood on my skin; I could smell it, that iron-like unmistakable smell.

I scrubbed myself, like Lady Macbeth, trying to rid myself of the last vestiges of horror but I just couldn't get rid of it. Eventually I gave up. I got out of the shower and wrapped my hair in a towel, put on my dressing gown and slippers then went back downstairs.

I made myself a cup of tea and sat at the counter in the kitchen thinking about the events of the day. Once again, I started to shake and I noticed that my skin was covered in goose bumps. I thought about the doctor squeezing my hand, the way he had looked at me just before he'd died, my lie to the police. Why had I lied to the police? What had I possibly gained from that? I had no answer to those questions. I could not fathom it really, except that the doctor had been there, dying on his living room floor, and had implored me to make sure that I took his notebook to someone called Stephen, or I talked to Stephen, I couldn't remember exactly. He had been struggling to speak and I had been desperately trying to save his life. Despite having absolutely no clue what he'd meant I had gone along with it. He had seemed so convincing. He had looked into my eyes and begged. He had turned to me as I'd taken up his lie, telling the police that it was his wallet I was returning. He'd died in the knowledge that I hadn't handed them his notebook. But I doubted myself.

I had to call Nash and confess. I'd tell him that I'd found the notebook in my pocket and forgotten that I'd picked it up with his wallet. That way I wouldn't need to tell him I was lying. That way I could fob it off as one of those 'details that people remember' after the event and hadn't given any significance to. I could say that I'd found the notebook in my pocket when I'd got home and must have forgotten it in the heat of the moment. The shock I was suffering from, after finding the doctor shot and dying, would surely account for a temporary loss of memory and if I rang straight away, as soon as I'd found it, that would sound convincing. Wouldn't it?

I reached over into my coat pocket and retrieved both my iPhone and the card that Nash had given me. As I pulled them from my coat, the notebook fell out of my pocket and hit the floor. I picked it up and flicked through the pages. There was hardly anything there. I could not begin to think why it had been so important to the doctor. The first page had his name and address in his elderly, loopy handwriting. Then there were a few pages that had been torn out. The next few pages were blank. There was nothing on them at all.

One page had one word written on it. It simply said, in the doctor's distinctive handwriting:

Champion!

That was it, just the one word, 'Champion!', nothing else. Champion of what? Had the doctor won something, I wondered. I shook my head.

After a couple of pages there was a short list of numbers.

43809760
63329916
72709588

A few pages further on there was what appeared to be a list. It consisted solely of what I took to be acronyms.

RSDI
KTMD
ADDI

I had no idea what any of those stood for.

One page contained some more numbers. Nothing else, just numbers in blocks of three.

215
762
879

I flicked through the pages and there was only one more entry. But it made me stop in my tracks. At the top of the page was written:

Stephen Ibbetson

Beneath the name, on the bottom of the page and in the corner were three letters.

LBH

Stephen. This had to be the Stephen that I was supposed to contact. *Shit, shit, shit.* A name. I had a whole name, not just a faceless request. I reached for my laptop and Googled 'Stephen Ibbetson'. It delivered 654,000 results. Great. I didn't even know why I was bothering. I was a recently widowed, poorly paid further education teacher. Who had just lied to the police. That was probably one of the most daring and exciting things I had done in my adult life. What on earth did I think this had to do with me? Precisely nothing, was my answer to that question. The imploring look in the doctor's eyes, as he lay dying in his living room, popped into my head temporarily preventing me from making the call to Nash.

I flicked back through the notebook; it was compelling. I wondered what it all meant. I tried the acronyms, maybe there would be something there. On Google 'RSDI' netted 263,000 results, most commonly related to some US Admin fund called Retirement, Survivors and Disability Insurance. 'KTMD' returned 411,000 results. Nothing of interest. Highest up on the page was some Texan TV station. Both US based. Was there an American connection? I tried 'ADDI'. That brought in over 16 million results. Bizarrely the majority related to knitting needles. Knitting needles? Hmmm. Not much to go on there. I put the notebook to one side and decided that I was clearly not cut out for this. I had no idea who Stephen was. I didn't even know if he was this Stephen Ibbetson that Dr Neasden had noted in his book. There had to be plenty of other Stephens in the world. Although, I had to admit, it was a coincidence that Dr Neasden had mentioned the name if it had nothing to do with the person in the notebook. I was unsure as to why I should continue lying to the police and resolved once again to call Nash and hand the notebook over to him. After all, that was the police's job. If there was anything in there that related to the murder of Dr Neasden, surely it was the police who were best placed to trace them? And if the notebook held clues then they should have it. Shouldn't they?

Except Dr Neasden clearly hadn't thought so. He'd been very clear, having been the recipient of the bullet wound, that he did not want the police to have the notebook. Maybe it had nothing to do with his death. I remembered his strong grip on my hands.

'Trust no one.'

I got out my sandwich toaster and made myself a quick cheese and ham toasted sandwich, poured a large glass of wine and went through to the living room. I ate my sandwich sitting on the sofa and leaning over the coffee table whilst watching some dreadful reality TV programme. A group of squealing young people had been taken to Ibiza or somewhere and given free rein in the local nightclubs and bars and then the host not only ridiculed their drunken behaviour but secretly showed it to their horrified parents. What was the world coming to? After I'd finished eating, I pushed my plate to one side, turned off the television, replenished my wine glass then picked up the phone and dialled.

-6-

After three rings, Collette picked up. It was just after 7 and I knew dinner time would be done and it would be a good half an hour before the girls went to bed.

"Vee, hi," she said on answering.

"Are you okay to talk?" I asked. "Are the kids occupied?"

"Sure," she replied, then instantly shouted through to answer one or other of them.

"Shall I ring back later?" I really needed to talk to someone about what had happened and I wanted her full attention. My words caught in my throat as I spoke and I struggled once again to fight back the tears. What I really wanted was John's arms around me, pulling me in and telling me everything was okay, but Collette was the closest I had. She heard the snag in my voice and instantly became concerned.

"Are you okay? Vee? What is it? Do you want me to come round?"

"No, no." I genuinely didn't. "I'm okay. It's just… Oh, God, it's been a horrific afternoon."

I filled her in on what had happened that afternoon. I explained everything – the mayhem, the discovery of Dr Neasden, the call to the emergency services, the interview with the police, everything. I had to keep repeating things for her, and she was constantly interrupting with exclamations of amazement and disbelief at what I had gone through. She was suitably intrigued and horrified at the same time. Asking questions, asking how I'd felt, what I'd done, what I'd said and so on. Every now and again I needed to take a breath. Remembering my fight to keep the doctor alive was hard. I didn't want to cry down the phone and I needed a few seconds from time to time to gather my thoughts together.

"Whoa, what a day you've had." She sounded genuinely concerned. "Are you okay? Are you sure you don't want me to come over?"

"No, don't worry, I'm okay, honestly, and it'll be the children's bedtime soon."

"That's not a problem, Marcus can put the girls to bed."

"No, it's fine. I'm fine. Thanks. It's just…"

"What? Just what? Anything. Just let me know."

"Well…." I hesitated. I didn't know how to tell her I'd lied to the police. It was completely out of character. I didn't know what she'd say.

"What? Verity, what is it?"

"Before he died, the doctor asked me to do something." I thought it might sound better if I got in there first with it being the doctor who'd asked. Almost like it wasn't my fault.

"He asked you to do something? Verity are you okay? You're making no sense at all."

I swallowed. "He asked me to take his notebook to someone." I didn't mention that at this point I wasn't even sure who I was supposed to take it to, or actually if he'd said take it, or talk about it; I didn't think sounding vague would be useful at this juncture.

She calmed down. "Okay, that's not so bad then, is it?"

"Well he also asked me not to tell the police about it. He asked me to tell them he'd dropped his wallet instead and that was what I'd brought back. So I didn't mention the notebook."

As predicted, this did not go down too well.

"Verity are you mad?"

I said nothing.

"You're not thinking straight," she continued, "it's perfectly understandable with what you've been through recently. Losing someone close can do that. I mean, it can make you behave in strange ways. Then finding that poor man like that, it's not surprising that you weren't thinking straight. You have to tell them, Vee, you have to."

But I was not going to change my mind. In fact, the more she implored, the more determined I was that I had done the right thing. She veered between anger at my stupidity and worry at what would happen if anyone found out. She cried with frustration when I refused to hand over the notebook to the police.

"Collette, you didn't hold him whilst he died. You didn't see the look in his eyes. He implored me. What else could I do? He made me promise. He was so…convinced that I shouldn't tell them"

"Lying to the police is a serious offence; you could end up in court." But I could tell she had softened a bit.

"Look, I'll take the notebook to the friend and see what he has to say. If he wants me to go to the police, I will. I'll tell them I found it in my pocket and had forgotten I'd picked it up with the wallet. The Sergeant said people forget and then remember things after incidents like that. Ok? I promise, if the friend doesn't pan out for any reason, or if he thinks I should go to the police, I will."

Silence.

"Collette? Is that okay? I'll keep you informed all the way."

More silence.

"Collette, please."

"Okay. I suppose," she sighed, forcing the words out. "But it doesn't mean I agree with what you did, alright?" She lightened up a bit. "You're a very naughty girl," she said in her 'cross Mummy' voice.

"I know. I don't know why I did it. But I've never sat with anyone who was dying before, let alone someone who's been shot in a house that's been ransacked. I can't believe it all happened; it's like a nightmare or something. I don't understand what's gone on and I guess it's for the police to investigate but the doctor seemed genuine, and he seemed so desperate for me to hide the notebook and take it to his friend."

"Okay, well be careful. Make sure you deal with it tomorrow or very soon. If you leave it too long and then suddenly 'remember' that you found the notebook it won't ring true."

"I will. I promise. Oh, and, Collette?"

"Yes."

"If the police contact you and ask what we spoke about, it was the wallet okay? Not the notebook."

"Jesus, Verity, what's got into you."

But I knew I could rely on her.

TUESDAY

I slept the sleep of the dead that night. I thought I'd be awake all night but it was quite the opposite. I kept dreaming vivid dreams of chases and guns that dissipated the moment I reached full wakefulness, and then I would drift back off again. I woke early, just after 7, so I showered and dressed and headed to the city centre for a coffee. I put on my coat and took my laptop in its bag and headed for Café Nero as I knew it would be open. I walked down the hill, the sun just rising behind me and casting a soulful light across the city.

I got to the café to find two other early birds ahead of me in the queue. I ordered a croissant and a large Americano with hot milk and asked for it in a takeaway cup, even though I was not going to take it away. I just prefer my coffee hot and it stays warmer longer in a takeaway cup. Grabbing the cup, I resolved to buy a reusable one soon, and I went and found a seat in the corner. I got my laptop out and fired it up, connecting automatically to The Cloud. I searched for news about the doctor, but there was nothing, not even a mention in the local paper. That was a bit unusual, wasn't it? Maybe it was because he had been shot. Perhaps they weren't giving any details. I Googled his name to see if I had missed something, but all I got was a newspaper article from a couple of years ago about his retirement and the send-off his patients had given him. It seemed that he was quite a popular guy.

I scanned a few of the dailies on my laptop. Not much going on really, the usual moans at the government for one thing or another, predictions of the weather turning bad in a few days' time, who was going out with who in celeb world. Pretty boring stuff really.

I fished the notebook out of my pocket and flicked through it again. Nothing in it made any sense at all really. I couldn't fathom the importance of it, but then I suppose all I had to do was deliver it to 'Stephen'. I didn't have to figure out what it all meant. I Googled Stephen Ibbetson again. Hundreds of Facebook and Twitter and LinkedIn accounts came up. I glanced at a couple but they told me nothing so I ignored the rest and moved away from social media. There were some firms, an accountant, a vicar. I spent ages ploughing through these, opening webpages and looking through to see if there was anything, anything at all that remotely might connect these different Stephen Ibbetsons with Dr Neasden. I couldn't come up with anything. I looked at a couple of newspaper articles but they were from ages ago and got me nowhere. Dejected, I took a swig of my now stone-cold coffee. I went up to the counter and ordered another one the same. I'd been sitting here for over two hours now and still had nothing. When I sat back down, I flicked through the notebook again and sighed. I didn't know what to do and would have gone home if I hadn't just bought myself another coffee.

The laptop had gone to sleep so I opened it up again and tried Googling the name Stephen Ibbetson together with some of the acronyms in the notebook. That also got me nowhere; there didn't appear to be any connections there at all. Nothing of any use came up. I looked back at the page in the notebook where the doctor had written the name. It was written right at the top of the page. And right at the bottom of the page were the letters LBH. They looked unconnected but I thought I would give it one more try and I Googled 'Stephen Ibbetson LBH'.

Bingo.

LBH, in this case at least, turned out to stand for the London Borough of Hillingdon. There was a Stephen Ibbetson who was an Assistant Director of Children's Services who worked for the London Borough of Hillingdon, or LBH. There was only the one person. At the top of the Google results' page there were quite a few references to him, but beneath those, the results were shown for 'similar searches' so I knew there was only one Stephen Ibbetson that went with the initials LBH. The entries mostly consisted of some minutes from meetings he had attended, presentations he had given and so on, but they didn't tell me much about him. In fact most of them just had his name listed as an attendee, or made a vague reference to 'Stephen Ibbetson suggested that…' or something along those lines. There was one PowerPoint presentation which had been delivered, apparently, to a group of London Boroughs and it was about changes to safeguarding procedures. It didn't look very interesting.

I looked on the website of the London Borough of Hillingdon. I wasn't even sure exactly which area of London it covered, but it turned out to be the very west-most borough and the headquarters were in Uxbridge. I found a staff photo of Stephen Ibbetson. He was smiling and had a rugged, round face with dark curly hair. I read his biography.

> *Stephen Ibbetson has worked in children's social care for almost thirty years. He qualified at the North London Polytechnic and started out as a social worker in West Berkshire, working in both child protection and looked after children teams. Since then, Stephen has held various positions in several London Boroughs including team manager, service manager and head of service. Stephen has been at the London Borough of Hillingdon since June 2010 having joined us from his position as head of service for child protection in the London Borough of Ealing. He has responsibility for children's specialist services,*

including children in need, child protection and children with disabilities.

That was pretty bland and didn't tell me much. He looked early-mid 50s in his photo, which I guessed tied in with the information in the bio.

I double checked by looking at some of the other London Boroughs which also began with the initial H, of which there were quite a few, including Hammersmith, Hounslow, Haringey and so on. None of these places had anyone called Stephen Ibbetson working for them. There was nothing else of any interest that came up when I just Googled LBH. This had to be Dr Neasden's Stephen.

On the website for the London Borough of Hillingdon, there were several contact details for certain members of staff, although not for Stephen Ibbetson. It was easy to figure out the formula for email addresses though. It went first initial, dot, surname and always had the ending lbhillingdon.gov.uk. I opened up my Hotmail account and wrote him an email.

> *From:*<Sugarandspice328@hotmail.com>

> *To:*<s.ibbetson@lbhillingdon.gov.uk>
> *Dear Mr Ibbetson,*

> *I am sorry for approaching you out of the blue, but I was asked to contact you by the late Dr Neasden of Lincoln. Would it be possible for us to arrange an appointment in the next day or two?*

> *I look forward to a swift reply.*

Kind regards,
Verity Spencer

I read it over. I thought about the doctor and his dying moments; his hand gripping mine. '*Trust no one*'. I looked at my name again and decided that it might be prudent to use a different name. I thought that I was being a bit paranoid, but what harm did it do to sign off with a false name, just in case? My Hotmail account didn't include my name so that wouldn't give it away. I changed my sign off to Miriam Nathan, a combination of mine and John's mothers' names, then pressed send before I changed my mind. I figured that if it wasn't the right Stephen Ibbetson he would dismiss it as a crank email, but if it was then I could have just made contact. What did I have to lose? I also thought that, unless he was on holiday, he'd make contact pretty quickly if he had any idea what this was about. I didn't get an out-of-office reply so I figured I'd hear from him soon if indeed he was the right Stephen Ibbetson.

I felt elated as I walked back up the hill in the sun. I had a sense of purpose. Hopefully, if I'd finally found the right Stephen, I was going to be able to fulfil my promise to talk to him on behalf of Dr Neasden about the notebook and its mysterious contents. Then I could tell Collette I'd done what I'd said I would and I could just get on with my life.

If only I'd known.

-8-

As I turned into Steeple Lane my stomach dropped. Something was wrong. The front door had been left open, at least half-way. I felt sick; I knew I hadn't left it like that. I stopped in my tracks, struggling to comprehend, and then I started to run. I ran along the road and up the front path and pushed the door open. I ran inside, dropping my handbag and my laptop bag as I went. For a while I just stood there, stunned, open-mouthed, gazing at my suddenly unrecognisable home.

The house had been completely ransacked. There were things everywhere. I walked from room to room in a daze. There was no one in the house but in my stupefied state it hadn't really occurred to me that there might be. Drawers had been emptied in the kitchen, in the front room, and in the bedrooms and all the contents scattered across the floor. Tables had been upturned, bookshelves emptied of their contents, clothes yanked out of wardrobes, bedclothes removed from beds. I walked back, once more, through all the rooms. Nothing seemed to be missing. My jewellery box had been emptied onto the bedroom floor, but it appeared that it was all still there. The television, the stereo, the expensive speakers John had insisted on buying because they 'enhanced the listening experience' had all been thrown onto the floor, but they were all still there.

I returned, dumbfounded, to the living room and looked around me, thoughts of the doctor's ransacked house racing through my brain. And then thoughts of the doctor dying in amongst the remains of his possessions. I looked at the floor strewn with smashed photographs, clearly just thrown on the floor with contempt. I trod carefully through shards of broken glass, and ornaments. I stepped over the television, pictures of loved ones smiling up at me from the floor as I walked. Most of the glass had broken and the photos were slipping out of the frames. One of me with my mum had miraculously survived and I picked it up and placed it on a shelf. I sighed heavily; it seemed like a futile gesture in all this mayhem. I glanced at the picture. There we were, smiling and unaware of the chaos around us, alone on a shelf that had once groaned with books and other photos and random things I'd picked up with John on our travels across the globe.

I looked around again. It appeared that everything had been gone through in a hurry, in a desperate search for something. *A desperate search.* Just like Dr Neasden's house.

I stopped. The notebook. *Oh shit. Oh shit.* Why hadn't it occurred to me when I'd first walked in? It had to be the notebook. It had to be connected with Dr Neasden; the way the house had been tipped upside down with nothing stolen, was exactly the same. This wasn't a random burglary, this was a search. There was no other explanation; it had to be the notebook. I'd had it with me so they wouldn't have found it.

But who would know that I had anything to do with it? I'd never met Dr Neasden before yesterday. And who would know where to find me?

I pondered this last point for a while. I went round and round, over and over it in my head. I hadn't told anyone about the notebook, apart from Collette, not even the police. Someone must have known about it and figured out that I might have it, or know about it, or know something about where it was.

The notebook; it was the only connection between me and Dr Neasden and thank God I had been out when they'd arrived or I might well now have been lying on the floor with a bullet in my stomach. Whoever was searching clearly didn't care about leaving bodies in their wake. I was frozen to the spot. Frozen with fear and I didn't know what to do. Someone must have known that I'd been to Dr Neasden's house. But only the police knew about my visit, only they knew that there was any link between the two of us. And Collette, of course, but I wasn't even going to entertain the thought that she had anything to do with any of this. I hadn't told the police about the notebook, but if someone knew it existed and was searching for it and knew I had been round to

Dr Neasden's house they might assume that I knew something about it. Or indeed, think that I had it in my possession. *They're right on that one.* I sat down on the floor, my back against the wall.

'*Trust no one'.*

No one knew about this except the police. Someone had to have found out that I had been at the house, and they could only have found that out that information from one source. Someone had to have got my address from the police. I reached for my phone, instinctively wanting to call Nash and tell him what had happened, that someone had got information from them, somehow. But how could they have? Who would have access to that? Nobody could have accessed that so quickly unless it was actually someone on the force. Whoever had done this, whoever was looking for that notebook had someone working for them inside the police. Either that, or they were the police. Perhaps that was why Dr Neasden had been so keen to hide the notebook from them.

I put the phone down. I sank further into the floor, my shoulders slouched. I reached for a broken photo frame. It contained a picture of me and John on holiday in Spain a couple of years' ago, smiling against the crystal blue sky, unaware at that point that he would be alive for only another eighteen months or so. I clutched the photo to my chest and sobbed.

I sat there, crying, wishing more than anything that I had not picked up the notebook, or that I'd chosen to run after the doctor and been a couple more minutes late for Collette. But I couldn't turn back time and, as I surveyed the damage around me, I realised that I would have to do something. And fast. Whoever had done this would be back. They had killed Dr Neasden and I certainly did not want them to find me with a gun in their hand, whoever they were.

I left the house; I didn't know where I was going but I needed to think and to do that I needed to walk in the fresh air. I grabbed my coat and handbag and headed towards Steep Hill. There were a few people about and I was suspicious of everyone. Everyone seemed to be looking at me. Everyone looked shifty. I hurried along with my head down, but I felt uneasy. Something wasn't right. I tried to shake the feeling off, telling myself that I was just shaken by what had happened to the house. People milled about and turned away, into the cathedral or the castle, or into the shops. I kept looking round nervously. I was mentally kicking myself for leaving the house but I was here, out in the open, now. I wanted to hide; I didn't know what to do so I slowed down and let several people walk past me. They chatted animatedly as they walked along. *You're being silly, paranoid.* But I couldn't get rid of the feeling of unease. I dipped into one of the little shops that line Steep Hill, it sold quirky shoes and normally I would love to stay and admire the display. Today though I nervously peered out of the window from the back of the shop.

The street was quite busy outside with people going about their business. Some walked straight by, up or down the hill. Others took time to browse, looking through the window to admire the display of shoes.

And then a man sauntered into view, looking for all the world like another tourist meandering down the hill. He peered through the window and into the depths of the shop and although I turned my head away as fast I could, there was a brief moment when our eyes met. And I knew straight away that he wasn't shopping for shoes. He was looking for me.

I thought my heart had stopped. Everything stopped. Then suddenly it started pounding, loudly and quickly in my ears. The blood rushing through my head and making me feel nauseous. Sweat poured down my back. I had been followed and I had no idea how to handle it. I was into something I didn't understand, and I was way out of my depth. I tried to breathe more slowly. *Get a grip, Verity, you can deal with this.* My mind was spinning, though. How was I supposed to lose someone who was following me? I struggled to even think of where to begin.

I glanced around the shop at the shoes, hoping that my unease wasn't evident for all to see, and tried to figure out if there was any way I could gain the upper hand. Well, for a start, he clearly wasn't very professional because I had spotted him almost straight away. I had to lose him. And I had seen enough movies to know that the best thing to do would be to find a crowd. It was much harder to spot someone in a crowd.

I came out of the shop and headed towards town. I tried to look as if nothing was amiss, sauntering slowly past the shops and glancing in the windows. All the time I could sense him behind me but I didn't turn round, I didn't want him to know he had been spotted.

I wandered down the hill and past the High Street shops, stopping here and there for a look and checking the reflection in the windows to see whether he was still there. It was a Tuesday so it was not as crowded as it sometimes was at the weekend, but the High Street shops were always quite busy. I headed for Boots. That was a big store and there were lots of different isles, nooks and crannies, places to get lost. And, most importantly, it had a side exit towards the back. Just before I got to Boots, I upped my speed so that I would arrive a few paces ahead of my follower, hoping to catch him unawares with my sudden change in pace. I wasn't sure how close he was.

As soon as I got to the shop I went in through the first door. I walked quickly through the shoppers, brushing them out of my way and ignoring the impatient tuts. It was actually really busy and, luckily, being fairly average in height with shoulder length brown hair, there was nothing too distinctive to make me stand out from all the other people. I tried to slow myself a little as I didn't want to draw any attention to myself. I attempted to mingle so that anyone looking across the top of the pool of heads would find it hard to pick me out. Then I dipped through the opticians at the back and out of the side entrance. Once out in the open I ran as fast as I could across City Square and into the old, horrid 70s shopping centre building, now almost empty apart from the Post Office. I ran through the building and out the other end towards the bus station, jumped into a taxi waiting in the rank, then went straight back home.

9

I knew I had to work fast but I'd been formulating a plan. I was guessing that there was probably only the one guy who'd followed me, but if I got home and there was someone else lurking around waiting for me then I'd have to reformulate. As the taxi drew up outside, everything looked just as I had left it. I figured I would have maybe half an hour before they'd fully realised that they'd lost me and would have to come back to watch the house and wait for me. I had the upper hand, but not for long. If they returned and saw that I was already back, there would be nothing to stop them coming in and beating me up, or worse, here where no one would see. I needed to get a move on and leave the house before they realised I was inside. Once I was in the open there would be too many people around for them to try to attack me. Or shoot me. My heart leapt back into my mouth at that thought and a fresh wave of nausea swept over my body. I didn't want to leave my house, but I had no alternative. I didn't want to end up dead either. I would have to shake them off and find somewhere else to be until it was safe to come home. Hopefully once I'd met up with Stephen Ibbetson everything would be sorted out and I would be able to return, but I wasn't sure how long that would take. I guessed I'd need to be prepared to be away from the house for a few days at least.

I ran in through the front door, leap frogging over the debris strewn across the floor, trying to avoid any broken glass and definitely trying not to notice John's prized vase; 'the only thing in my family that's worth anything' he had said when he had inherited it from his Grandma. It was now laying in pieces across the floor, but I'd have to think about that later; there was no time for sentimentality now. I dashed up the stairs, taking them two and three at a time then ran into the bedroom. I grabbed a small holdall from the floor. It had been on top of the wardrobe but was now in the midst of a pile of clothes, bedding, toiletries and jewellery. I found a handbag that I hadn't used in years and put my current handbag inside it. It was quite garish, made from leopard print faux leather. I had bought it on the beach on holiday one year. It was a terrible copy of a Vivienne Westwood and I'd hardly used it since we'd got back. I'd thought about taking it to the charity shop so many times but it always reminded me of what a good time we'd had on that holiday, and I could never quite bring myself to part with it. It was perfect for what I needed now, so I said a silent prayer to the gods of charity shops zipped the notebook into an inside pocket and put the handbag inside the holdall.

Next I searched through the pile for a tracksuit. I had so many clothes they formed quite an enormous pile in the middle of the room. John had always commented on how often I bought new clothes, but I did like to look nice and I had been lucky enough to inherit a decent figure, so why not make the most of it? Every now and again I had a blitz but the clothes I gave away soon got replaced with new ones. The good thing about this was that, whoever had pulled everything I owned out of the wardrobe would be pushed to recognise anything in particular.

I located the tracksuit. It was unlike anything else I possessed. It was bright pink and made of velour and had been a really cheap purchase from Primark. A few months before John had died we had been invited to a fancy dress party at a friends' house. After overcoming my initial reluctance on the 'chavs' theme, feeling it wasn't terribly politically correct, I entered into the spirit and bought this shocking pink tracksuit. I'd also bought a long hairpiece and some garish makeup and I found these on the bathroom floor, picking them out from the remnants of the bathroom cabinet which now covered the bath, the floor and also the toilet bowl. I stuffed all these things into the holdall.

I unearthed a pair of black sheepskin Ugg-style slippers which I also took, some massive hoop earrings and some pretend gold bangles. I looked on the floor near the bedside cabinet and picked up some discarded £20 notes. At least the person who'd done this hadn't stolen my money. I found about £200 altogether. I knew I'd need more and I knew I'd have to go to the bank to get it but I hoped my plan would allow for this. Finally, I found my passport on the living room floor and put that in the handbag, inside the holdall.

I studied what I was wearing in the bedroom mirror—this would do, they'd already seen me in these clothes and would be looking out for me. I was wearing leggings and a blue tunic dress. I changed my knee-length boots for a pair of shoes I didn't really like and took a breath. I hoped this would work. I had to disappear from view. I needed to buy some stuff to tide me over the next few days and I had to lose my tail in order to do so. I had shaken them off temporarily, and I hoped they'd be thinking the house was the best place to relocate me.

I looked out of the window. If somebody was outside waiting for me to come back home, in order for them to be absolutely sure they saw me enter the house they would have to stand at the front. They would either need to wait by the corner which led to Steep Hill or a little bit further down the lane on the other side of the house. I could walk to and from town either way, although I almost always walked past the cathedral and down Steep Hill just because it was more interesting. But they didn't know this. They would have no idea which way I would approach the house. There was nowhere to hide, if someone wanted to see me arrive they would have to leave themselves exposed. I prayed that they hadn't realised I had actually noticed I was being followed. I was hoping that they thought they'd just been unfortunate to lose me in the crowd. Because if that was the case, they wouldn't know I was home and would have to think that I'd come back to the house at some point.

And there he was, standing on the corner smoking a cigarette, looking for all the world as if he had just left the corner shop and was having a well-deserved smoke. On any other day, I wouldn't have given him a second look. It certainly wasn't uncommon for people to stand there, leaning against the wall, smoking. But I knew it was him. It was definitely the same guy I had seen peering into the shoe shop earlier. Good, I would take him by surprise when I left the house. I was fairly sure that he wouldn't realise I was inside; I had stayed well away from the windows and he would be expecting me to be walking back home. I gathered my things together, grabbing the holdall but leaving my coat behind. Then, taking a deep breath, I left the house.

10

I walked purposefully past my follower and didn't look in his direction. I wasn't sure if it was the right thing to do to pretend I hadn't noticed I was being followed or not, but it seemed the most sensible thing to me. I marched down Steep Hill for the third time that day and headed straight into town. There were no stops off this time; I strode into town as if I had things to do, my quick steps covering up the feeling of terror that was brewing inside me. Luckily it was a lovely sunny autumn day and I wasn't cold, especially as I marched along all the way into the city centre. It didn't take long, ten minutes or so, and on a day like this it would normally be a pleasurable walk. Today, however, I had things to sort out.

Firstly, I stopped off at the bank. I had no idea how much money I was going to need. I was rather hoping that I would take a quick trip to London, see

Stephen Ibbetson, and then this would all be sorted. I knew I couldn't go back home until I was sure that it was safe, though, and I knew that, after this, I wouldn't be able to withdraw any more cash without potentially giving my location away. I had to overestimate. So, I thought I'd play safe and withdrew £5000. Luckily the payment from John's pension had gone into the bank a couple of weeks' before, so I could spare the cash. I had to provide ID in the bank which necessitated rummaging through my holdall to find the passport in my handbag. It was hard not letting the panic that was rising in my throat take over. I tried to hide my leopard print handbag within the holdall and started worrying that my follower would notice. But when I looked over my shoulder he wasn't there. He had to be lurking outside waiting. I took a couple of deep breaths and handed over my passport.

I put the money in my handbag, inside my holdall. I put the strap of the holdall over my head and around my arm so that it couldn't easily be grabbed and walked out of the bank and into the sunlight. The guy was there, smoking another cigarette, lurking by the hotdog stand. I caught him out of the corner of my eye throwing his cigarette onto the ground and hurrying after me. I thought hard. I had my money, I had the notebook, but there were other things I needed and I had to throw him off. I'd got the plan in my head, but now I was going to have to put it into practice. So I steeled myself, took a deep breath and headed straight for Marks and Spencer.

I deliberately walked through the crowds and tried to blend in. He lost me briefly as I mingled with the people and headed for the stairs. I climbed the stairs and quickly glanced behind me. He was there, turning this way and that, and then he spotted me and came after me, pushing past the shoppers. I walked briskly across the first floor and down the escalator again to the ground floor. He came up the stairs just in time to see me disappear down the escalator at the other side of the store. I moved quickly, running down the escalator as fast as I could, and then darted into the changing rooms which were just around the corner from the escalator. I knew he hadn't seen me go in; I'd jumped off the escalator before he had appeared at the top. Luckily the lady at the entrance to the changing rooms, who should have asked me how many items I had, was turned away, and I ran past and into a cubicle where I shut the door.

"Hey!" She shouted after me. "Are you okay?" But I ignored her and kept quiet.

I very briefly looked at myself in the mirror before taking off my clothes. I thought I didn't look too bad for 42 – being about 5'5" and a slim size 8 helped. I'd left home with no make-up on and I quickly applied a little of a rather bronzy coloured foundation I'd got in a free promotion and only ever used once. I added my bright pink lipstick and blue eye shadow, before rubbing more rouge than necessary over my cheek bones. I pulled off my clothes as quickly as I could and put on the pink velour tracksuit, then scraped my hair up into a tight knot on the top of my head, securing it with a band. I attached the long hair piece, which matched my hair colour really well and I now looked as if I had almost waist-length hair. Pulling my hair back so severely changed the shape of my face a bit. It accentuated my cheekbones, which I plastered with a bit more rouge. I put the black sheepskin slippers on my feet, put on the large hooped earrings and fake gold bangles then looked in the mirror. I was almost unrecognisable. Certainly, if you were scanning a crowd and looking for me you would not have noticed that I was the same person who had run into the changing rooms earlier.

I stuffed my old clothes and shoes into the holdall along with the make-up and left it on the floor. Someone would find it later and assume it had been left by mistake. It would be taken to a lost property office for a while and then, eventually, taken to a charity shop or thrown away. I didn't really care. The tunic top was quite nice, but I'd had it a few years and the leggings were wearing out at the waist. The shoes I didn't really like anyway.

I sat on the bench in the changing room and unlocked my iPhone, copying down some of the important numbers. I picked up the leopard print handbag and double checked that the money and the notebook were safe. Taking a few deep breaths, I looked at myself once again in the mirror and then walked out of the changing rooms. I headed towards the exit via the food store and left the shop through the back entrance. I felt incredibly self-conscious, but nobody else took any notice and probably assumed I always dressed like that.

When I reached the outside world beyond the back door I stood by the wall for a while. After a couple of minutes the door opened. I thought my heart was about to explode as it began to hammer in my chest, but it wasn't my follower. An elderly couple came out. Then nothing. After another couple of minutes a very fat man came out. Nothing more. I breathed a sigh of relief. I'd shaken him off and I didn't believe for one second that he would look twice at the woman in the pink velour tracksuit. I took my iPhone out of the bag. It was fully charged and I turned off all the apps but left the phone on. I glanced around and saw just what I needed. Across the car park was a delivery van, its back door swung open, with the slogan 'We deliver to the four corners of the country, every day' painted down its side. Perfect. I walked around the back; the driver was nowhere to be seen. I hid the iPhone in the back of the van. The police had my mobile number and if someone in their ranks was trying to find out where I'd gone by tracking my phone that should throw them off the trail, at least for a while.

I walked back into the High Street, feeling nervous and forcing myself to not glance around and look for my assailant. I tried to act as nonchalantly as I could. I called in first at Boots. I bought a pair of scissors, deodorant, toothpaste, a toothbrush, some plastic food bags and some hair dye. Then I went up the High Street to CEX, a shop that bought and sold secondhand phones, electrical stuff, DVDs and so on. I looked at the tablets that they had for sale; they had some iPads, iPad minis, Samsungs and so on. I spent some time talking to the, very helpful, sales assistant, positioning myself so that I could see the door, just in case I needed to suddenly run or hide. In the end I bought a second-hand iPad. Maybe it was just my imagination but I thought I saw a look of suspicion cross his face when I paid in cash. But he took the money without saying anything.

The iPad was similar to my iPhone in terms of operating it so it wouldn't take me any time to get used to it. I had them set it up for me and show me the basics of how to access the Internet, email and so on. I knew I would have to be careful, and not link it to my iPhone in any way. I'd have to use the email via the Internet for example; I didn't want to run the risk of being traced even though I had dumped my precious iPhone. I also bought a cheap Sony Erikson phone. I got chargers for the phone and the iPad as well as some earphones. I then crossed the street and went into Black's and bought a rucksack, some trainers, socks, light trousers and tops, some pants, a zip-up jacket and two of the only type of bra they had which was a sports bra. I rushed back down the high street and called in at a phone shop to put £100 of credit on the phone.

I then walked hurriedly over to the Premier Inn, which was the nearest reasonable hotel I could think of, and booked myself into a room under my new pseudonym, Miriam Nathan.

11

As soon as I was in the room I flopped onto the bed. I had bought myself some time, thankfully, but I needed to move fast, so I forced myself upright, quelling any notion that I might be in danger, or should be scared. I made myself concentrate on what needed to be done. Firstly, I turned on the iPad and checked my Hotmail account.

From:
<s.ibbetson@lbhillingdon.gov.uk>
To: <Sugarandspice328@hotmail.com>
Hello Miriam,

It's interesting to hear from you. I have a slot at 2pm on Wednesday if you would like to meet then?

If you come to the Civic Centre in Uxbridge we can talk in my office. Just ask for me at reception and someone will come down to meet you.

Kind regards,
Stephen
Stephen Ibbetson
Assistant Director, Children's Specialist Services
London Borough of Hillingdon: Civic Centre: High Street: Uxbridge: Middlesex: UB8 1UW
Tel: 01895 254215

Wednesday, wow, that was tomorrow. He had to be quite keen to see me, I thought, I imagined being an Assistant Director to be quite a busy job. I rattled off a quick reply saying that I would see him at 2pm on Wednesday. That meant that I would have to travel to London in the morning so the next thing I did was open the Trainline page and look at train times. I almost booked online, but then realised that if whoever at the police had accessed my address was trying to trace me through debit card transactions that would give them an easy trail. Stupid. I needed to keep my wits about me. It would be more expensive but I'd have to turn up the following day and pay cash at the station. The 7.20am was a direct train from Lincoln so I resolved to get that one.

By now the light was beginning to fade. I got out the notebook and took some photos on my iPad of every page. I took photos of whole pages, close-ups of the writing, a photo of the outside of the book, the name and address, everything from every angle that I could possibly think of. Then I tore out a page from the back of the book and wrote everything down again on that, only all bunched together and mixed up. I folded the page several times so that it was tiny and zipped it into an inside pocket of the new jacket I'd bought. It was a pocket within a pocket. Just in case the iPad got stolen. I then put the original notebook in a plastic bag and wrapped it tightly. I put that bag into another bag, and that one into another. I wished I'd thought to buy some Sellotape but I hadn't so that would have to do.

I left the hotel still wearing my pink velour tracksuit. It was dusk and the traffic had slowed and the streetlights had come on. I scanned around carefully before crossing the road but I was sure that no one had seen me, or recognised me and I still had the dreadful make-up and pretend long hair. I walked across the road and down by the side of the river, past the Waterside Shopping Centre and along to the steps which led up from the river to the High Street. I bent down behind the steps, carefully checking that no one had seen me. It was almost dark and there was little light in that corner. If someone came down the steps from the High Street they wouldn't even notice me. If someone came the other way, from the river, they would but I'd have to pretend I was ill or drunk or something. I looked again, no one was coming so I had a good minute or so at least.

I tapped and pulled at a couple of bricks until I found a loose one and I carefully pulled it out. I put the notebook into the hole and then pushed the brick back into place. With the notebook flat against the back of the brick the difference in the level of the bricks was barely noticeable. They were all uneven and worn anyway; nobody had replaced the pointing for about three hundred years so there were several loose bricks. It had been a hiding place I'd used with a friend when we were young. We'd thought it was great fun to leave notes or little gifts for each other in turn, in a hiding spot that no one else knew about. Sometimes we would write the letters in code or in invisible ink so that if they were discovered they would stay secret. Sometimes we'd leave a map, or clues, or instructions to find something else and then hide a sweet or a chocolate bar in another location. No one ever seemed to find our notes then, and I was pretty sure no one would think about looking in that particular place for the notebook. I was still reluctant to leave it, though.

When I got back to the hotel I cut off all the price tags from my new clothes and put them in the rucksack. I left out a pair of pants, a bra, a pair of trousers and a long-sleeved top for the morning. They wouldn't be what I would normally wear, but they would be comfortable and they were very light and easy to carry around.

Then I took off the tracksuit and the hairpiece. I had a shower and washed my hair using the hotel toiletries. When I had finished in the shower I wrapped myself in a towel. I looked at myself in the mirror. I knew I would have to change my appearance if I could, as much as possible. If anyone was looking out for me they would be looking for someone with shoulder-length brown hair. I had to do something drastic. I wasn't going to get away with a hairpiece and terrible make-up for long. I looked at my face in the mirror. It wasn't a bad face; I'd often been described as attractive although having known every fault in it for so long I sometimes wasn't so sure. I wasn't model glamorous. But it was a face I lived with every day and I was quite pleased with how it looked. I could pass for several years below my actual age. I scraped my hair up and back once again into the ponytail, high on my head and turned my head upside down. I took the scissors and cut off my hair as close to the band as I could. When I took the band out I was amazed at the change in my face. There were a few strands longer than others which I evened out and, after cutting away at this bit and that, I was left with a reasonably neat pixie style hair-do. I'd never really liked my hair short, but looking in the mirror now, I thought it quite suited me.

I then took the hair bleach and dyed my hair blonde. I waited for the required 20 minutes before washing it off and whilst doing this I took out my new phone. It was clunky and difficult to navigate after my iPhone and I spent the 20 minutes familiarising myself with it and putting in the numbers I had copied from my iPhone. I managed to work out how to set the alarm, so I set that for 6am as I didn't want to miss the train in the morning. I rinsed off my hair and stood looking in the mirror whilst I blow dried it. I was amazed. Even I would have had difficulty recognising myself. The change was incredible. I was very pleased.

12

I got undressed and climbed into bed. I took out the iPad and re-read the email from Stephen Ibbetson. '*It's interesting to hear from you.*' *What does that mean? Interesting?* It sounded like he wasn't too surprised. I closed the iPad down, feeling a mixture of frustration but also an anticipation that going to London might, just, bring this thing to a close and enable me to return home to my house. My house. My heart sank as I thought about the ransacked place that I used to call home. I wouldn't be able to face going back to it and cleaning it all up on my own. I tried hard not to think about the broken photos, shattered memories of a life that had been taken from me only a few months ago. I was determined not to cry, not to sink because of this. I had to fight. I had to get to London and talk to Stephen Ibbetson. I'd decided not to actually take the notebook, for one thing I didn't want to lose it somewhere and for another I thought it was too dangerous. I'd check out this Ibbetson guy, see if he was the right Stephen and fill him in. If he needed the notebook it was in a safe place, and anyway, I had all the photos on my iPad containing the same information.

My mind kept racing back to the house. I fought back the tears. I was determined that whoever had done this was not going to beat me down; I couldn't give in. But I couldn't face going back to the house in the state it was in. I thought carefully about what I could do, what I could say to anyone about what had happened, and how I could make sure that nobody else got involved. I took out the new Sony Erikson and dialled my friend Robert. He answered on the second ring. Not a surprise - he was seldom more than a couple of feet away from his phone.

"Hello?" He clearly didn't recognise the number as it was a different phone.

"Robert, hi, it's me, Verity."

"Oh, hello, darling, how are you? Have you got a new phone?"

"Yes, I do. It's a long story. But... Look, Robert, I need you to do me a big favour."

"Ask away."

I decided to be a little economical with the truth "Well, I've been burgled."

"Oh! My Good Lord. Are you okay? Do you want us to come round?"

Robert Timpson had been a good friend of mine for years and together with his partner, Keith, and Collette of course, had scooped me up pretty well after

John's death. Collette and some of my other friends were amazing but most of them had kids now. Robert and Keith had been there whenever Collette had other commitments. They'd made me do normal things, and even made me laugh sometimes, gradually piecing me back together.

Robert and I had worked together years ago, but had always kept in touch and had remained good friends. I'd already met and married John at that point but Robert had just been coming to grips with his sexuality. When he'd met Keith and settled down a few years later, Keith too had become an integral part of our circle of friends. I knew I could rely on them but I didn't want them to get involved. There was clearly someone, if not more than one person, watching my house and they might not yet realise that I wasn't planning on returning anytime soon. I was sure they'd be keeping an eye on it for any signs of life. If anyone saw either Keith or Robert at the house they might assume they knew something and I really didn't want anything happening to either of them. I had to tread a careful line.

"I'm not at home at the moment. I've gone to stay with a friend. The house is a bit of a mess."

"Bless you, are you sure you're okay?"

"I'm fine, honestly, but I'm going to stay away for a few days. Listen, I was wondering if you could arrange for a cleaning firm to go in and sort everything out. I'll settle up when I'm back. It's too much of a mess for someone to do it alone, it needs professionals. Can you call someone and ask them to go round?"

"Of course, I'll supervise them myself. I'll make sure it's all spick and span for when you get back."

"Robert, there's something really important. I don't want to worry you, but the burglars were looking for something in particular and they didn't find it. It's really, really important that you don't go to the house. I don't want anyone seen at the house except a bunch of professional cleaners. Just ask them to pick up the spare key at yours and then let them go on their own."

At this Robert became quite distressed. He clearly wanted me to be safe and he wanted to make sure the cleaners were honest and did a good job. I managed, with some difficulty, to persuade him that it wasn't a good idea to go to the house right now. I hated not being honest with him, but what could I do? He was worried for my safety. And sanity probably, but we could cross that bridge later. If anyone was watching, they'd think it natural that I'd have the house cleaned up and, hopefully, wouldn't think they were involved in any way. I cajoled and persuaded and, exasperated, was on the verge of explaining the doctor's sticky end but luckily he came round and I didn't have to.

"Okay, okay, enough! You've persuaded me. Cross my heart and hope to die, I promise I won't go anywhere near. You take care, sweetheart." He was breathing heavily. "And let me know as soon as you're home."

"Rob, can you ask a locksmith to change the lock too?" I didn't know if I needed a new lock, they seemed to have just forced the front door open, but I was taking no chances. "Can you organise for the locksmith to put the keys in the key box? You know the code."

"Of course, and don't you worry about anything. I'll pay; we can settle up when you're back home."

"Thanks, Robert, give my love to Keith."

"Sweet dreams, sweetheart. Say 'hi' to Collette."

I didn't put him right when he assumed my 'friend' was Collette and not the Premier Inn. I turned off the phone, feeling a mixture of sadness at having to lead my friend on and relief that the house would be returned to something approaching normal when I got back. I knew everything would be in the wrong place, and I'd have to get new photo frames and probably new crockery too, but that would be the least of my worries.

I went back to the iPad and spent some time searching on the Internet for information that might relate to any of the acronyms in the notebook but drew yet more blanks. I kept returning to the photo of the page with the word 'Champion!' What did that refer to? I shook my head with frustration. I looked back at Ibbetson's email. '*It's interesting to hear from you.*' I played this over in my mind but couldn't really come to any firm conclusion.

It was then that I noticed his phone number. The last three digits were 215. That corresponded to one of the numbers in the first group of three digits listed in the notebook. I double checked the photos. It was definitely the same. Coincidence? But what use were the last three digits of a phone number? The rest had to be there somewhere. I scanned through the photos again. I looked at the set of longer numbers that had been a few pages further on. There were eight numbers in each list. Eight plus three made eleven. I counted how many numbers were in Stephen Ibbetson's phone number. Eleven. There had to be a match. I looked at all the numbers again but I couldn't find anything that corresponded. There was no way that any of the numbers in the second list would complete Ibbetson's number. I tried them backwards and scrambled but I could not make any of the second set of numbers correspond to the first three numbers. Maybe it was a coincidence that the number ended 215? There had to be many numbers, hundreds, possibly thousands that ended with that combination of numbers.

I gave up. I was absolutely shattered. I made a cup of tea using the tiny kettle provided and turned on the TV. I woke up at 4 in the morning with the TV still on and a half full cup of tea on the bedside cabinet beside me.

WEDNESDAY

-13-

I dozed for a bit, in and out of a fitful sleep; wondering how on earth I had landed in this mess, and missing the calm orderliness of my life. The alarm on my phone went off, although I was already awake so I didn't really need it, and I got up soon after. I showered then checked myself once again in the full-length mirror; I looked like some relative of mine. The short hair which, overnight, had developed a kind of spiky appearance and the bleached-blonde look, coupled with the sporty attire made me look like someone on the way to the gym. In truth I hardly ever went to the gym, although I did belong to one. I usually went for the sauna, though, not to actually exercise. Walking up and down Steep Hill kept me quite fit and I was lucky to have a relatively fast metabolism. It was freaky seeing this strange person staring back at me. The whole sporty, spikey appearance was so different and I was fairly sure that even people who knew me well would walk past me without a second glance.

I put on my zip-up jacket before picking up my rucksack and slinging it over my shoulder. I stuffed the pink velour tracksuit into a carrier bag along with the sheepskin slippers. I couldn't see that I would ever wear the tracksuit again but I quite liked the slippers. Still, they were too cumbersome to carry around with me; and they had needed replacing anyway. When I left the hotel there was no one at the reception desk so I left my key card on the desk and walked out. I dumped the carrier bag into a waste bin and found a coffee shop on a nearby corner which was open and, surprisingly, had a small queue of bleary-eyed commuters waiting. I joined the queue, got my usual large Americano and went and sat down. I grabbed The Times from the rack and read that whilst I waited. A steady stream of people came in and out of the café; I was surprised there were so many people up at that time of the morning. Where were they all going? Mostly to work I guessed. A lot of them had briefcases and seemed like businessmen and women grabbing a coffee to drink on the train.

At 7am I put the paper back where I had found it and then left and headed for the train station. I booked a first class ticket which, because I was buying it on the day, cost me well over £100 but a standard would have been £78 so I opted for sitting in relative comfort and quiet. I found a seat with a table and hoped that no one would come to join me. I wasn't in the mood for small talk. I glanced around nervously at my fellow travellers, but no one seemed to be taking any interest in me. Although I knew anyone would have to look quite closely to realise it was me, I felt suspicious of everyone. I didn't want to take any chances. I tried listening to people's phone conversations but no one was saying anything remotely interesting. There was a group of giggling middle-aged women who looked as if they might be on their way to a trip somewhere, maybe London for a show or to catch the Eurostar to Paris or something. They all seemed excited and one kept laughing really raucously. *Too much for this time of the morning.* I took my iPad and the charger out of my bag, plugged the charger in so that the iPad would stay fully charged and put my rucksack and jacket on the rack above the table. I had a bacon sandwich, some toast, copious cups of coffee and a muffin for breakfast. I hadn't realised how hungry I was, but then it dawned on me that, what with everything that had gone on, I had barely eaten the day before.

I arrived at Kings Cross at almost 9.30, having spent much of the train journey puzzling over the photos of the notebook, still none the wiser. I had briefly spent some time doing the Sudoku in the free copy of The Times but I had found it hard to concentrate. Luckily it hadn't been a particularly challenging one. I walked across the road from the station and headed down Gray's Inn Road. I booked into a small hotel not too far from the station, once again using the name Miriam Nathan. I booked in for a night and paid up front with some of the cash that I had, hoping that I would get things sorted at my meeting with Stephen Ibbetson and be able to head straight back home the following day.

Luckily, they had a room ready. It was on the fifth floor so I took the lift. It was quite small but it had everything I needed. There was a small recess behind the door, of about a foot or so, with a hook for coats and a small fixed box for putting your bag on. From the door there was a corridor of about five feet leading to the bedroom. There was no need to put a card into a slot to operate the lights, which I liked; I could leave the lights on when I left the room. Off the corridor on the right was a bathroom with a small bath with a shower over and all the usual toiletries. Walking down past this you came to the bed area which opened out to the right at the end of the small corridor. The bed was a king size with an iron frame and there were small bedroom tables with lamps on them at either side of the bed.

I sat down on the bed and got out my iPad. I figured out the route I would need to take to Uxbridge later. According to Transport for London, it would take about 45 minutes on the tube. Uxbridge was the very last stop on the Metropolitan line, but I could pick it up at Kings Cross which meant no changes. I looked at my phone, it was now 10.30. I wanted to arrive in Uxbridge by 1.30 at the latest to give me time to orient myself. Google maps informed me that the London Borough of Hillingdon Civic Centre was only a 5 minute walk from the station. I switched to street view – the Civic Centre looked quite an impressive building, all red brick but an interesting design. I'd sooner get there early and have to have a coffee somewhere than risk being late. I could not afford to miss this meeting. So, I decided to get to the station by midday in order to be doubly sure that I'd get there on time. That gave me an hour and a half and, as there was little else I could do before meeting Ibbetson I decided to go for a walk.

I hadn't picked the most picturesque area of London to stay, and it wasn't an area I was very familiar with. Normally, when John and I had come down to London for a show, or a weekend break visiting art galleries and museums we'd stayed in the centre, somewhere near the British Museum. I gathered up my iPad and phone and put them in my rucksack, made sure I had everything safe, put on my jacket then headed out.

I grabbed the 'Do not disturb' notice and put it over the handle on the outside of the door. I didn't know why, but I always did this when I left hotel rooms. Perhaps I just thought it would make a rogue staff member think twice before entering the room with a thought to steal something. It didn't really matter in this instance that I had left absolutely nothing in the room, apart from my toothbrush and toothpaste which they were welcome to, it was more a case of old habits die hard. As I closed the door, the notice blew up and caught upside down in the door. I opened the door and reclosed it but the same thing happened. I left the notice trapped upside down.

-14-

I turned left out of the hotel and walked for about 5 minutes before turning left again and wandering through some streets, and past some parks before ending up on Clerkenwell Road. It had all become incredibly trendy since the last time I had been there which, granted, was probably twenty years before. It was full of über-trendy furniture stores filled with white cabinets and colourful, strangely-shaped chairs. There were estate agents with flats for sale for £2million and lots of incredibly swish cafes. I walked around Clerkenwell for a while and then headed towards Farringdon. I wandered north up the Farringdon Road, turning off occasionally and then turning back at the next junction just seeing what was around. I pulled out my phone and checked the time. It was 11.30 so I started walking more purposefully up the Farringdon Road and towards King's Cross. My stomach was tying itself in knots – a little bit of excitement mixed with a little bit of trepidation. I hoped that by meeting Stephen Ibbetson I would be able to quickly return to my normal routine. But I wasn't really sure what to expect and I didn't have a clear strategy, other than to see how it went. '*Trust no one.*' I had to be cautious.

I found the right platform for the Metropolitan line, bought a trashy magazine at a W.H. Smith and a cup of coffee from a Costa stand and waited for the train. At midday the train was not too busy and I easily found a seat. I flicked through the magazine I'd bought. There were pictures of celebrities I didn't know, articles about TV programmes I didn't watch and stories about film stars I knew of but didn't really care about. I read about high-street fashion and laughed inwardly at some of the pictures of 'fashionable' members of the public dressed in outrageous, clashing clothes. *Good to be an individual.* I glanced at an article on hair styles. Apparently, the pixie cut was 'in'. I glanced at my unfamiliar reflection in the train window and wondered if my self-administered haircut would count as fashionable. I somehow doubted it.

It was almost one o'clock when I emerged from Uxbridge station. I wandered down the High Street and into the shopping centre. I went into a café upstairs in one of the Department stores, which looked out over the entrance to the Civic Centre on the other side of the road. I ordered a coffee and a ham and cheese toastie and sat in the window watching the people coming and going. It was a busy place. People with identity badges hanging around their necks came in and out, mostly to stand on the pavement and have a cigarette, chatting to colleagues before heading back inside. A whole host of other people – couples, families with small children, older people – came and went. Some disappeared and I never saw them again, but others entered and re-emerged within a few minutes. Everybody busy going about their business.

At 1.50 I walked across the road and into the reception. I was given a 'visitor' pass and asked to wait in a room through some double doors. I sat on a chair watching BBC news 24 on a TV on the wall. The sound was turned down and there were no subtitles. The headlines were scrolling past along the bottom of the screen but I had to guess what the newsreaders were talking about. It seemed a pretty futile exercise to have it there really, with no sound or subtitles. Pictures of unrest somewhere played on the screen, with rebels and government forces firing weapons at each other and civilians running for cover. *Nothing changes.* I watched the silent images and then after a few minutes Stephen Ibbetson appeared. I recognised him instantly from his staff photo. He was shorter than I'd expected, about 5'9" or 5'10" and also fitter; he clearly worked out. He was wearing a suit with an open-necked shirt and tan coloured shoes. The suit looked reasonably expensive but was a bit tired and worn.

He smiled and held out his hand. He had a cheery, friendly face with creases appearing around his eyes as he smiled.

"Miriam, good to meet you," he said as I shook his hand.

It took me a while to register my pretend name and I hoped he didn't notice my hesitation. "Likewise," I replied.

We walked to the lifts and he pressed the button for floor 4. When we emerged it became apparent what a bizarrely designed building the Civic Centre was. The sign on the wall near the lift said 'Centre Core'. We walked along the edge of a room marked 'East' full of busy people sitting at desks. To our left was another room full of busy people, but at a half-room level lower. It was all open plan and the people would have seen our feet walking past but not our top half. Also visible to our left was a room a half level higher, but you couldn't really see much of this as it was above head level. Weird. We turned a corner and along the edge of another identical open-plan room, this one marked 'North', and it also had the strange half-level rooms to one side. We then went down a few steps and into a small office. Stephen Ibbetson held open the door and gestured for me to go inside.

"Can I get you a drink? Coffee? Tea?"

"Just a glass of water would be good, if that's okay?" I'd had enough coffee to float a boat and couldn't face another.

He went off to get a glass of water, and I sat down. My legs started to shake and my mouth became dry. I didn't know how to play this. I suddenly felt completely out of my depth. I didn't want to give too much away too soon, so I needed to play it a bit safe. The doctor had implored me to find this man, although I wasn't really sure why yet, but the words '*trust no one'* resonated through my head like a beat on a drum. *Trust no one, trust no one.* I was reserving judgement.

15

Stephen Ibbetson came back into the room, carrying two plastic cups full of water. He put them down on the desk and closed the door, before sitting down at the opposite side of the desk and smiling his crinkly-faced smile again. After the usual niceties about the weather, the tube journey and the relative merits and demerits of public transport, his smile dropped and a more serious look clouded his face.

"So, tell me, you have had some dealings with Dr Neasden?"

"Yes, he asked me to come and visit you."

"I see." He smiled again. "In relation to…?"

I lied. "He told me about the work you were doing together." They must have had dealings with each other, so I thought the term 'work' would cover a range of options and I was hoping for the best.

"The paper?"

Writing a paper together, of course, an academic exercise. "Yes. I think he thought you might be able to help me out."

"Help you out, in what way? What do you do then?"

I remembered about Dr Neasden's work with those who had no recourse to public funds. *Quick, Verity, think of a lie, a lie, a believable lie. Shit, shit, shit.*

I carried on without a blink. A smile. "Yes, I work at the local college in Lincoln and we have some young people who needed help. That's how I met Dr Neasden." Well, part of that was true. A lie is easier to maintain, surely, if it is based in truth. I surprised myself at how believable I sounded. And Dr Neasden, unfortunately, was no longer around to refute the point that we had met in those circumstances.

"And why did Dr Neasden suggest you came to see me?"

"He thought you might be able to help." *I'm being too vague, I've already said that.* I decided to take a leap – if he was writing a paper on something, whatever it was, he had to know something about the subject. "You being something of an expert in the field; he said you were highly regarded." *Careful, Verity, don't push it.* But flattery will get you everywhere.

A tilt of the head in recognition of the compliment. "Yes, well, with Heathrow in our patch, becoming an expert is, unfortunately, something that is hard to avoid. It's a relatively common occurrence and some of the children and young people—" He paused. "And vulnerable adults too, who are brought to this country are subject to terrible abuses. Well"—he looked off to his left—"I'm sure you've read about some of the cases in the newspapers." He arched an eyebrow, and I thought he was going to carry on, but he just stopped.

I nodded. He was making an assumption that I knew what the paper was on. My mind whirred and I hoped he couldn't see me trying to figure it out as we spoke. I had to keep up the pretence or I thought he'd stop talking to me. He thought I knew more than I did. *Think. Heathrow, children and adults being brought into the country. Dr Neasden's voluntary work. Shit. I was reading about this the other day. What is it called? What is it called when people are brought here against their will, or under some pretence?* Trafficking. I dragged the word up from the back of my brain somewhere. It suddenly dawned on me. He was talking about trafficking and he thought I knew something about what they had been working on. Or what Dr Neasden had been working on, at least. *Should I mention the notebook?* I thought about this, quickly, before carrying on. I still couldn't remember if Dr Neasden had asked me to talk to Ibbetson or take the notebook to him. What I could remember was the desperate '*trust no one'.* I decided discretion was the better part of valour, and I carried on; I was in enough shit as it was, I couldn't afford to dig myself into more danger by being indiscrete.

I had read about cases of trafficking in the newspapers; it was only a couple of weeks ago that some poor young woman from Romania, or Bulgaria, or somewhere had been rescued from a family after years spent as a domestic slave since she had been brought here aged about ten.

"Would it be possible to see the paper you were working on?" I asked.

He straightened up in his chair. He suddenly seemed cautious, almost suspicious. "It's confidential, I'm afraid. Still in draft form. There's plenty of stuff on trafficking on the Internet if you want generic information. I'm not quite sure how Dr Neasden thought I could help."

I'd pushed it a bit, and he was closing up. I paused. He seemed to suddenly realise he had sounded defensive and he instantly loosened up once more. That smile again.

"The young people at your college. Where are they from?"

A stab in the dark. "Eastern Europe." Time to bite the bullet, I thought. "Dr Neasden said you could help and now he's dead. And I'm not sure what to do now."

He stared back off to the side. "That's very sad, I agree. Dr Neasden and I had worked closely together for some time. He was a good man; very dedicated to helping people that no one had ever bothered to help. Not everybody wants to help people who are brought to this country, or realises that they are often made to come, against their will. A lot of people would prefer to punish them for being here in the first place." He stopped and looked up at me. That hint of suspicion had come back. "The work that Dr Neasden did wasn't popular with a lot of people. We'd published a couple of papers together but they weren't universally applauded." He paused again, softened. He returned his gaze to the table. "But I didn't realise he'd died until I got your email. When did it happen?"

It seemed like about three years' ago. "Monday," I said.

He appeared a little surprised, so I went on, "Mr Ibbetson, Dr Neasden pointed me in your direction and now he is dead. I don't know what to do, so I've come to you as he suggested. It's more than the young people at the college." I decided I had to lay a few of my cards on the table. "On Monday Dr Neasden was murdered. Shot in his home. He told me to find you."

A shift. I noticed a shift in his eyes, it was subtle and he tried to hide it. I guessed it was the shock – he clearly hadn't known that Dr Neasden had been murdered. He closed up again.

"I'm really sorry, Miriam, but I don't know what I can do to help."

Miriam; the pretend me with the blonde spiky hair and new found ability to lie through her teeth. "I was there just after Dr Neasden was shot. I tried to keep him alive but I couldn't."

Ibbetson said nothing, just shook his head.

I carried on, "I gave a statement to the local police."

I wasn't getting anywhere. I sighed. I couldn't go home, this was nowhere near solved. I thought about the notebook, the acronyms, the fact that I had got Ibbetson's name from the notebook. He hadn't mentioned anything about it and so neither did I. I still had the notebook and somebody badly wanted it but I decided to play a bit dumb. I needed to get things sorted, and I desperately wanted to go back home, but I wanted to do that alive and, it seemed, that someone or some people would do anything to get their hands on the information I had, even though I had no idea what it all meant. '*Trust no one.*'

"Mr Ibbetson, after Dr Neasden suggested I came to see you he was murdered and then my house was turned upside down. I have absolutely no clue why that was." Okay, not strictly true but Miriam seemed quite good at maintaining a lie. "But I followed his advice and came down to see you. I'm worried about what this is all about." I paused. "I'm worried for my safety and I don't know what to do. Why do you think he asked me to come and see you?"

He was still silent. Lost in thought. The smile had gone and had been replaced by a glum stare off to his left.

"Please, please help me. The only people who knew where I lived after Dr Neasden's death were the police. I can't go to them. I think someone in the police used the information in my statement to come to my house."

His gaze shifted back to mine. He looked profoundly sad. I felt for him; if he and Dr Neasden had worked closely together it had to have been a big shock to find out he had been murdered. It also dawned on me that perhaps he was worried for his own safety, if this was anything to do with the paper he and Dr Neasden had been writing.

"I work very closely with the police here in London, the National Trafficking Unit." He raised his eyebrows and gesticulated towards his computer as if to indicate where the information he needed was held. "I can put you in touch with a good policeman. I could arrange for you to meet and you can explain your situation. He might be able to help make sure you're safe when you get home. This has nothing to do with you, right? You weren't involved in Dr Neasden's death in any way?"

"Absolutely not."

"Then there's no reason for you to not go home and be safe. If the local police are using information in a way that they shouldn't, this guy will be able to help, I'm sure. He'll make sure they're exposed."

I nodded. "Can you email me the details? You've got my email address." I was beginning to feel as if my much-hyped meeting with Ibbetson had turned into a crushing anti-climax.

"Sure. Where are you staying?" The smile was back. A sense of self-assurance had crept back into Stephen Ibbetson's demeanour. He stood up and opened the door.

"Over near King's Cross." I hoped that was vague enough. I wasn't about to give my location away to anyone.

We walked to the lift together. I would never have found the way out of that maze of a building by myself. Everywhere looked exactly the same. It felt like something out of a Kafka book. I wondered how on earth the people who worked here knew where they were. At the lift we said our goodbyes and shook hands.

"Good luck," he said. "You'll be fine, don't worry."

16

I left the Civic Centre and turned onto Uxbridge High Street. The weather had shifted whilst I'd been inside and I shivered in the cold. I crossed the road and went into the shopping centre, dipping into Dorothy Perkins to pick up a scarf. As I looked at the display, the red tartan one caught my eye, but I decided instead on a plain grey. I didn't want to be wearing anything distinctive. I also bought a grey woolly hat, partly to keep out the cold – my neck was feeling it since I'd cut my hair – but also in case I needed to cover up my blonde hair at any point. A grey hat would blend into a crowd nicely. I paid in cash and headed for the tube station.

I spent the 45 minutes heading back to King's Cross deep in thought. Dr Neasden and Ibbetson had been working on a paper to do with trafficking. Child trafficking I assumed given Ibbetson's position; I didn't really know much about the crime, apart from what I'd read in the newspapers. I knew that people had been brought into the country to work as domestic slaves, as prostitutes, and as pick-pockets but that information was well known. Would it be worth killing someone over? It didn't make any sense. I thought of the people involved in bringing the people into the country and spiriting them away when they arrived. Perhaps Dr Neasden had been about to expose someone? Perhaps there was someone fairly high-profile involved? Would someone kill so that they weren't brought to justice? People had killed for less, I thought. I had a sinking feeling that, rather than things resolving themselves after my visit to Ibbetson, they had become more complicated. I was desperately disappointed. Nothing was resolved, far from it. I didn't want to be in the middle of all this. It had absolutely nothing to do with me. But I knew that I couldn't extricate myself from it now. I felt helpless and, not for the first time, out of my depth. Hopefully, meeting Ibbetson's police friend would give me a way to get back home and back to normality.

I wasn't quite sure why I hadn't mentioned the notebook to Ibbetson. It just hadn't felt right, somehow. He didn't seem aware of it, and if it had to do with the paper they were working on then surely Ibbetson would have asked about it? He had become a little guarded when I'd asked him if I could see the paper. But surely if he knew there was an important notebook around he would have, at least, alluded to it. Perhaps Neasden had wanted me to show it to Ibbetson and he would have been the right person to deal with whatever information it contained, but it just didn't seem that way. I was sure I'd done the right thing. Ibbetson had seemed nice enough and maybe I was being a bit too careful. Dr Neasden had wanted me to find Ibbetson, which I had now done but he had told me to trust no one. He hadn't said trust no one but Ibbetson. I thought back to Dr Neasden's blood-soaked body, the bullet wound, the impassioned look on his face. No, I couldn't be too careful.

When I got back to King's Cross it was almost 5pm so I walked straight to the hotel and took a shower. I dried my hair with the hotel hairdryer, getting used to my appearance in the mirror now. I grabbed my rucksack, jacket, scarf and hat, then headed out to find some dinner. As I pulled the door closed the 'Do not disturb' notice did its flippy thing and ended up trapped in the door again. This time I didn't even bother to try to untrap it.

I walked for about ten minutes before finding a lovely pub-cum-restaurant and I ordered a large glass of rioja and some fish and chips. Whilst I was waiting for my dinner, I fired up the iPad and checked my emails. Nothing yet from Ibbetson. The rest of the inbox of my Hotmail account was full of junk because it was the address I always gave when I knew I would be bombarded with offers and unsolicited crap. When my fish and chips arrived I ate them slowly whilst browsing the online daily papers and catching up on national and international news. Nothing of note really; uprisings in the Middle East, protests about government cuts: it was all becoming a bit predictable. When the waitress came to take my plate away I ordered another glass of wine.

I Googled 'trafficking' and was amazed at how many results I got; well over 40 million. That would take some sifting through. I concentrated initially on the hits that were more specific to child trafficking, as that seemed most likely to be Ibbetson and Dr Neasden's focus. I then scanned a few bits here and there, not reading anything in depth. People were trafficked for all sorts of reasons, sexual slavery being the most common. People were also trafficked for the removal of kidneys for kidney transplants or for use as a surrogate. Children were trafficked for child pornography. Jesus. Could Dr Neasden's work have had anything to do with that kind of thing? I couldn't understand why he would keep a separate notebook, though, if he was writing a paper about it. Perhaps he was working on something that Ibbetson didn't know about? That would make sense. Ibbetson had seemed shocked to hear of Neasden's murder. Although why would he have implored me to talk to Ibbetson? Maybe he was the only person Neasden thought would be able to figure it out. Maybe I should have told him about the notebook. I was going round in circles and getting nowhere. I went back to the Google search.

According to Wikipedia the human trafficking industry was worth $32billion per year. *Bloody hell.*

But there were whole areas of the police dedicated to dealing with trafficking, and they were all well aware of the sort of activity that took place. Why hadn't Dr Neasden reported what he was working on to the police? Maybe he had tried the local police. I knew there had to be some corruption there because of them using my address details. But why not go through Ibbetson to the Met? If the people were coming through Heathrow, as Ibbetson had suggested, that would make more sense. I was getting lost trying to think about it all.

My thoughts were interrupted by the 'bling' sound that signified an email had arrived. I opened Hotmail.

> *From:* <StephIbb54@gmail.com>
> *To:* <Sugarandspice328@hotmail.com>
> *Miriam,*
> *My colleague Sam Charlton, DI will meet you at the Urban Kitchen on Farringdon Road at 7.30pm tomorrow.*
> *Good luck*
> *Stephen*

He'd sent it from his personal email address not work. I had a look on Google maps—the Urban Kitchen was only fifteen minutes' walk from my hotel. I sent a quick email back acknowledging receipt.

I packed up my belongings and walked back to the hotel. I booked in for tomorrow night and was told I could keep the same room. I paid cash up front and no, I still didn't want to use a card to set up an account. If I had any extras I'd pay for them as I went. I took the lift up to my room on the 5th floor and cleaned my teeth, got undressed and went straight to bed.

THURSDAY

17

I didn't wake up until 10am on Thursday morning. It was light outside although it was dull and windy. I quickly showered and got dressed, then took my rucksack and left, leaving the 'Do not disturb' sign in its usual upside down position. It was chilly out and several degrees colder than it had been recently, I zipped my jacket up under my chin and pulled my scarf tightly around my neck. I fished out the grey hat and pulled it over my ears. I walked up to the Euston Road and found an Internet café where I could browse and print stuff if I wanted to.

I started by Googling Detective Inspector Sam Charlton who, surprisingly I thought, had a LinkedIn account. I knew, or suspected, it was the right guy as I didn't think there could be that many Sam Charlton's working for the Met, although the profile didn't mention that he worked for the Human Trafficking

Unit. I couldn't view the full profile as I only had the free version and I wasn't 'connected' to him, but the short version had a photo showing a forty-something attractive black man. He had worked for the Metropolitan Police for 20 years. Apart from that there was little information. I looked at the Met website but they didn't have information on individual members. That wasn't a surprise I supposed.

I moved on. I did another search of information about trafficking.

I found a recent report from the Children's Society called *Still at Risk: A review of support for trafficked children.* I printed off the full report.

I had a brief look at the United Nations report *Global Report on Trafficking in Persons* but decided not to print it as it had been written in 2009 and there was a lot more recent stuff.

I printed off Andrew Boff's 229 page tome *Shadow City: Exposing human trafficking in everyday London* as it was both recent and local.

Lastly I printed off the *Second report of the Inter-Departmental Ministerial Group on Human Trafficking.*

Then I googled 'Neasden and Ibbetson trafficking' and I found a reference to a previous paper they had written in 2011. It had been entitled *Child victims of trafficking: victims, not illegal immigrants.* I could only read the excerpt, though, as it had been published in a journal that had to be subscribed to to read. However, the brief told me little more than the other papers I'd printed off, and I noticed that some of the citations were in the reports that I'd been able to access, so I hoped that if there was anything significant it would be summarised in them. I paid up for all my printing and put it into my rucksack.

Next, I found a Phones4U shop and bought another pay-as-you-go phone. I wasn't quite sure why but I just wanted to be really careful and also have some options. I stuck to the same model Sony Erikson so I knew how to use it. Once outside the shop, I sat down on a bench and copied the few numbers I had across from the old phone to the new one. I took the battery and SIM card out of the old one and put them in my rucksack. Then I walked down to the British Library and found a spot to sit and read through everything. I made notes on my iPad as I went, and although I wasn't sure how it might be relevant to my current situation, by 2pm that afternoon I had learnt an awful lot.

I had learned that nobody seemed to know exactly how many victims there were due to the hidden nature of the crime but certainly there are many victims of human trafficking in the UK, with around a quarter of these being children.

I also now knew that many of the child victims, if they are found, are placed in care, but they often go missing from their care homes due to being scared or being coerced by the people who brought them into the country. Others are met by people who will spirit them away for whatever purposes they want. Some of the young people who had been interviewed for the research gave reports of feeling terrified and suspicious of everyone.   Often, they said, nobody properly explained to them what was happening. I thought about these poor young souls without anyone to care for them, being used for sexual servitude, or working on cannabis farms or undertaking other illegal activity. Many said that they were brought to the country with promises of jobs or an education or had been forced to come here to work to pay off debts that their family owed and which they will never be able to repay. Some of the young people they had talked to had escaped but then had run back to the people who had been maltreating them. They believed that they had nowhere else to go.

According to the various reports and charity estimates there are between one million and 27 million victims of trafficking worldwide. The government report I read stated that there were an estimated almost 2,600 victims of trafficking in the UK. Non-Government Organisations working with the victims of trafficking in the UK stated that this estimate is a tip of the iceberg. Yet according to Boff's report there were only 18 convictions across London for trafficking offences in 2012-13 and this had been the most for the last three years.

18

I was hungry when I left the British Library and feeling empty and sad after reading so many horror stories. I walked across the road and found an Eat cafe to sit in and bought a slice of carrot cake, a banana and a cup of coffee, taking them off to sit down on a spare sofa. I took out my iPad once again and looked at the photos of the cryptic numbers. I tried to imagine what Dr Neasden would have been thinking if he'd wanted to keep a few key phone numbers but didn't want them being instantly recognised.

I spent some time trying to work out how he might have hidden the numbers within his notebook. He clearly had written the last three digits separately. I decided to try to work on the principle that Ibbetson's number was definitely here, somewhere, and that I might as well spend the next couple of hours trying to figure it out. I didn't have much else to do. I wouldn't be in a worse position if I couldn't find it. And if I could I might well have two other phone numbers to give me a clue as to what this was all about. I realised with a sinking feeling of dread, that I wasn't going to be able to rely on Ibbetson or anyone else to get me out of this mess and that I probably needed to do something myself. So, working on my principle that Ibbetson's number was in here somewhere meant that it had to be written in some sort of a code; at least the first part of the number. Dr Neasden, I guessed to try to make them look less like phone numbers, had split the numbers into two lists. Well, that had worked. I hadn't realised they were phone numbers until I had actually seen Ibbetson's number and realised that the last three digits were the same as one of the numbers in the list. In fact, I wasn't 100% convinced still, but that didn't fit with my principle so I soldiered on.

If I was going to be working out a code I figured that it would be easier to do this with a proper pen and paper rather than on the iPad, although it did occur to me that, if I knew where to look, there was probably an app for that somewhere out there in the ether. I finished off my cake and walked a little further down Euston Road until I found a small newsagent's shop. I bought a small spiral bound pad and a couple of ball-point pens and took them off in search of somewhere to sit. I found another café, ordered another coffee and sat down to think. I opened up the photos of the numbers and copied them into the notepad.

I started work; if the last three numbers of Ibbetson's phone number were 215, I had to find the beginning of the number in amongst the three numbers in the first list, the list where the numbers had eight digits. I knew that none of the numbers corresponded to the actual phone number, even when I had tried scrambling them up, so I had to assume that they were in some kind of code. I guess that this would have given a bit of added security as the formula for phone numbers with the '01' or '07'prefix is fairly easy to spot. I imagined that it wouldn't need to be a hard code, just enough to prevent the list looking like a list of phone numbers. And as they all began with a different number I assumed that, once coded, the numbers had been shuffled around a bit, so I would need to figure that one out too. That would obviously be easier if I could work out which of the three was the code for Ibbetson's number.

Okay, so I started with the first eight digits of Ibbetson's phone number 01895259. I sorted out these eight numbers into a list.

99

55

8

1

2

0

Then I looked at the three coded numbers and wrote them out in similar lists so that I could compare.

00	88	99
9	77	33
7	9	66
3	5	2
6	2	1
4	0	
8		

That told me that the coded number for Ibbetson was 72709588 as it was the only one with two sets of double digits and 4 single digits. I looked at all the lists. The only number common to all the numbers was '9'. So, 9 must correspond to 0. All the numbers would have to start with a 0. So I began my decoder.

Real   code

0   =   9

It was a start.

Next I knew that either 9 or 5 in the real number had to be equal to 8 in the code and either 9 or 5 in the real number had to be equal to 7 in the code. Ibbetson's number contained two 9s and two 5s and the coded number contained two 8s and two 7s. I started with what I knew, $0 = 9$, so how did you get from 0 to 9? That looked like it could be a fairly simple manoeuvre. If you looked at the numbers as if they were on a circle you could minus 1 and 0 would equal 9. That would be a really simple code, just moving back one each time. Would that work for the other numbers? It would for 9, if that was equal to 8. Nine minus one equals 8. But that would mean that 5 would have to equal 7 and even with my limited maths I knew that 5 minus one didn't equal 7.

I tried all sorts of ways of getting from 5 to 7. Add two. That didn't work for getting 9 to 8 though. I could double 5; $5 \times 2 = 10$ then minus 3. But if I did the same sum with 9 it came to 15.

Okay, I thought I'd try it from a different angle. What if it was 5 that became 8 in the code? How could I get from 5 to 8? Well, I could double it; $5 \times 2 = 10$ and take away two to equal 8. Or I could minus one; $5 - 1 = 4$ and double that and that would also equal 8. That was essentially the same sum. Would that work for getting 9 to 7? $9 \times 2 = 18$ then $18 - 2 = 16$. Hmmm. Sixteen didn't fit the code at all. And you couldn't have two digits replacing one. But what if I added those two together to get back to one number?

1+6, that would equal 7. And doing the sum the other way, got me the same result 9 − 1 = 8 then 8 x 2 = 16 and 1 + 6 = 7. But the 0 presented a problem. 0 x 2 = 0 and even if I went back two from 0 on a cycle I'd come to 8 and not 9. I tried it the other way. 0 − 1 would equal 9 on the continuous cycle. 9 x 2 = 18. Then if I added 1 + 8 that brought me back to 9.

I smiled. I had it. I did the same sum with all the numbers from 0-9 until I had the finished code and I added them all to my list.

Real		Code
0	=	9
1	=	0
2	=	2
3	=	4
4	=	6
5	=	8
6	=	1
7	=	3
8	=	5

9 = 7

It was a simple code, but effective. The coded numbers did not end up being sequential but the sums all produced a different code for each number. I compared my code to Ibbetson's number and also the way it had been written in the notebook. I wrote them one above the other.

0	1	8	9	5	2	5	9
REAL							

9	0	5	7	8	2	8	7
CODED							

7	2	7	0	9	5	8	8
SCRAMBLED							

I looked and my heart sank a bit. Because of the double numbers, the order of scrambling could be done in a few different ways. The first seven could have been moved from the end of the number or the middle. There was no way of knowing. That would mean when I decoded the other numbers there would be several potential scrambled combinations. I'd end up with a list of *possible* numbers rather than two definite ones. More work.

19

I packed everything away again in my rucksack, feeling a little depressed both about the amount of work I would need to do to decode the phone numbers and also about the plight of trafficking victims. I headed back to the hotel. I showered and changed into clean clothes. The clean clothes were almost identical to the ones I'd taken off, but at least I felt cleaner. You didn't have to walk around London for long without feeling as if you were covered in grime and dirt.

I thought about the person I was going to meet. Ibbetson had introduced us. Ibbetson had been Dr Neasden's research partner and had been the person he had implored me to contact. But a policeman? Would the police in Lincolnshire have contacted the Met? No, I didn't think so; I didn't think they knew I was down here for a start. Could the Met be involved in whatever it was Dr Neasden had uncovered? Again, I didn't think so, but I couldn't be sure. The Met seemed to be involved in lots of trafficking related issues, but if whatever Neasden had been working on had anything to do with the London police, I thought Ibbetson would have been aware of it, and he didn't seem to be. Unless he was bluffing? He could have been. But I hadn't had the sense that he was. To be honest, I hadn't had the feeling that Ibbetson would have been bright enough to have bluffed about it. He had given no hint that he knew anything about the notebook. He hadn't asked if I had anything that belonged to Dr Neasden or tried to make me give him any information. He'd seemed shocked. Shocked at Dr Neasden's death and shocked at what, perhaps, he might be involved in by proxy. Perhaps he was worried for his own safety?

I decided that, if I wanted to get home and leave all this behind me then I really only had one option and that was to go and meet this Detective Inspector. I hadn't actually done anything wrong, and if he was involved? Well, I thought I would have to deal with that when it arose. I would have to take my chances. What was the alternative? To stay in a hotel in London forever, afraid to go home?

I left the hotel at about 7.20, knowing that it would take me fifteen minutes to get to the Urban Kitchen and hoping that DI Sam Charlton would get there first. I closed the door, smiled at the upside down 'Do not disturb' notice and walked briskly down to the pub.

I recognised DI Charlton straight away from his LinkedIn profile picture, although his hair had grown quite a bit since then. In his picture he'd had a really short buzz cut, now he had inch-long dreadlocks covering his head. He was tall, about six feet, and slim. I walked up to him. He smiled as I approached – Ibbetson must have described me to him and he clearly recognised the description. He had a broad smile and he tilted his head back as I approached.

"Miriam?" He held out his hand.

"DI Charlton?"

"The same," he said. "But, please, call me Sam." He gestured towards the bar. "Want a drink?" He was holding a pint of beer. The fact that it was almost full told me that he hadn't arrived long before I had. He was wearing a suit; I couldn't tell in the dimly lit pub whether it was dark blue or black, but I could tell it was reasonably good quality. He wore a pale blue striped shirt with silver cufflinks and a red tie which he was loosening. He removed it from round his neck and put it in his pocket before undoing the top button of his shirt.

"Red wine, please; a small rioja if they have it."

He signalled for me to go and sit down. I found a table in the corner, with a wall behind one seat and a window behind the other. The windows were mostly obscured by the window boxes outside which contained still-flowering geraniums and overflowing ivy. It was an old-school pub with a polished wooden floor and bar. Wooden bar stools lined the edge of the bar and little brass hooks hung beneath the bar for hanging your coat on. The tables were like old style kitchen tables and with an assortment of leather-lined chairs pushed up against them, some of which had lost their stuffing a long time ago. There was a blackboard on one wall with 'today's menu' written in a fancy chalk script, and a log fire midway along the wall, underneath the blackboard. It was a cosy, traditional place. The log fire hadn't been lit, I guessed it was a bit too early in the year, but there was a stack of logs next to it, looking as if they were well prepared for the inevitable cold snap.

DI Sam Charlton came over to the table, carrying his pint and a glass of red wine. "No rioja so I got a tempranillo. I hope that's okay?"

"That's fine," I said, taking the wine and trying a sip. It was, it was lovely. I liked Spanish wine.

"Now, how can I help you?"

"Well," I said, thinking. If I was going to ask this policeman to help me with going home and sorting things out there was no point him continuing to believe that I was Miriam Nathan. I'd thought about this over and over. The mantra '*trust no one*' had played round and round my head. I'd have to blow my cover, but I desperately wanted this to be finished and to get back home and he appeared to be my best hope. If he knew anything then he would know it wasn't my real name anyway. I thought I could suss him out whilst I was being a little cagey, see if he fished for any information, try to get a sense of where he was coming from. I bit the bullet. "I ought to tell you first that my name is not Miriam Nathan."

"Not Miriam Nathan?"

"No."

He seemed to be mildly amused at this, raising one eyebrow and smiling, before running the fingers of one hand over the corner of his mouth. He looked up at me, raising both eyebrows this time, as if soliciting an explanation.

"I was scared," I spluttered, unexpectedly thrown by his amusement. "My home had been ransacked. I felt like I was on the run."

"And now?"

"Well, I'm hoping that's where you will be able to help me."

"Okay, well I suppose you ought to start by telling me your real name."

I hesitated. '*Trust no one.*' Oh, hell. I had to do something. "Verity," I almost whispered it, "Verity Spencer."

"Okay, Verity. So tell me what happened."

I started on the story of what had happened, except that I stuck to the version where I had found Dr Neasden's wallet rather than his notebook and I also, without explicitly saying it, carried on the impression that Dr Neasden had suggested Stephen Ibbetson would be able to help me in some way. That way I wouldn't have to reveal that I had his notebook or that it even existed. I said I'd found Ibbetson's name in Dr Neasden's wallet and that Neasden had wanted me to talk to him, but I didn't know why. I told him I hadn't really taken it seriously until I'd come home the next day and my house had been ransacked. I admitted that I'd lied to Ibbetson in that I hadn't met Dr Neasden before he'd dropped his wallet. I told DI Charlton that I'd said that to Ibbetson because it sounded more believable. If I'd told him I'd found his name written in Dr Neasden's wallet and had to Google it until I found him, he might have thought I was some kind of mad stalker. I rather hoped that my story was a good enough blend of truth and fiction that if Charlton were able to access the police records then he wouldn't notice any discrepancies. But I was still hiding the fact that I had the notebook and that I was fairly convinced that there was something in there which someone badly wanted. I wasn't going to give that piece of information to anyone.

It was half an hour later, and we had both finished our drinks, by the time I'd finished my story. It was my turn to buy so I went and reordered, before returning to the table a few minutes later with replenished glasses. Just as I was putting the glasses down, Charlton's phone rang. He looked at the number, pressing 'answer' whilst simultaneously gesturing that he needed to take the call. He stepped outside, and I could see him, huddling by the door, pulling his jacket up around his ears.

Whilst he was gone, I thought about what I'd told him. Once again, I'd been suitably cagey about what I knew. I wasn't giving any information to Charlton apart from the very basics. I was playing it a bit dumb, but I thought that's what I needed to do. I'd guessed if anyone was suspicious that I had the notebook they would try and get the information out of me. But Charlton, like Ibbetson, seemed blissfully unaware of its existence, let alone the meaning of its contents. He had asked questions and given prompts throughout my narration of what had happened, and he had given no indication that he was aware of the notebook, or for that matter, Dr Neasden.

Charlton was only gone two minutes before he came back, apologised and sat down. He sighed and took a swig of his beer. "I'll be honest," he said, "I'm not sure I'll be able to help you."

I must have looked crestfallen because he quickly followed that statement up with, "But I will do what I can."

I nodded but said nothing.

"I should be able to access the police records on the national database so I can have a look and see if there is anything in them that might give us a clue." He took another slug of beer. "If not then I can ring up the investigating officer. What did you say his name was?"

"Mike Nash. But, like I said before, I'm a bit suspicious about how the house-ransackers got my address. It must have been through the local police. I don't want to make it worse."

"I'll be discreet. You said that Dr Neasden and Ibbetson were working on a paper? About child trafficking? Anything else on that?"

"No, Ibbetson was quite cagey on the details. I know they've published at least one paper in the past, in 2011, but I couldn't print it off because it was in a journal." It struck me then, that I'd been in the British Library all morning and could have more than likely looked at the journal there. Damn.

"Well, I can always use that as a shoe-in. If I need to ring this Nash guy I can always use that as an excuse."

I kept quiet about the research I'd read on how poor the Met were at picking up cases.

He carried on, "It also provides a legitimate excuse to be looking at the local records. If I think there might be a connection to local trafficking it'll be a good enough reason to look."

I gave him the number of my new mobile phone. We chatted a little whilst we finished our drinks. He seemed like a pleasant man and I asked him about working for the Human Trafficking Unit and the kind of work that he did. He was easy to talk to and he had a good sense of humour, making me laugh out loud on more than one occasion. It was good to forget the mess I was in. Then he looked at his watch and apologised that he would have to dash off. He asked if I was okay to walk back to my hotel, which I assured him I was, and then rushed off into the night.

It was heading towards 9pm. I thought about sitting and having another glass of wine but decided against it, and instead walked the fifteen minutes back to my hotel, leaning into the wind and wondering when it would start raining.

20

I took the lift up to the 5th floor, turned the corner to the right outside the lift and walked towards my room. I had my key card out and ready to use but as I lifted my head to use it I stopped, a horrible tension was rising in me, gripping me from the legs upwards. *Oh my God, oh my God, someone has been in my room.* In fact, they had to still be in there because I knew it was almost impossible to close the door from the outside without the 'Do not disturb' sign turning upside down. How the sign had managed to right itself when it was closed from the inside was a puzzle I wasn't about to try and work out. All I knew was that when you closed it from the outside it always flipped itself over. And yet there it was, the right way up. *Shit, shit, shit.* I started to run away, back towards the lifts, but halfway along the corridor I stopped. Where would I go? I sank to the floor, leaned against the wall and considered my options. I didn't have many – face whoever it was in my room, or run. Maybe it was the couple of glasses of wine that were giving me extra bravado, maybe not, but one thing was for sure, I couldn't face running anymore. If they were after me, whoever they were, they would most definitely keep coming.

I stood outside the door, trying to think, trying to imagine what it was they were doing. *Waiting for you to come back, you idiot.* They still thought I had the notebook of course. Well, they were right there but they couldn't know for sure. I hadn't mentioned it to anyone. No one, not even DI Charlton. Nobody knew for sure that I had the notebook. I thought about the room. Where would they hide if they were waiting for me to return so that they could ambush me? The bathroom wouldn't work because the door opened so that when you walked into the room you could see into the bathroom. There wasn't room to hide behind the door because it was so close the bath, and it was frosted glass anyway, so you'd notice anyone behind it. In the main area of the bedroom the massive mirror on the left hand wall meant that you could see almost the entire bedroom from the door. Anyone hiding round the corner would be noticeable in the mirror as soon as you came in, meaning someone coming through the door would instantly be able to back out and run away. Unless they hid under the bed? But that would make no sense either because by the time they'd crawled out I'd be able to run away.

The only logical place I could think of, that made any sense at all if you were waiting to pounce on someone, would be in the recess behind the door. That made the most sense because the door would hide you as it was opened and then, as someone came through the door and went to close it, you could grab them before they had even seen you.

I realised that I was breathing really quietly, subconsciously trying not to alert anyone to my presence. I'd have to be really quick and really sharp. My build wasn't up to much in terms of strength so I'd need to make up for that by being fast and decisive. I put my rucksack properly on my back without making a sound. I could have put it on the floor near the door to give me a bit more agility but I was reluctant to leave it. It had everything in it; all my notes, the photos, everything; if anyone ran out of the room before I got to it they could easily pick it up and run away. No, it was safer on my back. I looked at the door and took a deep breath as quietly as I could. I reminded myself that I had an advantage – they didn't know about the 'Do not disturb' sign and they wouldn't realise that I knew they were in there. I put the key card in the door. That would mean they would be aware of me returning. Then, as swiftly and as hard as I could I smashed the door back into the wall with all my force and weight. I heard a groan and something skittled across the floor. I grabbed the door again, adrenaline pumping through my body, and smashed it another time as hard as I possibly could into the wall. Except it didn't go as far as the wall this time, as something, or rather someone was in the way. As fast as I could, I turned on the light, pulled the door towards me as I came round it and into the room, and took a wild kick round the door, swinging my leg as fast as I could.

I realised at this point that what had been stopping the door was the man's foot. He'd wedged it against the door to stop it hitting him again. He had blood on the side of his face though; his head had clearly hit the coat hook when I smashed the door open the first time. There was quite a gash and the blood was running down his cheek. He looked extremely pissed off and as I swung my leg to kick him, he grabbed my ankle and twisted me round sharply. A stabbing pain pierced through my ankle as he twisted it. I fell on the floor with a thud and had no time to put my arms out to stop me. My chest hit the ground and for a second I was winded completely. All the breath left my chest and a searing pain ran through my lungs as I gasped to refill them.

He dug his fingers into my skin as he yanked me towards him by the ankle.

"Where is it?" he shouted. "Where is it?" He continued to pull me towards him as I struggled to regain my breathing. "Cow, I'm talking to you."

I twisted round as quickly as I could and kicked backwards at his hand with the heel of my other foot. I caught him sharp on the wrist with the heel of my trainer. It wouldn't have done much harm but it was enough to make him shout out. He let go of my ankle, and I scrambled away towards the bed. I saw then, that what had rattled across the room was a gun, a small handgun, and as I crawled across the floor I pushed it under the bed and to the other side of the room as far away from my assailant as I could.

"Bitch!" he shouted and he came at me again, kicking me in the back, just below my rucksack. His foot hit the small of my back with such force that I fell forwards sharply on the ground and crashed my face into the floor. A pain exploded in my mouth from my tongue, or my lip, I wasn't sure. I pushed myself quickly to my knees and watched through my legs as he geared up to attack me again. As he ran towards me, I kicked my leg back as hard as I could and caught him in the stomach. He was a big but pudgy man with pasty white skin and a reasonably fat tummy so my kick didn't do much damage but it slowed him down enough for me to stand up. He immediately came at me again and punched at me, hitting me hard in the shoulder. He pushed me onto the bed, the rucksack digging painfully into my back. He rushed at me and I slapped him across the face, but it barely touched him although it stung the palm of my hand. He grabbed me by the throat with his left hand and started to squeeze. He slapped my face with his right hand, hitting me with such a force that for a second the room went completely black. A wave of nausea washed through me; I wished I hadn't had two glasses of wine to drink.

He put both hands around my throat and squeezed even harder. I struggled to breathe and pinpricks of light exploded in the corner of my eyes. I clawed at his hands, gasping, desperately trying to get air through a non-existent gap in my throat. I clawed again at his hands, trying to pull them off my throat. I was feeling dizzy from a lack of oxygen and tried in vain to pull his hands away.

"What have you done with it?" he shouted. "Bitch! Tell me what you've done with it."

I couldn't have answered even if I had wanted to. I couldn't breathe, I was clutching, clawing at his hands, but there was no hope I could pull them away from my neck. I didn't know what to do; I was struggling, I couldn't move and he had a good grip. From the depths of somewhere I vaguely remembered a self-defence course I had attended a year or two ago at work after the college had become worried about female staff walking home late and in the dark. The male instructor had talked about jabbing people in the eyes as this was an area that would really hurt. I lifted my right hand up to his face and began to push my thumb into his left eye as hard as I could. He cried out, reaching up to his face and grabbing my hand to pin it down on the bed.

The release on my neck was a relief; with only one hand around it there was enough room to just about breathe. The air rushed in, feeling like fire against the sides of my throat. I glanced up at his flabby body looming over mine. He was on all fours on top of me. I was lying beneath him, my legs beneath his body. I looked at my leg and took aim. I pulled it up, with all the force I could muster, sharply between his legs. There hadn't been enough space to get a full swing but I caught him straight between the legs with my shin and it was clearly enough to hurt. He let go of me, clutching his balls and writhing on the edge of the bed.

He turned to me, enraged, snarling, "I'll teach you, whore." He reached behind the bed for the gun. It was inches from his grasp. I moved as quickly as I could and grabbed one of the ceramic lamps. It was a solid square, hard enough to do some damage, but not too heavy to get a good swing. I yanked the plug out of the wall as he bent down to pick up the gun and crashed the lamp down on his head with as much strength and force as I could gather.

It worked. He sank to the edge of the bed, and then rolled off and onto the floor. He was overweight and he was wearing slacks and a tracksuit top which had risen up revealing his flabby tummy hanging over the top of his trousers. I aimed another kick at his balls and this time my foot connected with a mighty crunch.

It was only when his response to my kick was little more than a soft moan that I realised the man was actually unconscious. He was bleeding from the head but breathing rhythmically and softly so I figured he would be okay. Hopefully when he came round, the pain would be enough to keep him occupied for a while. To be honest, the adrenaline was flowing so freely at that point I could quite easily have smashed his skull with my bare hand and not worried, but I restrained myself. My foot felt as if it had exploded on impact with him—there was a searing pain in my toes but I ignored it. My lip and face were also swelling up but I didn't have time to worry and I think the adrenaline was beginning to numb any pain I was feeling.

I looked around the room. Things had been turned about a bit, he'd clearly been looking for something although there was a limit to the damage that could be done in a hotel room, I supposed. The gun was behind his head, luckily it had been just out of his reach. Once again my heart began pounding and a fresh wave of adrenaline rushed through my body. If I'd chosen that moment to run a marathon I reckon I'd have done it in world record time. I picked up the gun and calmly aimed it at his head. The main thing preventing me from pulling the trigger was that I thought it would alert people. That, and I had no idea how to handle a gun. I kept the gun pointed at his head in case he came round and I bent down to fish in his pockets. I pulled out a phone and a wallet, which I put in my jacket pocket. He had some handcuffs attached to his belt, clearly meant for me, so I took those, put one end round his right wrist, pulled his arm high above his head to the top of the bed and attached his arm to the iron frame of the bed. I rummaged through his pockets again for keys, which I eventually located in one of his tracksuit jacket pockets along with several £20 notes, which I also took.

I checked the gun. I had no idea what sort of a gun it was, and I wasn't about to fiddle with anything. I took my rucksack off and placed the gun inside. In a rather paranoid fashion I made sure the barrel was pointing at the ground and away from my back just in case guns were capable of firing themselves without anyone pulling the trigger. After hurriedly gathering my things together, I took a last quick glance at the podgy man still sprawled on the floor. He was breathing gently. He'd no doubt have a sore head and sore balls in the morning but he'd be fine. He'd be a surprise for whoever found him, that was for sure. It would take him a while to work himself free and I figured he'd rather pretend that he was trying a kinky game or something than admit the real reason he'd ended up handcuffed to a bed. I turned off the light and pulled the door closed, leaving the 'Do not disturb' sign back in its normal upside down position.

Just as I was leaving the room, a woman in a receptionist's outfit came, almost running, out of the lift and up the corridor. "Is everything okay?" she said hurriedly. "Someone rang and said they thought there was a disturbance."

"No, it's cool," I said, keeping the swollen side of my face away from her. My voice was thin and scratchy from being strangled and I tried hard to sound as normal as I could. "Sorry, I must have had the TV on a bit too loud. There was some fighting in a film. I'm sorry. I'm off for dinner now."

"Okay." She looked nervously over her shoulder at the door of the room so I engaged her in polite and sparkly conversation all the way back down to reception. I waved her a cheery farewell and left the hotel. Then my legs started to shake. I paused and leaned against the wall outside the hotel to keep myself from falling over, my legs buckling underneath me. Images of the man's face so close to mine, and memories of his heavy breath played in my brain as I tried to steady myself. I wanted to lay on the ground, to curl up and hide, to escape the feeling of those hands still clutching at my throat. But I knew I had to get as far away from the hotel as I possibly could.

-21-

I didn't know where I was going. My foot was throbbing from the kicks I had administered, my ankle ached from being twisted, and my legs would barely hold me up they were shaking so much. I was sure I must have broken a bone at least. I just walked and walked, resolving to take up self-defence lessons when I got home. My face and lips were swollen and sore, and my throat felt as if I had drunk acid. I'm not sure how long I was walking for but I ended up somewhere near Covent Garden station. I walked with a furious pace, fuelled by the adrenaline and unable to think clearly, just wanting to put as much distance between me and that creep as I could. I wondered if it was the same guy who had turned over my house, or whether this was a special London 'hit man'. I walked up and down streets turning this way and that, making sure that it would be impossible to follow me, just in case anyone had been waiting outside the hotel. It was pouring with rain and I was soaked to the skin, even my 'weatherproof' jacket proving to be inadequate against the driving rain. I had no umbrella, but even if I had it would have been little use against this rain. It was bouncing off the pavements, soaking everybody's socks and jeans. I was freezing cold. At some point as I was wending my way back and forth through the streets, I hit Oxford Street and walked past Primark. It was still open, despite it being nearly 10 o'clock. I went in, adding my drips to those that were already on the floor. It was almost closing time and the place was pretty much deserted. I went to the 'sleepwear' section and quickly browsed the selection on offer. There were nighties and pyjamas and nightshirts of all sizes, colours and designs. I wanted the warmest, cosiest pyjamas I could find. I chose a pale blue fluffy pair that was a couple of sizes too big. They had pastel coloured hearts all over the top. I also picked up a pair of woolly socks. There was no queue and I got straight to the till, a bonus for shopping so late in the evening. The young girl took my money with an air of utter indifference, as if she were already sitting on the sofa in front of the television, mentally if not physically, and then I rushed out once more into the cold, wet evening.

I found a reasonably smart hotel in Covent Garden and checked in for the night, this time dreaming up a name from nowhere, Carrie Davenport. I stood, dripping, in the foyer and the receptionist took pity on me, offering to tumble dry my clothes once I'd changed out of them. I went straight up to my hotel room on the 9th floor. It was a comfortable room, much more in the traditional style than the last one. The room was square with one corner taken up by the bathroom. There was a king-sized bed, a modern desk and chair, an easy chair and coffee table, and a couple of bedside tables. The lamps in this room were screwed to the walls, so I hoped I didn't need to hit anyone over the head. The television was fixed to the wall opposite the bed and there was a small mirror over the desk. The wardrobe had a full-length mirror on the inside of the door, but I kept that shut. I looked dishevelled and my lip was swollen, although the rain had rinsed any blood away. My foot ached, my ankle ached, and my throat ached and I was shivering quite dramatically.

I stripped off my wet clothes, left them on the bathroom floor and had a shower. There was no bath but the shower was a big one, with an oversized shower head. I stayed in the shower for what felt like hours, letting the hot water warm up my frozen skin. Eventually I emerged, feeling calmer and warmer. I assessed the damage to my foot. It was swollen and would bruise, but there didn't appear to be anything broken. My lip was also swollen and I could see where my teeth had been pushed into it. There was a red mark around my neck which I hoped would fade fairly quickly. I looked exactly as if I had been in a fight with a pudgy, pasty man.

I put on my new, soft fluffy pyjamas and socks. I hardly ever wore pyjamas; John and I had always slept naked. In fact, pyjamas had been the cause of one of our most spectacular arguments. We didn't argue often,

141

but when we did we didn't hold back. I couldn't really remember how it had started now, but it had had something to do with me deciding to wear a pair of pyjamas in bed one freezing winter evening and John deciding that this was a sign I didn't want my skin against his. At least that was my memory of what had been said; John would probably tell it differently if he could. Anyway, we'd screamed and shouted and I'd thrown a shoe at him which had caught him on the head and caused a gash that bled profusely. We had made up and ended up snuggled in bed, both wearing pyjamas as something of a compromise, I supposed. I glanced down at the fluffy pastel hearts covering my body and smiled. Even remembering the bad times didn't seem to dull the ache of missing him.

I scooped up my wet clothes, put them in the laundry bag and left it in the corridor outside my room. I shut the door and made sure the deadbolt was engaged. And then I flopped down onto the bed. It was only then that I started to slow down, the adrenaline leaving my body and I began to shake again, tears appearing unbidden in my eyes. Instead of fighting them back, I let them flow, building up as the emotions erupted within me. I wasn't sure if I was crying for John, or for my house, or for almost being strangled. Or maybe it was for all three. I sobbed, great heaving sobs, tears pouring down my face and I lay hugging one of the pillows for a while until my body started calming down. Eventually I got up, made a cup of tea and then picked up my rucksack and sat on the bed.

I emptied the contents of the rucksack onto the bed. My clothes had got a bit wet through the fabric, but it had proven surprisingly water resistant. I arranged the clothes around the room so that they would be dry in the morning. I put my trainers on top of the radiator to dry out the insides and examined the items I'd taken from the intruder. I put his phone to one side and looked through his wallet. His credit and debit cards named him as Kevin Lambert but there was no driver's licence and nothing to suggest where he came from. His wallet also contained a couple of loyalty cards for coffee shops but they were chains like Café Nero so nothing there to indicate where he had come from either. There were a couple of ten pound notes, a fiver and some change. Nothing personal at all. Where had he come from and how had he known where I was? Who had tipped him off?

I picked up the gun. I'd never held a gun before and I was cautious with it. It was a stubby looking, black gun. Along the side of the barrel it said Sig Sauer P229 so I guessed that was the make and model. There was a small lever just below the barrel and another at the top of the handle. I left them well alone. There was another lever at the back, which looked like you would pull it down with your thumb when you were holding the gun. I had no idea what any of these things did and I wasn't about to start experimenting. I picked the gun up carefully, still worried that it might fire itself, and put it in the drawer under the television.

Next I looked at his phone. It was an old fashioned one, similar in style to my little Sony Erikson but made by Nokia. There was no passcode entry so I turned it on and scrolled through the list of calls. He had received a call at 8pm that night. *Shit.* That was the time that DI Charlton had gone out to accept that call. Had this man been ringing, asking for a description or a location? No, it couldn't be that. Charlton didn't know where I was staying. And the guy was already in my room when I'd got back so he couldn't have followed me. Plus, Charlton had received his call and so had Lambert, so it couldn't have been the same call. And, looking back, I was fairly sure that I had seen the photo of a smiling, attractive, blonde pop up on Charlton's phone when it had rung.

The number that had called at 8pm had not been identified so there was no way I could ring it but there were other numbers in the call list. I couldn't be bothered to ring them at that time, I was too exhausted; I'd do it in the morning. I had a quick look through his texts but as he had neither sent nor received one this evening, I switched his phone off. I took out the SIM card and battery to make doubly sure that there would be no signal being transmitted. I'd have another look tomorrow.

I got in bed and lay there thinking about the intruder. I couldn't see, however I played it, that it could have been Charlton that had alerted anyone to my whereabouts. He didn't know where I was staying, plus he hadn't had enough time. That left Ibbetson. It had to be something to do with him. Perhaps he had used Charlton as a decoy but it had to have started with him. He had asked where I was staying and although I hadn't told him, I'd said near King's Cross so it wouldn't have been too difficult to ring around hotels. And I'd used the same false name I'd given him to check in. Stupid, stupid mistake. That *bastard*. What was he thinking?

As I lay there wondering how and why Ibbetson had led them to me, my eyelids started to feel heavy and began to drop.

And then I'm walking round the Civic Centre in Uxbridge with the gun that I took from Lambert. I stride calmly round the building, holding the gun out in front of me. No one is taking any notice of it, or me, they are just carrying on with their work as if it is a perfectly normal occurrence. I find Ibbetson's office easily and walk straight in. He's sitting there, his head bowed over some paperwork, but he looks up as he hears me enter. As he sees the gun he starts to panic, scrambling to get away from his desk. I don't say anything to him, I just aim the gun and shoot him through the head. I walk out of the office, carrying the gun down at my side but I can't find my way out of the building. I start running but I'm going round in circles and every time I take a turn it leads to a dead end. I turn another corner and I'm back at Ibbetson's office. He's still there with a hole through his forehead, and panic begins to rise inside me. I run faster and faster, past all the workers, up and down the strange half level floors but I'm going nowhere. I can hear the blood thumping in my ears and bile is rising in my throat. I open my mouth to cry out, but nothing comes.

FRIDAY

I was tangled up in the sheet and lying perilously close to the edge of the bed. I opened my eyes and a flood of relief passed through me as I realised I had been dreaming. A smile crept unbidden across my face as I jumped out of the bed, leaving the memory of Ibbetson behind. I was actually in a bit of a sweat, not just because of my night-time shenanigans but as I reached the bathroom I realised the heating was on full blast. I'd been so cold the night before that I had turned it up. At some point in the night I must have taken off my pyjamas but I didn't remember doing that. They were lying in a heap next to the bed. I showered then dried my hair. I looked in the mirror. My face was red and my lip was still swollen. I put on the clothes that I had placed around the room and were now, thankfully, dry. My trainers were still a bit damp but I put two pairs of socks on to protect myself from them. I looked out of the window—it had stopped raining but the trees were being buffeted by a strong wind, and people were scuttling along the road with their collars pulled up round their necks. I put my scarf on, which I wrapped tightly round my neck to cover up the red mark, and pulled my hat down over my ears. Then I remembered the gun. What was I going to do with that? I didn't want to take it with me, but I also didn't really want to leave it in the hotel room. I took a chance. I wrapped my pyjamas round it and stuffed it back into the drawer. If anyone came to clean my room, despite the 'Do not disturb' sign, and opened the drawer they would just think it was clothes. Hopefully.

I left the hotel and went to buy coffee and a pain-au-raisin at a local café. My foot hurt as I walked along and the cold air bit into my tender throat as I breathed. I sat down in a corner and ate my pastry. Between mouthfuls, I got out my phone and called Ibbetson's number. It was early, about 8.30, but I figured an Assistant Director would be there at that time. It answered on the second ring.

"Good morning, London Borough of Hillingdon, Dorothy Chambers speaking, how can I help you?

"Could I speak to Stephen Ibbetson please?"

"I'm afraid he's in a meeting. Can I take a message?

"Yes, thank you. Can you tell him that Miriam Nathan called? Can you ask him to call me back, please?" I gave her my new mobile number. "Can you tell him that it is urgent, please? I need to talk to him as soon as possible."

"I'll give him the message," she said curtly, and I imagined a piece of paper with only my name and number being passed to him or put into a tray with several others, never to see the light of day.

I disconnected and turned on my iPad. I went straight to the photo of the eight-digit numbers. I wrote down the numbers, as they were in the lists and began to use my decoder on them. I started with the top number, just because it seemed logical. Once I'd decoded the numbers I sorted them according to the way Ibbetson's number had been scrambled up. Because there had been two sets of double digits in Ibbetson's number this meant that there were four possible ways of scrambling which led to four combinations that the number might end up being. I wrote them all down.

01974513
01931547
01971543
01934517

Plus there were two possible 3-digit endings 762 and 879 so that would leave me with eight possibilities.

I moved on to the last number and went through the same process, coming up with the four possibilities. I added these to my list. They could also be attached to either of the three-digit endings. So far, then, I had 16 possible combinations of phone numbers.

02076744
02044767
02074764
02046747

An hour had passed and there had been no response from Ibbetson so I tried again. The same, rather officious, woman answered. I assumed she was his PA, or something. I told her who it was.

"I passed on your message but I'm afraid Mr Ibbetson is in another meeting now."

"Well, can you tell him I called again? It is really urgent that I speak to him."

I hung up and ordered another coffee. I also got a slice of coffee cake. I went back to the numbers. I knew that 0207 numbers were for inner London. I Googled 0204. *Hooray*; something helpful at last. Without even having to open any of the links I read the first result '*There are no numbers in the UK that start with the prefix 0204, although there are plans to introduce this as a new prefix for London area numbers later in the year.*' That meant it was currently not in use, so I could cross out some of my numbers. It at least got me closer. And because that meant that the scrambling method I had used to make the 0204 numbers was wrong, I could cross out two of the other numbers as well. I revisited the list.

01974513
~~01931547~~
01971543
~~01934517~~
02076744
~~02044767~~
02074764
~~02046747~~

I knew 0207 was a London number so I left them for the time being. I Googled the area code 01974; it was for a place called Llanon in Wales. That made no sense. Why would anyone from a tiny place in Wales be involved? I tried Googling 01971; this came from Scourie, a place I had never heard of before but which is, according to Google maps, almost as far north in Scotland as you can go. This was making no sense at all.

Then my phone rang. I answered without even looking at it.

"Verity, it's Sam. Charlton."

It threw me a bit, I'd been expecting Ibbetson. "Sam. Hi." My voice still sounded a bit ropey from the night before and I hoped it wasn't too obvious.

"I've only done some of the work, but there is definitely something strange going on. Someone has added something to the record of your account of Dr Neasden's death."

All the hairs on my back stood up and goosebumps appeared down my arm. I said nothing.

"You didn't speak to anyone else, did you, after leaving Dr Neasden's house?"

"How do you mean?"

"Did a policeman come round to your house and talk to you?"

"No. I haven't spoken to the police since Monday." They'd have a job, I thought and wondered how many missed calls my iPhone had received on its trip round the country.

"The record shows that a Detective Inspector Adrian Darnold came to visit you on Tuesday morning. I won't bore you with the details but he has more or less discredited you as a witness. Says you were hysterical and that as you were recently widowed." He paused. "Well, basically, in not so many words he is saying not to believe a word you say."

I breathed out sharply. "No, shit." I wrote the name down Adrian Darnold DI. "A DI; so he's superior to Nash, yes?"

"Yes, but hang on. There's more."

"More?" What more could there be?

"I read the report on Dr Neasden's death. It's not far off what you said to me. Except…"

"Except what?"

"There's no mention of a bullet wound. Nothing at all."

I didn't know what to say. Bloody hell. Someone had changed the account of what had actually happened.

Charlton continued, "I don't know if that is the way the report was written, or if it has been altered by this Darnold person after Nash filed his report. You need to be careful, Verity."

"I'm not going anywhere very soon." Then I started to fill him in on the events of the night before, although I didn't mention that there had been a gun, which I had taken and was now in my new hotel room. There is a limit to what you can say to a policeman. He asked questions about the man, so I told him what I knew, which wasn't much more than a name and a description.

He sounded duly concerned for my well-being. I said that I was okay, although my foot continued to hurt and, although the swelling in my face wasn't too bad, there was a nasty gash on my lip and a red mark around my neck.

"I can find you a safe house to go to whilst I carry on investigating."

I was touched by his concern, but I stayed silent. I probably would have leapt at the chance of a safe haven only a couple of days ago, but I was determined now. I had come this far, and I really wanted to find out what was going on.

"I'll be fine, Sam. I really will. I'm sure my hotel is as safe as anywhere."

"Just let me know if you change your mind, okay?"

"I promise."

I hadn't told him about the notebook, and I wasn't about to. I had to try to figure that bit out myself. I couldn't rely on anyone else. '*Trust no one*'. I'd been discredited as a witness and I needed to stay sharp. I knew Charlton was trying to help but police could talk to each other and I felt safer out here, where no one knew where I was. I could stay on my toes much more easily if I was in control of what I was doing. He gave me his mobile phone number.

"Be careful, and don't do anything rash. Stay in touch."

I put the phone down and instantly picked it up again. I was incensed now. I called Ibbetson and when the woman answered again and said he was still in a meeting I just lost it. I didn't believe that he was in a meeting. I thought she was lying. I didn't shout, just very calmly and determinedly said, "Well, go and get him out of his meeting. I don't care how important it is, if he doesn't phone me back *instantly* I will personally come in and drag him out myself. Okay?" I hung up.

Ten minutes later the phone rang again. I recognised the number. I jabbed at the answer button with my finger.

"Ibbetson, you *prick.* You nearly got me killed. *"*

"What are you talking about?" He was trying to sound as if he knew nothing. He wasn't being very convincing.

"You know damn well what I am talking about. I'm talking about the *twat* who was hiding in my hotel room when I got back from seeing Charlton last night."

He sounded uncomfortable. "Miriam, what is it?" He was stuttering. "What…what happened?"

"*You* happened. That's what happened. I come down to try and get help and you send round the

156

moron flabby hit-man to wait in my room and *shoot* me. *That's* what happened."

"I had nothing to do with that." His attempt at bravado was almost amusingly feeble.

"So why did you send the fat man round to my hotel room?"

"I didn't…I didn't…I didn't do anything like that. My God. Are you alright? I rang Charlton, that's all… I didn't send anyone round. I don't know people like that." He sounded so nervous; he sounded genuinely shocked and disturbed but he had clearly done something other than just ring Charlton. I could tell it in his voice. Something that had led them to me.

"Ibbetson, you are lying. I can tell." I was on a roll and I was steaming angry. I was not going to let him get away without telling me what he had done. "Who else did you tell about our meeting? Did you ring anyone other than Charlton?"

He didn't say anything but his breathing became increasingly fast and the heaviness of it carried down the phone.

"Ibbetson, stop behaving like a twat and tell me who you told. That pudgy bastard that came for me last night is still chained to the bed with a bedpost up his arse." Okay, not strictly true, but I wished I'd thought of doing that. "I took his gun. Which I still have. I didn't shoot him, but I am quite warming to the idea of coming after you and trying it out on you. Now. Tell me. Who did you tell?"

"I'm sorry….I didn't…" He was gibbering. "I didn't mean…"

I changed tack a bit. I quietened down, not least because people were beginning to glance in my direction and my paranoia once again rose to the surface. "What's this all about, Stephen? What have you got involved in?"

"I don't know," he said. I genuinely thought he really didn't know. "I don't know. Neasden was doing some extra research. He said he'd found something big, scarily big. But I don't know what. He wouldn't tell me. He didn't tell me what, and now he's dead." He was scared, it was all over his voice.

"So, you were worried? After I'd been to see you?"

"Yes. And then…" he swallowed several times, coughed, tapped what I assumed was a pen against the phone. His anxiety was evident. "I called Charlton, but then I…I didn't know they'd… I mean…I didn't mean for…" His voice was barely a whisper now. "I was scared."

I slowed right down and tried to sound as sympathetic as I could. "I understand that you didn't mean for me to get killed. Luckily for you that hasn't happened because I've kept copious notes which would now appear to implicate you if I did." Another lie. They were becoming easy now. "Just tell me what you did." I lowered my voice even further and said calmly, "Ibbetson, just tell me what you did. I know you didn't mean to do anything bad, but please, just tell me."

He took a deep breath. I could tell he was struggling. I didn't think he'd be returning to work that afternoon. "I didn't think…I didn't think it would hurt. I mean, I didn't think it would matter to call

158

them. I just thought they would know what had happened to Neasden. I was just trying to find out."

"Who, Stephen? Who did you call?"

"The police."

"Other police? Other than Charlton."

"Yes." He was almost inaudible. "The Lincolnshire police."

"The police I told you I didn't trust?"

Silence.

"The police I told you had been round and ransacked my house?"

"Yes."

Jesus. I closed my eyes and sighed. "Who? Who did you talk to?"

Nothing.

"Ibbetson. It's important. Was it Darnold? Did you ring Adrian Darnold?"

Nothing. Just heavy, anxious breathing.

"Ibbetson. Was it Darnold?"

Click. The line went dead. I looked at the phone. Great, now Darnold would have my pseudonym too. And possibly a description of what I looked like with bleached hair. Thank God I'd used a different name to check into the hotel this time.

-23-

I gathered my stuff together and went for a walk, wandering through Covent Garden towards Holborn and then back along Oxford Street where I dipped back towards Covent Garden and from there to Seven Dials. A little independent coffee shop seemed like a suitable place to stop. It was in a secluded little yard off the main shopping area. I ordered a decaffeinated coffee this time and another cake- a strawberry confection with loads of cream and icing sugar, thinking that the sugar boost was just what I needed. I was hoping no one was tracking what I had been eating for the last few days. I didn't think I'd be getting any awards for a healthy diet. I seemed to have been existing mostly on cake.

I fished out my iPad and the notes I had been making. I got out the phone and started ringing the number combinations. I worked my way down the list of numbers, trying each one twice, once with the 762 ending and again with the 879 ending. The first three were met with the familiar rising *beep, beep, beep* and a woman in a posh voice telling me that the number I had dialled had not been recognised and to please check and try again. The fourth number actually rang. On the fifth or sixth ring it was answered. What I thought was a man, but couldn't be definite, answered and spoke with the thickest Scottish accent I could ever have imagined.

"Scourie Birdwatching."

"I'm sorry?" I struggled to understand what he was saying.

"Scourie Birdwatching."

"Sorry, are you are a nature park?"

"No, lassie. We organise trips to the nature reserves. To watch the birds."

"Okay, thanks. I think I must have dialled the wrong number."

"Nae worry." The man, or possibly woman, said and put the phone down.

I made a note next to the number and moved on. Only one of the other numbers rang. It was one of the London numbers. The lady who answered it sounded about 126 years old and kept asking me to repeat what I'd said. After two attempts at apologising I just put the phone down.

I was feeling a bit dejected. After having eventually worked out Neasden's code I was, actually, no further forward. I reached for Lambert's phone, putting the battery and SIM card back in. I opened the call list. I wrote down every call that had been made or received in the last two weeks. Some came up only as names, so I noted down the name and then cross referenced the names to the contacts in the address book. I wrote down all the other numbers in the address book. There were only a few. I guessed that this was a 'work' mobile as there were only a couple of calls made and not that many received. As well as the address book not containing many numbers there were no familiar numbers, no women, no 'Mum' and no 'home'.

I cross checked the list of numbers I had with the decoded numbers from the notebook. None of them matched. Although…I looked again. There was one number that was almost a match except one number was different. I checked again. One number, which had been a received call on Tuesday, was identical to one of my decoded numbers except that instead of starting 01 it started 07. I began to get excited. Perhaps Neasden had added an extra decoy in case someone else, like me, had figured out his code. He'd disguised the number as a landline when in reality it was a mobile. It was probably just a complete coincidence that the same landline number had led to a tiny village in the north of Scotland.

I pondered which mobile to use. If I used one of mine, and it was an important contact then they would have one of my numbers and I'd potentially have to ditch the phone. On the other hand, they would, in all probability, be aware that I had taken Lambert's phone and if I rang would know that I was on the trail. I wasn't sure if that would be a bad thing, but I guessed it probably might be. I decided to use the new phone. It was only cheap and I could buy another SIM card for next to nothing if I needed to. I wondered who it might be and what I should say. I thought I'd have to play it by ear, really, it could be anyone.

I picked up my phone and dialled the number. It was answered almost immediately.

"Darnold."

Shit, shit shit. I was suddenly shaking violently. I pressed 'end' and almost threw the phone across the table, as if Darnold might be about to climb out of it. Some of the people in the café turned to look at me. I took some deep breaths and calmed myself down. It was a breakthrough. Neasden had written Darnold's phone number in his notebook. He had to be significant. He had to be involved in this, and not in a good way. He had changed the information in the police report. What was he trying to cover up? Was it just the fact that Neasden had been shot or was there something else? He clearly wanted to discredit me. If I had already been painted as a hysterical widow then they could easily paint me as someone who couldn't be believed. I could imagine them in court suggesting that I'd been mistaken when I'd seen the bullet wound. My brain whirred, there was something. Something there that I thought was important but I couldn't quite figure out. Whatever it was deep in the recesses of my mind, my brain was not grasping hold of it.

I looked back at my list of numbers and underlined the number and wrote Adrian Darnold DI next to it. Another feeling of a strange sense of recognition was just sweeping over me when I jumped out of my skin as Lambert's phone vibrated its way across the table. I recognised Darnold's number and my heart started pounding again. I pressed answer and held the phone to my ear, trying not to breathe.

"Lambert? Lambert, what's going on? Where are you and why didn't you call me yesterday?" His voice was gruff and deep as if he'd smoked twenty cigarettes a day for the last thirty years.

A brief pause.

"Lambert. You are in deep shit." The phone went dead.

So, Darnold didn't know that Lambert hadn't succeeded in his mission. And they didn't know I had Lambert's phone. It suddenly dawned on me that this was a very good thing as I had just put the battery and SIM card back in and if they had realised, and they had been tracking Lambert's phone, then I would have just given away my location. I kicked myself mentally; I couldn't afford to make any stupid mistakes. I'd taken the SIM card out early on but hadn't thought when I'd put it back in—I had been so keen to look at the numbers, lost in what I was doing. *Stupid, stupid.* But I couldn't afford to wallow, and it appeared that Darnold, at least, thought that Lambert still had his own phone. I wasn't sure if Darnold had intended for him to kill me, or if he was just going to use the gun to intimidate me into telling them where the notebook was. Whatever it was he was meant to have done, he was clearly supposed to have let Darnold know. I wondered if it was Darnold who was in charge of everything and, if so, what it was he was protecting. Lambert, assuming he had escaped by now, had either

164

not wanted to tell Darnold he'd messed up or not been able to. I quickly took the battery and SIM card back out of the phone and put it in my rucksack.

24

I had outstayed my welcome at the café. I could sense the woman behind the counter glaring at my empty cup. I couldn't face another cup of coffee so I gathered my things together and headed back to the hotel. As I walked I remembered the sense of recognition when I'd written Darnold's initials down. I couldn't quite bring to mind what it was that had given me that feeling but I thought I'd ponder it a bit more from the hotel room. I took the lift up to my room, and outside the door of my room, in a laundry bag, were my clothes all clean and dry. I picked them up and took them into the room.

The first thing I did when I got inside was to check that the gun was undisturbed. There it was, still wrapped up in my pyjamas. I breathed a sigh of relief. I sat down at the desk in the room and took the first phone I had bought out of the rucksack. I put the battery and the SIM card in and switched it on. I had 32 missed calls. *Bloody hell; what was going on?* Twenty-six of them were from Robert. The others were mostly from Collette's number and there were two from an 0845 number, which I guessed would be unsolicited marketing calls. I had six voicemail messages so I listened to them. The first one was from Robert.

"Verity, it's Robert. Just to let you know that I've organised for the cleaners and the locksmith to go round. I've stayed away." He paused. *"Honestly, I haven't even peeked. Anyway, the house will be sorted by the end of Friday so you'll be able to come back then. Okay? See you. Bye."*

The next one was from Robert too.

"Verity! I know you are not staying with Collette because I saw her in town today. You were supposed to be meeting her for coffee but didn't show up. Are you okay? Verity, let me know what's happening and where you are."

Damn! Of course, coffee with Collette, I'd completely forgotten that I'd said I'd meet her on Thursday morning. My mind drifted for a moment to an alternative reality, one where I'd been on time for coffee on Monday and not even seen Dr Neasden, or where Dr Neasden had dropped his notebook higher up the hill, and I hadn't got embroiled in all of this. In that reality I would have carried on unawares and would have been meeting Collette on Thursday morning and hearing all about her meeting with the headteacher. *Bugger.* Collette had been so good to me and I hadn't even let her know that I couldn't make it. A wave of guilt came over me. Tears appeared in the corners of my eyes and I blinked hard to stop them, wiping my cheeks with the sleeve of my top. I felt so alone, and so far away from everyone I loved. I had a strong urge to dive under the duvet and curl up on the bed to try to escape from it all for a while. I wanted one of Robert's reassuring hugs.

I stood up and made myself a cup of tea, deciding that I couldn't afford the time to sink into a mire of self-pity. I took a few deep breaths, picked up the phone and carried on listening to my concerned friends.

In the next message Robert actually sounded a little exasperated.

"Verity, it's me again. Where are you? I'm getting worried."

Then one from Collette. She spoke in a high, shrill voice and gasped between words.

"Darling, how are you? Are you okay? Oh my God, Vee everyone is worried about you. Rob gave me this number, he said you were burgled! Vee, what happened? What are you doing? Where are you? And why did you tell Rob you were staying with me? What's going on, Vee?"

My guilt deepened.

The next one was nothing, just the sound of a phone being put down. The last one was Robert again. He sounded really concerned.

"Verity, darling, we are worried about you. Are you okay?"

I sighed. It was nice that my friends were concerned about me, but I felt a million miles away from them at the moment. And I knew I couldn't be distracted by trying to keep other people happy. I didn't want to ring them; I couldn't face all the questions and I knew I'd have to lie, which I didn't want to do. I didn't want them to be worried about me, though, and mostly I didn't want them going round to the house. I tried not to linger on the feeling that I had somehow let them down by getting involved in this situation and running away without even attempting to explain. I picked up the phone and wrote a quick text to Robert.

Everything ok. Lots to explain. Pls tell C all is fine. Will be back soon. Lots love V xx

I pressed send and then removed the battery and SIM card quickly before I got a reply, which I knew would set the guilty feelings off again.

I took out my iPad and looked through the photos again. I wasn't sure why I was bothering, I knew them all off by heart, I was sure there was nothing new to be seen. But then it dawned on me what the connection had been. I'd felt it when I'd

169

written down Darnold's name but hadn't been able to grasp hold of anything concrete. Now it jumped out at me. The list of acronyms. The bottom acronym was ADDI. Adrian Darnold, Detective Inspector. Not an acronym after all, it was a name and a position.

I scoured the list again. Did this mean that the other letters on the list were also initials and jobs? RSDI. Could that be another Detective Inspector? And what about KTMD? MD? Doctor of Medicine? There were too many questions and my head was spinning. I thought about Darnold again, ADDI. But there was something else. There was something niggling in the back of my head which would not come forward. I shook my head as if to try to free it then went back to the photos and my notes. What did 'Champion!' mean? I shook my head. I had no clue.

I revisited the phone numbers, looking again at the second decoded number. The one that had started 0207. It had led me nowhere and I wondered if Neasden had used a 2 in that number in place of a 7. It would make sense to use a 2 because it would make the number look like a London landline. Once again, I searched the numbers that I had noted down from Lambert's phone but still none of them matched the numbers in my list. So, using my new phone I started dialling the numbers again but this time using a 7 instead of a 2. The first and second numbers drew a blank but when I dialled the third one on the list it rang. It rang about six times, then stopped. I thought someone had picked up so I held my breath but instead there was a click and a pause, then a deep, male voice said,

"This is Richard Sanderson's phone. Thank you for calling. I'm sorry I can't take your call but if you leave a message, including your name and number, I will return your call as soon as I can."

I hung up without leaving my name or number, or a message.

Richard Sanderson. Could that be RSDI? It began to feel as if I might be getting somewhere. I rang the other number combinations just to be sure but they were all 'incorrect' or 'unavailable'. It took me by surprise how many number combinations you could ring that didn't belong to anyone. It seemed that there were so many mobile phones and landlines in the country that I'd have thought every combination possible had been taken. It appeared not.

25

Next, I tried calling Sam Charlton. He answered almost immediately.

"Charlton, it's Verity. I think I might be onto something. I'm not sure what, but you may be able to do some checking."

"Go ahead."

"Well, it was definitely Darnold who sent Lambert over to my hotel last night."

"Okay."

"And it was definitely him who Ibbetson rang. Or someone, but I think it was Darnold, which is what led him to me. I don't think Ibbetson really knew what he was doing. He sounded really flustered when I told him what had happened."

"Any idea what it is all about?"

"No, Ibbetson was really nervous, almost gibbering, and he wouldn't say. But I have another name. I think it's another policeman."

"From Lincolnshire?"

"Well, I guess. That's what I'd thought, but actually I don't know for sure."

"What's the name?"

"Richard Sanderson. I think he is a DI too."

Charlton whistled through his teeth. "Okay, I'll check it out and get back to you if there is anything. How are you holding up?"

"I'm okay," I said.

I suddenly felt weary, and not at all okay. My throat still hurt as did my lip and my foot. I looked around at my hotel room and instantly felt very homesick. The messages from my friends had brought home to me how much I had been relying on them lately and I missed them.

"I'll be fine. Let's get this sorted out, though." I gave Charlton the contact details I had for Sanderson and hung up.

I looked at the time on my phone. It was just after 6.30pm. I couldn't believe where the time had gone. I felt exhausted. I undressed and got into the shower in the hope that it might revive me. I considered getting straight into bed; I was so tired I thought I would easily sleep through until the morning. But I was hungry again so I put on my freshly laundered clothes and headed out. I had wanted to work through the texts on Lambert's phone but I didn't want to turn it on again, just in case. I was looking around for a likely place to eat dinner and then it struck me; I bought a ticket and went down into the depths of Covent Garden tube station. There would be no signal down here. I sat on a bench, double-checked that the 4G network hadn't reached this station yet, then fished out the phone and put the battery and the SIM card in. There was absolutely no signal at all. Good. I worked through the texts, noting them all down in two lists - those that had been received and those that had been sent. I wrote the date and time down next to each message as well as the number it had been sent or received from, these were mostly the same couple of numbers so I shorthanded it to a, b, c and so on. There weren't that many texts, which was lucky as it was laborious work and, because it was an old style phone, it didn't keep texts as conversations like an iPhone did, which would mean cross checking sent messages with received messages when I later came to read them in more detail. That was something to look forward to then.

It took me the best part of an hour, but at least I could feel that I had avoided at least one way of being traced. I emerged from the station, headed towards Shaftesbury Avenue and into the nearest decent-looking restaurant, which turned out to be a quirky French bistro on a corner just a few minutes' walk away. The waitress was French, or she was effecting a very good French accent, and I ordered a large glass of bordeaux and a bowl of beef bourguignon. It was a small restaurant; there couldn't have been more than eight or nine tables. About half of them had people sitting at them, even at this early hour, although many of them were dining alone. People in London on business I assumed. All the tables were covered in gingham tablecloths, and the menus for the day, with today's date, were all handwritten on headed pieces of A4 paper. The kitchen was off to one side of the room where the chefs could be clearly seen cooking, preparing dishes and talking to each other in French. The whole place had a homely, and very French, feel. It seemed very authentic, and reminded me of some of the places John and I had been to when we had been holidaying in France. Not the more sophisticated and upmarket restaurants of the south coast that catered for moneyed, international tourists; more the rustic, country restaurants in proper French villages used by the locals. Those had been the places we had preferred to go to. We had been to St Tropez once, for a long weekend, but everywhere was so expensive and everyone seemed to be competing with everyone else to be the best dressed, drive the poshest car, own the biggest villa and so on. We hadn't ever returned.

The waitress came back with my wine and some bread. I took out my notes detailing all of Lambert's texts. The texts only went back about six weeks and many were just very short messages giving a time, a date and a location. That had to have been for a meeting, or a rendezvous of some sort, or to pick something up, or drop something off. Maybe Lambert was dealing drugs? Maybe this was all to do with drugs. There was huge money to be made there and, I guessed, people would be involved who wouldn't stop short of shooting someone in the stomach. I imagined there would be some policemen who would be easily bought off too, with the promise of extra cash, who would then turned a blind eye to certain 'goings on' in their area. Could Neasden have stumbled across something involving child trafficking and drugs? I remembered from my research that dealing drugs, tending cannabis farms and so on was one of the major reasons that people were trafficked to the UK. It was a possibility, and would make sense in the context of Dr Neasden's specialism.

My dinner arrived, so I pushed the texts to one side whilst I ate. The food was amazing. It was fresh and tender and delicious. I was starving. I'd only eaten a couple of pieces of cake today. Probably very calorific, but not very substantial. I wolfed down my bourguignon and vegetables and all the sautéed potatoes, then wiped the plate clean with my bread. Then I ordered a bowl of tiramisu. Not very French, but homemade. I had a glass of French brandy with my tiramisu, which was creamy and divine and just what I needed. I felt as if I hadn't had a proper meal in days and I felt better for it, less weary as well.

I ordered a cup of peppermint tea and sat and drank that in peace, watching people coming and going. Most of the business diners had gone and had been replaced by groups of friends, couples and families. The place was full and I wasn't surprised. I paid my bill in cash, leaving a sizeable tip then walked back around the corner to my hotel. I opened the door cautiously, but there was no one in the room. I went in with the intention of working further on Lambert's texts. I wanted to know what he knew and what the connection was between him, Darnold and Sanderson. I put on my pyjamas and cleaned my teeth. I took my iPad and my notes out of the rucksack and got into bed.

SATURDAY

-26-

I woke with a start. I was lying across the top of bed, my neck aching from being at an angle it wasn't intended to stay in for a prolonged period. I glanced at my phone, it was 4am. I had clearly fallen forwards from a sitting position and gone to sleep where I had landed. The light was still on and the iPad and notes were still on the bed. I moved them to the bedside cabinet, turned off the light and went back to sleep.

I woke again at 9am, feeling well rested and alert. I got showered and dressed then gathered all of my stuff together ready to go out and find some breakfast. I caught sight of myself in the mirror. The swelling on my lip had all but disappeared and the red mark around my neck had faded. I wondered if I should dye my hair a different colour. Maybe red? I thought about whether Ibbetson, or Lambert, had given Darnold a description of what I looked like now.

I had got quite used to the blonde, though, and I didn't think I would achieve much by dying it again. It might throw them off for a while, but what I really needed to do was figure out what was going on and stop them from wanting to chase after me. I couldn't just keep running away and changing the colour of my hair. I'd run out of colours soon enough. I wondered what John would think. He had always liked my hair longer, he'd thought it was more feminine, which I supposed it was; it did look quite boyish cut this short. A wave of sadness crept over me. I missed John so much. His death had come as such a shock. It wasn't like there had been anything to prepare us. One minute he'd been driving, alive, down the road and the next minute he'd been dead. I thought of our marriage, the ups and downs, the arguments and shoe-throwing, the good times and the bad; it had been a normal marriage full of trials and tribulations like anyone else's. But now he was dead, snatched so suddenly away from the life he should still be living.

Hang on. The niggling was back, but this time the thoughts were bubbling to the surface. I pushed the sad thoughts away as I struggled to hold on to the bubbles before they dissipated once again. Death, something to do with death; dying, somebody dying; the cause of death; a certificate. A death requires a death certificate. The police could alter their record of what had happened at Dr Neasden's house but the death certificate would state what had been the actual cause of his death.

I zipped up my jacket and put my grey hat on my head. I quickly re-wrapped the gun in my pyjamas and left it in the drawer under the television. I put the rucksack, with all my belongings inside, over my shoulder and left the hotel. I headed for a different café this morning and ordered a coffee and a croissant. The man behind the counter instructed me to sit down and said he would bring it over to me, so I paid him and then went and found a sofa. I was just taking my rucksack off my back when I felt my phone vibrating. It was Charlton.

"Morning, Sam, how are you doing?"

"Hey. You sound a bit brighter this morning. Listen, let's meet up this evening. I'd like to catch up on stuff but I don't want to talk too much on the phone."

"Okay." I wondered if he was worried his phone was being listened to. "There's a cool little French restaurant near here, I went there last night and it was great. If that is okay?"

He agreed that it would be.

I told him the name and location. "Oh and, Sam?"

"Yep."

"Dr Neasden must have had a death certificate."

"Well, yes, but…"

"It will state his cause of death. Which was clearly a bullet in the stomach. It might help prove that Darnold is tampering with the records."

"I'll do a little digging. See you later."

My coffee and croissant arrived. I fished out my copies of Lambert's texts and studied them in a bit more detail. I went through them all, checking the number they had come from or been sent to and cross checking this against the time and date they had been sent or received. It was boring work. There were no real conversations; in fact almost all of the texts seemed to concern arrangements to meet. There were some vague references to 'pick ups' and I, once again, wondered if there was some drug connection. It seemed that, looking through the messages, it was Lambert who was telling others where to be and at what time. Most of the replies were 'ok' or 'got it' or 'message received'. It was all very bland.

I checked the numbers. All the texts relating to these meetings had been sent to just two different numbers. Only two. This phone was clearly only used for making arrangements. I cross checked the numbers against the list of calls that Lambert had made and received. One of them was in the list. It had been called a few days previously. I picked up my phone and dialled. After a couple of rings someone picked up. *Shit, I should have thought about this before dialling.* I didn't know what to say. I was completely unprepared. Then a deep, resounding male voice said, "Yeah? Who is this?" I couldn't think of an answer to that so I hung up.

Damn. I should have thought it through. I thought someone might have answered, giving me their name when they picked up, and that the loose ends would tie up. But things weren't working as smoothly as that. I went back to the texts. It was then that I noticed the date. The date on the last text. I'd completely lost track of the days and the dates over the last week but the text said:

> *Sunday 5th. Toddington. Northbound. 2pm.*

Shit. Sunday 5th. That was tomorrow. I thought about it, and it took me a while but, yes, today was Saturday. The text had been sent to the number that had never been called. It had been answered only a few minutes after it had been sent.

> *Got it. C.*

Who was C? None of the initials in the notebook had a C in them. I thought about ringing and taking a stab in the dark 'hello is that Charlie?' but it could be Clive, or Chris or probably a hundred other names that started with a C. It could be a Christine or a Charlotte for all I knew. Whoever it was, I knew I needed to be there, at Toddington at 2pm. I'd think about whether I needed to ring the number later, but now I had to get prepared. I made a list of things I would need.

Top of the list was a hire car; I'd need a car to drive to Toddington—it was miles up the M1. If I hired a car I'd need a driver's licence. I had mine in my bag, but did I really want to use mine? I sat and thought of a plan for stealing someone else's licence but it all seemed a bit speculative. What if I nicked someone's purse and they didn't have their licence in it? Plus I'd have to choose someone who was vaguely the same age as me, or with a picture that could possibly pass for me. In the end, I decided that the best thing would be to just go for it and book it in my name. I figured that, as long as I paid cash and didn't use my debit card, it wouldn't be too bad. Someone would have to be actively looking for me renting a car, and why would they suspect I'd do that? And they would have to ask every car hire place in the country, surely? I could see that they might be looking for debit card transactions and it would be stupid to use one of those, but as long as I paid in cash I didn't think using my driver's licence would be too risky.

I Googled car hire firms in North London; I figured I didn't want to have to drive through central London if I could avoid it. I tried a couple but they wouldn't let me pay cash, they said I'd have to pay in advance with a credit or debit card. I even tried telling them a sob story about having my handbag stolen and all my cards were in it, along with my train tickets and I just wanted to go home. They must have thought I was trying to scam them so I gave up and moved on. Eventually I found a firm in Highgate with an extremely helpful assistant who said it would be okay to pick up a car in the morning and pay in cash when I arrived. I fished out my driver's licence, which luckily I did carry around in my purse, and ordered a medium-sized family car. I wanted something that would blend in.

Then I paid for my coffee and croissant and went on a search for all the other things on my list.

27

I started by walking to Oxford Street. I headed westwards along the south side of the street. The weather had warmed up again to the point where it was almost unseasonably warm. I stopped and took off my jacket and hat. I folded my jacket and put it into my rucksack, along with my hat, but I kept the scarf round my neck. Then a few hundred yards further down the road I found exactly what I was looking for; Ann Summers.

I had never been in an Ann Summers shop before and I sauntered past the rows of fancy bras and pants towards the back of the shop. I glanced around, trying to look as if I was an old hand at this. I thought that the assistants were appraising my outfit; my outdoor wear didn't really chime with the notion of sexy underwear. Still, maybe I had hidden depths that my clothes didn't betray. I smiled, thinking of the big pants I had on that had been bought in Blacks. I held my head up and headed further into the shop. There was a display to my left of clothes to dress up in, including nurse's outfits, French maid outfits and one for a dominatrix, all for women to dress up in I noted. Most of them appeared to be PVC and didn't look very comfortable. In the middle of the room there was a circular display that you walked into. I looked at the array of objects in amazement. There were vibrators of all sizes and colours, some with variable speeds and some with all sorts of add-on pieces. There were also clamps, rings and anal plugs as well as a weird looking vibrator with two prongs. I picked it up curiously and was reading the back of the package when an assistant came up and asked me if I needed any help.

"No, that's great, thanks," I said sheepishly. "Just looking."

I put the strange double vibrator down and carried on through the display to the other side of the room. Here there were whips and leather bondage gear and copies of 'Fifty Shades of Grey' next to paddles and shackles. I marvelled at the vagaries of human proclivities; John and I had had what I had thought was a fairly active sex life, but it had been strictly normal, under the covers stuff. Should we have the lights on, or do it in the afternoon or on the kitchen floor was about as risqué as we'd got. Then I saw what I needed; handcuffs. I bypassed the pink fluffy ones, and the ones that could be attached to feet and hands at the same time and went for the boring metal handcuffs. I picked them off the display and studied them. They weren't quite as sturdy as the ones I'd used to attach Lambert to the bed in my hotel room, but they would definitely do; they would certainly hold someone up for a while if the need arose. I briefly thought about Lambert. I wondered when he had been discovered and by who and what he had said by way of an explanation. Maybe he was still there, shackled to the bed.

I picked three pairs of handcuffs off the hook and took them to the counter. The shop assistant smiled but said nothing as she put them in a bag for me.

"You never know when you might need to tie up more than one person," I said with a smile.

She just laughed, as if she was well used to the idea of handcuffing several people in one go and said, "Quite."

I walked further along Oxford Street, looking down side streets for secondhand bookshops. After walking for half a mile or so, I found a likely looking street off to the North side of Oxford Street. There was a quirky little book store a couple of hundred yards down the road on the right-hand side. I stepped inside and perused the shelves. Instantly a man came over and asked me if I was okay. He was thin and wiry and didn't look at all as if he should be working in a secondhand bookshop. I always imagined bookshop owners should wear corduroy trousers and sleeveless sweaters with collarless shirts and have shaggy, curly hair and wire-rimmed glasses. A bit like the Irish guy that had been in Black Books whose name I could never remember. This guy had none of those things; he would have looked more at home as a villain in a Harry

Potter book. He had straight hair slicked over a bald patch and plastered to his head with some kind of greasy substance, and he was wearing a suit that looked as if it was three sizes too large. He had a hooked nose, thin lips and rubbed his hands together when he talked. He reminded me of the child catcher from Chitty Chitty Bang Bang.

"Just looking thanks," I replied and carried on scanning the shelves.

"Were you looking for anything in particular?"

"No. No thanks, just browsing."

"Any genre you especially like reading?" He rubbed his hands together as if miming washing them.

I turned to look at him. I had a serious urge to shove him backwards into his bookcase and drown him under a pile of falling books. Instead I smiled curtly, said, "I'm fine," then turned away and carried on perusing the shelves.

He didn't say anything but I could sense him hovering behind me, hopping from foot to foot and rubbing his hands together.

I couldn't see what I wanted so, against my better judgement, I turned to the shop owner, or manager, or assistant, or whatever he was.

"Do you have a section for dictionaries and encyclopaedias?"

"Of course." He nodded and kind of bowed in the direction he wanted us to go. I followed him to the back of the shop where he indicated with a sweep of his arm a bookcase full of huge books. I pulled a couple from the shelf and held them, weighing them in my hands. The hovering man seemed to find this incredibly curious.

"Any particular kind you were after?" he asked in his thin voice. It matched his thin stature. And his thin hair.

"No, no." I kept pulling books off the shelf until I found one that was perfect. It was bound in that stuff that is like a cross between a paperback and a hardback; was it called softback? Heavy enough to really hurt if you swung it at someone's head but soft enough not to kill them. I didn't want anyone's life on my hands if things got tricky.

I took the book to the counter and paid. Then I returned to Oxford Street, turned right and walked almost to Marble Arch to find Selfridges. I went up the escalator to their homeware department and through to the kitchen section. I walked around for a while before finding an assistant and asking about the various knives they had on sale. It was Saturday and I wondered if the young man helping me was on a Saturday job and still at school. He looked about fifteen and, according to his name badge, was called Liam. Maybe it's me growing old, I thought. Anyway, Liam seemed to know his stuff. I explained that I wanted a knife that was not very long, but that could cut through really tough meat and wouldn't break easily. He selected a few and described the relative merits of each. I chose some that were made from Japanese steel – apparently really strong but also very sharp – I took two paring knives with 3.5" blades and two 6" chef's knives. That set me back almost £200 but I needed to be prepared. Liam wrapped the knives carefully and put them in a bag with the receipt and I thanked him and left.

I went through homeware to find the curtain section. There I selected several yards of clear curtain wire. Having had an intruder in my hotel room I thought it might come in handy in case I needed to booby trap another room. I went back down the escalators and returned to the street.

I headed along Oxford Street towards Covent Garden and called in at Jessops. There I bought a powerful torch and a pair of binoculars. I got the assistant to show me how to use them properly, how to focus them and change the focus for nearer, or further away, objects. I thanked him and left, carrying on along the road until I found a food store. I bought three lemons, some ground black pepper, some cayenne pepper, some extra-hot chilli powder, some Sellotape and some tabasco sauce.

As I continued my trip back towards the hotel I passed an outdoors store. I paused; shoes hadn't been on my shopping list, but I remembered how my foot had hurt after kicking Lambert, and I veered in. A young girl came to help and fetched a variety of styles to try. She asked what activities I would be using them for. I felt like telling her I was planning on using them to kick people in the balls, or on the shins, but I thought better of it. After trying on several pairs I decided on a pair of sturdy walking boots. I knew I would have to drive the hire car whilst wearing them and so I didn't want anything too clumpy, but at the same time I wanted something that would protect my feet and also hurt any adversary if I needed to swing my foot between anyone else's legs. I wondered what my long-haired self from a week ago would have thought about me preparing for kicking people, hitting them with heavy books or handcuffing them to beds. I imagined she would have taken a very dim view. I smiled at my reflection in the mirror as I left the shop, not just physically different now but mentally too. I knew I was getting involved with some very dangerous people, but I had found a determination that hadn't existed in me for some time and I was not going to give in without a fight. I knew they were going to keep coming for me and I was not going to sit around and wait. I had to take the fight to them.

Finally, I found a Boots and called in there. I wandered around until I found the holiday section, and there I located some empty plastic bottles that you can fill with your favourite toiletries when you go away without falling foul of the 'no more than 100ml' rule. I chose a couple that had a spray pump-action top and took them to the counter. I joined a long queue of people and eventually made my way to the front of the queue and paid. I walked out into the autumn sunshine and headed back to my hotel.

28

When I returned to the hotel I assessed my purchases. I spread everything out on the bed. The new shoes were good. If I kicked anyone wearing those I didn't think my foot would hurt quite as much as the last time. The pain had now subsided in my toes and I really didn't want to experience that again. I took the binoculars out of their box and put the box back in the carrier bag. I walked over to the window and surveyed London from the hotel window. There was a reasonably good view down the Thames if I peered between the buildings, and, once I got the binoculars focused, I could see one end of Tower Bridge quite clearly. I tried moving quickly to look at something closer and practised refocusing as fast as I could. I practised it a few times, moving and refocusing, until my fingers knew exactly where the dial was without me having to think about it.

I then got out the torch and went into the bathroom, which had no windows. I shut the door so that it was in darkness and turned on the torch. I surveyed the bathroom with the beam of light, noticing a couple of spiders that had escaped my attention until now. I let them be; spiders had never bothered me. Not like earwigs, or maggots, I hated those things but spiders were okay. The beam was sharp and focused, not spreading too far out either side. Perfect. I went back into the room and sat back down on the bed.

Then I gathered together the items I'd got in Sainsbury's. I unwrapped the cellophane from around the spices and grabbed one of the mugs that had been left next to the little hotel kettle. Using the mug as a mixing bowl, I poured some of the black pepper, extra-hot chilli powder and cayenne pepper into it, and stirred them all together. When I was satisfied, I tried a taste, just a little on the tip of my tongue. I could stand hot food, in my opinion the hotter the better. Whenever John and I had gone out for curry I would order the hottest meal on the menu. If it brought tears to my eyes, that was the sign that the heat was about right. John, on the other hand would always opt for the korma or some other fairly bland concoction. As I tasted my mix of spices, tears welled up in my eyes; not from sentimentality but from the heat. Wow, that was quite a hot mix. My tongue was on fire. I added a little more of each to the mug, just to be sure. Then I unwrapped one of my new knives, cut into one of the lemons and squeezed it into the mug. I did the same with the other two lemons and then added quite a bit of tabasco sauce to the mix. I stirred the whole thing together, with one of the hotel teaspoons to get a really good mix and then went into the bathroom. I fished out the plastic bottles and, over the sink, I carefully filled both of them with the lemon, tabasco and spice mix. I tried both bottles to see if the spray action worked. It wasn't quite MACE but it would be a good substitute.

I put all my new purchases, except the walking shoes, in the drawer under the television with the gun. Then I had a shower, dried my hair, dressed and got ready to meet Charlton. I looked at myself in the mirror wearing my outdoor trousers and long sleeved top; pretty much the same outfit I'd worn the last time I'd met him. I thought, briefly, that maybe whilst I was out I should have bought a dress so I would at least look like I'd made an effort. Then I told myself not to be stupid; it wasn't a date, for heaven's sake. Besides I still had a cut on my lip and a faint red mark around my neck. I wasn't at my most attractive.

I arrived a few minutes early, and Charlton hadn't got there yet, so I asked for a table for two. The same waitress who had been there the night before indicated a choice of a couple of tables and I chose one tucked away in the corner. I ordered a glass of wine whilst I waited and perused the menu. All the items were different to the night before, which indicated that they had to make them fresh each day. Just as the waitress came over with my wine, Charlton arrived. He ordered a French beer and sat down, surveying his surroundings.

"I've never been here before," he said as he glanced at the menu. "Looks okay, though."

I told him I'd eaten here the night before and had been impressed.

"Are you okay?" he said, staring at my cut lip with a frown of concern.

"I'm fine. You should have seen the other guy," I joked. But it didn't really sound funny when I said it out loud and I'm not sure Charlton was too impressed. The waitress brought his beer over, along with some bread and olives, and so we ordered. He asked for the escargots to start followed by Sole with lemon; I had soup of the day and chicken fricassee. We nibbled the bread and exchanged niceties. Hadn't the weather improved? What about current politics in America? We chatted away as if the death and mayhem that had surrounded me for the best part of a week didn't exist. The conversation came easily and before I knew it we'd finished our starters and were waiting for the main courses. He was good company, an intelligent and thoughtful man. The time slipped easily by.

"So what have you been up to today?" he asked after a brief pause in the conversation.

"Shopping," I replied with a bright smile.

"Oh, that's a good idea. It's good to try and relax when you're in a bit of a stressful situation."

I nodded. A bit stressful? That was an understatement.

"Did you get anything nice?"

A few homemade weapons, I thought, but I kept that to myself. I hadn't mentioned anything to Charlton about the texts on Lambert's phone or the arrangements for tomorrow. Or the fact that I planned to hire a car and see what I could find out. I thought that he might be less than enthusiastic about my plan and try to talk me out of it. "I got some new shoes," I said brightly.

The main courses arrived and the conversation moved on. Once we had finished our food, declined desserts but ordered coffee and brandy, I said, "Anyway, lovely as this is, shall we compare notes on how we are getting on with things?"

Charlton kicked off with what he had found out earlier that day.

"Richard Sanderson is a Detective Inspector with Nottinghamshire police," he explained. He told me about his digging around and how he had found this out, double checking with the phone number I'd given him to make sure it was the same guy.

I nodded. That made sense; Nottinghamshire bordered Lincolnshire so it wouldn't be a surprise if people from that force were involved too. It might even have made it easier to cover things up.

Charlton carried on, "There is a connection between Sanderson and Dr Neasden."

"Oh, really? Interesting."

"Yes, it is." He paused to take a slug of his brandy. "Dr Neasden was doing some work with a young man who was being prosecuted by Nottinghamshire police. "

"I think he did voluntary work with people who had no recourse to public funds."

"He did. This young man was an illegal immigrant. His name is Ndeye Ndawayo. He came, originally, from Rwanda. Sanderson was in charge when the young man was arrested for burglary. He claimed to be 16years old but that was disputed, because apparently he had papers saying he was twenty-one."

"What happened?"

"He was convicted of burglary and he was sent to an adult jail."

I thought about that, but said nothing.

"What I did find strange was that there were no other police involved in the arrest."

"Is that unusual?"

"Well, it's not completely impossible, but it is unusual for a Detective Inspector to be the arresting officer for a burglary. I'm a Detective Inspector myself. I know that these days I spend most of my time doing managing and administrating. Obviously I get involved, but more as the chief investigating officer, I'm not often out on the front line."

"Maybe he got lucky? Just happened to be there when the lad ran out with a bag of swag over his shoulders?"

"It's a possibility," he conceded.

"And what was Dr Neasden's involvement?"

"He was helping the young man access medical treatment."

"Medical treatment?"

"Yeah, not sure what for though."

"Blimey."

We sipped our coffees and brandies in silence for a while.

"So, tell me a bit about the other guy. The one who ended up looking worse than you." Charlton pursed his lips and rubbed his finger along his jawline, as if he wasn't sure whether to be concerned, impressed or amused with my hotel room antics. He asked a few more questions, what had he looked like, what had he sounded like, how I had managed to overpower him and so on. I somewhat overplayed the effect that crashing his head into the coat hook had had, and rather underplayed me kicking him in the balls when he was unconscious. I still made no mention of the gun. We asked for the bill, paid, leaving a hefty tip, and then Charlton got up. He offered to walk me back to the hotel, but I was reluctant to give away my location to anyone, even this charming man. '*Trust no one.*' I let him leave first, making the excuse of needing the bathroom. He promised to be in touch if he had anything relating to Dr Neasden's death certificate. He had put some feelers out but had got nothing back yet.

I waited ten minutes after he'd gone. I didn't know why but I walked around in circles for fifteen minutes, through the streets of Covent Garden, which were still teeming with people, before returning to my hotel. I was pretty sure that nobody had followed me, and that if they had I would have lost them by darting in and out of the busy little streets.

It was 10.30pm when I got back to the hotel. I took the lift up to the 9th floor. I had had a pleasant evening. Despite the circumstances and despite the danger I knew I was in, I'd had an enjoyable few hours in the company of Detective Inspector Sam Charlton. I cautiously opened my bedroom door, double checked that there was no one there, made sure the gun was still safe, put the deadbolt on the door and then got changed and went to bed.

SUNDAY

29

I got up early on Sunday morning. After showering, I took all my purchases out of the drawer. I put the heavy book in the carrier bag that had come with the spices and lemons and I laid it down sideways. I wrapped Sellotape around the bag, just above where the book was so that it wouldn't slip and tried swinging it a few times to check it was secure. Everything stayed in place. *Good.* I placed the two bottles of my homemade pepper spray in one of the front pockets of the rucksack and put two of the knives in the other front pocket, and two in the side pocket. I put the handcuffs on top of all my clothes. I wore the walking boots and left the trainers in the hotel room as there was no room for them in the bag. I looked at the gun. I hadn't a clue what to do with it, but I didn't think I should leave it in the hotel room. I picked it up and, after carefully trying a couple of the levers, I figured out how to take the handle apart so that I could take the bullets out. This fascinated me. How could you put the bullets in the handle and yet they came out of the barrel? I assumed there had to be some mechanism for pushing them round the corner but I wasn't going to investigate. I stuffed the bullets into a zip-up pocket in the back of the rucksack, and hid the gun in amongst my clothes. I gathered up all the packaging from the purchases I'd made and also the spices, lemon peel and everything. I distributed them across a couple of the carrier bags and took everything with me.

I went to reception, settled my bill and checked out; even though I had had no extras on top of the room rate, the bill was eye-watering. You couldn't stay cheaply in London. As I left the hotel, I picked up a free copy of the 'i' newspaper and walked to Tottenham Court Road tube station, grabbing a cup of coffee on my way there. I dumped the carrier bags in different litter bins as I walked along. I thought that I was, perhaps, being a little over cautious but you never can tell. I recalled that when I hadn't been too careful, like using the same pseudonym twice, it had backfired. I decided that there was no such thing as being too cautious and I didn't want anyone figuring out that I had been making pepper spray in my hotel room, even if I had used a made-up name to check in that even I couldn't remember. *'Trust no one'* had become my mantra and I repeated it as I walked along, to the rhythm of my steps.

I took the northern line all the way to Highgate, which took just under twenty minutes; almost enough time to read through the paper. I arrived at the car hire place as they were opening at 8.30 and hung around whilst they brought the car to the front, took my money, checked my driver's licence, explained the terms and conditions and so on. I paid extra for the super damage waiver insurance and took the keys.

It was a slate grey Vauxhall Insignia. Pretty bog standard and nothing special at all. It was perfect. It was alright to drive, although I really didn't like the press button handbrake. I felt suddenly incredibly nervous and it dawned on me that I hadn't driven a car since John had died. Ours had obviously been written off, and although the insurance firm were going to pay me a decent amount for the loss of it, I hadn't even thought of buying a new one. In the first weeks after John's death I wouldn't have been capable of driving and if I'd needed to go anywhere recently, I'd usually got a lift off Collette. I hadn't done that often as the thought of being in a car had started to scare me. It felt strange and unnatural to be behind the wheel. I couldn't stop myself from thinking about John's last moments, driving along, not knowing what was about to happen. I'd often wondered what his last thoughts had been and whether he'd realised the lorry was heading for him. I had been assured that he would have died instantly as the lorry impacted with his car, but there must have been a few seconds when he'd seen the lorry heading his way and had known there was no way out. I wondered what had gone through his head at that point. I shook my head, trying hard to concentrate on the here and now, and pulled out gingerly before heading up the Archway Road and joining the M1 just after Brent Park.

The motorway was reasonably quiet as it was relatively early on a Sunday morning and I made good time getting to the services at Toddington. I turned into the northbound service station and parked in the furthest corner of the car park. I looked around. It would be a good spot. I could stand behind the car and remain relatively hidden, but I could see the entrance, and the whole of the car park. I took out my binoculars and scanned the car park. I watched a few cars coming in, people getting out and going in to use the services, people coming out and driving off. I was fairly sure that I could cover the majority of the car park from where I was standing. The only problem would be if it got busy and there were too many people milling about. I went into the services and bought a coffee and a cake and sat down by the window. I was early but it gave me time to think.

I pulled out my iPad and checked the copies I'd made of the texts that had been on Lambert's phone. I double checked the message, and double checked the date. I was definitely in the right place and on the right day. It was 10.30am so I had three and a half hours to wait. I hoped the weather stayed fine.

My phone rang; it was Charlton.

"Verity, are you in your hotel?"

"No. I'm not. I'm a bit busy today, actually." I cursed myself for sounding so on edge. I hadn't meant to sound quite as abrupt as I did.

"What are you doing?" He paused. "Verity what are you up to?" He had obviously picked up on the anxiety in my voice.

I wouldn't tell him. "I'm just checking something out. Don't worry, I think I might be onto something and I'm just doing a bit of digging, that's all."

He sounded unsure and kept urging me to be careful. I got the sense that he thought I might be getting into something that was well over my head. He was absolutely right.

"I probably shouldn't be telling you this, but I got hold of a copy of Dr Neasden's death certificate."

"Oh, well done. And?"

"Apparently he died from cardiac arrest caused by advanced heart disease."

I was stunned. "What? But that's…"

"Also a cover up. Yes, I know."

"I think the cardiac arrest was more likely brought on by having no blood left."

"Verity, be careful. I'm telling you this because we are dealing with some very dangerous, and clearly very devious people. Think very carefully about what you are doing won't you?"

I tried to push his concern to the back of my head. I needed to find out what was going on.

"But how will that tie up with the police report? The report that said there was a break-in?"

"I imagine the report will now conclude that the stress of the break-in, coupled with Dr Neasden's 'advanced heart disease' was what caused his death."

"But what about the investigation?" I asked.

"If Darnold is in charge then it will probably be quietly dropped. How many burglaries do you know where the burglar is never caught? I'm sure he will have manipulated this so it doesn't show up as manslaughter or murder. It'll be an unsolved burglary that unfortunately led to the death of a man who was very ill anyway and not much longer for this world."

I remembered Dr Neasden striding up Steep Hill, looking anything but very ill, and as if he was going to be in this world for a long time to come.

"Do you know who signed the death certificate?" I asked.

He paused. I got the sense that he was weighing up what he should and shouldn't tell me. He sighed at the other end of the phone and I imagined him running his finger along his jaw as he thought about whether it was more dangerous to answer my question or to keep me in the dark. I resisted the urge to push him for an answer, and after what seemed like a lifetime he responded. "Yes, it was a doctor called Kenneth Townsley."

Kenneth Townsley. Why did that ring a bell? I struggled to grab hold of the memory that was trying to push its way to the front of my brain. The acronyms. *Oh shit. KTMD. Kenneth Townsley Medical Doctor. The last of the acronyms.*

"Verity?"

"Yes."

"Whatever you are doing, be careful. Don't get involved in anything you can't handle. These people are clearly dangerous and not afraid to cover up whatever it is they're doing. A woman, alone, with nothing…well, I mean no exp…well, all I'm saying is to be careful. Okay?"

I thought about my makeshift armoury. I didn't tell Charlton I was heading out equipped and ready to cause some damage if I needed to. I didn't want to be in danger of being arrested before I'd even done anything and I thought if I told him what I had in my possession he would really think I was getting into something over my head. I thought it was best to keep that to myself. I just said quietly, "I will, I promise. You too."

Immediately after I had put the phone down I got out my iPad and Googled Kenneth Townsley MD. It turned out that the initials MD were a bit of shorthand on the part of Dr Neasden as Kenneth Townsley, or should I say *Professor* Kenneth Townsley had many initials after his name including BM, BCh, PhD, FRCP and FMedSci. I hadn't a clue what any of those meant. Bachelor of medicine, I guessed. But BCh, what was that? Bachelor of something. But what, chemistry? Chemotherapy? Could you get a degree in chemotherapy? PhD I knew was Doctor of Philosophy as I had thought of studying for one of those myself in the past. Then Fellow of something or other. Professor Townsley, it appeared, was a very well-qualified doctor at Lincoln County Hospital and was a specialist in cancer. I went onto the hospital website and read his biography.

It appeared that the professor had qualified in the mid-70s and had undertaken several specialist qualifications. I guessed that would account for all the letters then. He had worked in the states for a period in the early 90s where he had been undertaking research on how cancers grew and changed in the body. He had worked at Lincoln since 2000 and apparently was 'currently leading on a number of national trials for cancer treatment development'.

But why had he signed Dr Neasden's death certificate? Unless Dr Neasden had been suffering from cancer and had been seen by Townsley recently I couldn't think why a specialist at a hospital would sign a death certificate. Dr Neasden had died at his home. Surely they wouldn't have taken him to A&E at the hospital? When John had died, he'd apparently been rushed to Hull Royal Infirmary and had been declared dead on arrival at the hospital. Because his death had been sudden it had been reported to the coroner for an investigation. It hadn't really needed much of an investigation—his death had been caused by the massive trauma of being hit head-on by a lorry. So the coroner had agreed to issue the death certificate reasonably quickly. But with Dr Neasden, there had clearly been no hope of reviving him, they had done all they could in the house. They hadn't even turned on the sirens when they'd left with him in the ambulance, but his death was certainly sudden. I assumed they would have taken him straight to the mortuary. Surely they would have done a post-mortem? So who would have certified his death? And why would a cancer specialist have been involved? Townsley had to be involved in the cover-up. His were the last initials along with Sanderson and Darnold. They had obviously been covering this up together. If Neasden's

212

death was explained away as due to natural causes then perhaps the coroner wouldn't have been involved. There would be no investigation. Maybe they hadn't even done a post-mortem. What the hell was going on?

30

Dr Neasden had written Townsley's initials in his book. Townsley was a cancer specialist; I couldn't conceive of a connection. I searched a little more on the Internet and found a couple of articles about, or by, Townsley. The ones written by him all sounded very medically orientated and were mostly to do with the rate of the growth of cancer within the body. There was one article I discovered in a newspaper archive, but it gave me no clues. It was from two years' ago, almost to the day. It was about the research that Townsley was doing at the hospital. He had won some kind of prestigious award from the Royal Society of Medicine and had been given grants from the European Research Council and the Medical Research Council to enable him to continue his research, which was described in the article as 'ground breaking'. The article was full of platitudes from hospital staff, both managerial and lowly, as well as from the Royal Society. There were even pictures of him with patients, all full of both smiles and gratitude. It seemed that Professor Townsley was not only well qualified but also well renowned and well respected.

What could the connection possibly be? I stopped trying to think about it and instead I did some research on Sanderson and Darnold. I started with Sanderson. I dug around for about half an hour but I couldn't locate much on him. There were a couple of very brief articles in the local press reporting trials at Nottinghamshire Crown Court and a little piece about the Christmas drink-driving campaign from a couple of years ago. There didn't appear to be a picture.

I went and got myself another coffee and then started on Darnold. I got luckier there; I learned a bit more about him. He seemed to like getting his picture in the paper. There was one, very clear, picture of him at a fundraising event for Children in Need. It had been for the previous year and the local police had apparently been 'rowing around the coast' in a rowing machine, taking turns to do so many miles each. There was a picture with a young man rowing and another man standing next to the machine. The caption said, '*Detective Inspector Adrian Darnold watches PC Ian Lenton complete his stint at the rowing machine.*'

Darnold was standing next to the rowing machine, looking into the camera and smiling broadly. He looked about average height, judging by the things around him, and was a stocky build. I guessed he was around 45 but could have been 5 years either side of that. He had a full head of short hair with a little quiff at the front and was wearing shorts and a stripy polo shirt. He had rosy cheeks and a hint of a double chin, as if he struggled to keep excess weight off.

I flicked through a couple more articles. Darnold seemed to enjoy courting the local press. Maybe part of his job was to engage with the public. There was another shot of him, standing with an elderly lady, accompanying an article about home safety. He looked sturdier in this photo. I checked the date; it was more recent than the rowing picture. Maybe he'd put on some weight this year. I scanned through some reports that didn't have pictures and were about local crimes where the police were appealing to the public for more information.

I was getting bored. I had an idea of what he looked like now and was about to call it a day, but then something caught my eye. There was an article about an award ceremony for local youths. I read through it.

'Detective Inspector Adrian Darnold of Lincolnshire police was joined yesterday by Lincs FM presenter Stewart Calder, to hand out awards to local young people. The annual 'Get Real!' Awards Ceremony for local youth was held in the ballroom of The Lindum Hotel, which was donated to the event without charge. Recipients of awards are chosen each year by a panel of young people who also organised the event. Awards were given to local heroes such as James Dawlish, 16, who rescued his elderly neighbour from a

fire. Others were for succeeding against the odds, such as Emily Wilkinson, 20, who has just been accepted to do a law degree at Cambridge University following a period in a drug rehabilitation centre.'

The article went on to list other award winners. There were several photos; photos of Darnold and Calder shaking hands with various young people, beaming at the camera, their smiles not flagging throughout the ceremony. There were photos of the young people with their awards and photos of the young organisers. Then, at the bottom of the article, there was a photo of the young people who had organised the event with a man. He was a very tall black man, towering over the young people. He must have been 6'4" at least and looked as if he was in his late twenties or early thirties. He had very dark black skin and was flashing a huge, sparkling smile. He was wearing a T shirt and had his arms spread around the shoulders of the young people. Arms that sported muscles that can only be gained by spending long periods lifting weights. And possibly taking steroids. He had long hair in braids tied behind his head and falling over his back and shoulders. He was leaning down and over the young people, some of whom were looking up towards him and smiling. The caption underneath said '*The young organisers of the Get Real! Awards with Young People's Advocate Champion Obote who helped them bring their ideas to life.'*

'Champion!' The word in Dr Neasden's notebook. I laughed out loud and sat back in my chair. *Champion!* It was a person. I wasn't sure why Dr

Neasden had put the exclamation mark there, perhaps because it was an unusual name, or maybe because he couldn't believe this young person's advocate was involved. Maybe he wasn't involved. Ibbetson's name had been in the book and I doubted he knew much. I looked back at the smiling face of Champion Obote. He looked for all the world like a likeable, friendly, outgoing person; exactly the sort of person who would be great as a young person's advocate. I could imagine they would easily get along with him, and looking at the eager faces smiling up at him I didn't doubt for one minute the trust in their faces.

31

I looked through the iPad and reviewed all the photos of Dr Neasden's notebook. I knew now, or was fairly sure that, the word 'Champion!' referred to Champion Obote, the young people's advocate. He clearly had a connection with Darnold, working with some of the same young people. I had all the names to go with the initials. I had figured out the phone numbers and I had found Stephen Ibbetson. I had worked it all out. Yet, somehow, I felt hardly any further forward than I had when I'd first looked through the notebook and understood none of it. I had no idea how Richard Sanderson and Kenneth Townsley fitted into any of this. I didn't really understand what Darnold was doing. I knew that between them they were covering up the fact that Dr Neasden had been shot but I had no idea why. I had figured out who the players were, according to the notebook, but I didn't have any idea what it was they were 'playing' in. I was shooting in the dark. Dr Neasden had given no clues as to exactly what was going on, just the people involved. Did they know what was in the notebook? Had Dr Neasden confronted one of them maybe? And told them he had made notes. Clearly they wouldn't want their names to be connected with each other as that could lead a trail, a trail I was following. But perhaps they also thought that there was more in the notebook than just the names?

I went back to the counter and bought a revolting motorway service station sandwich. I forced myself to eat it, against my better judgement, as I hadn't a clue when the next time would be that I would get to eat, and I needed to have my wits about me. I needed the energy. I still had an hour to wait, so I picked up the Daily Mail that someone had left on the table to my left and read that. That was a distraction; I hate that paper, always having a go at some group or another for not being white and middle class. I flipped past most of the propaganda and went more or less straight to the Sudoku and completed the easy one and the hard one. I left the really difficult one on the basis that I probably wouldn't finish it in time. I went to the toilets, and then steadied myself as I washed my hands and looked in the mirror. I was incredibly nervous. I had no idea what it was that I might be getting into, or where I might be going or what I might see; everything was an unknown. I took some deep breaths then headed out to my spot at the top of the car park.

It was a good day for staking out. Well, I had never staked anything out before, but I assumed it didn't get much better than this. I looked up at the clouds. They didn't look like rain clouds but they also didn't look like they were going to clear away at any point that afternoon. Perfect.

I stood behind the car and wondered what someone would think if they saw me scanning the car park with a pair of binoculars. I was fairly well hidden behind the car. At 5'5" I was taller than the car, but just enough so that I could rest my chin on the roof and not be too conspicuous. I put my grey hat on and pulled it down over my ears. That way I would blend in even more with the car and the grey sky behind me. I took out the binoculars and focused on the entrance to the car park. Cars were coming in at a reasonable pace, but there was generally a gap between each one. I practised watching certain cars, watching them empty out and watching the driver, and sometimes passengers, getting out and going into the services. I tried it by looking through the binoculars and I tried without. I discovered it worked best if I watched the entrance without the binoculars to start with and then focused in on a particular car as they drove around and found somewhere to park. That way, I had time to note the registration number whilst they were finding a space, and then pick them out again with the binoculars as they were parking. I practised doing this with several cars until I had the timing down to perfection.

I wasn't really sure what I was looking out for. I could miss something completely. It could be that they, whoever they were, would go into the services and I would be none the wiser. I'd thought about this whilst I had been inside eating my horrible sandwich. I had thought about watching from the window of the services. I'd decided against that on the grounds that it would be much harder to be inconspicuous inside. I was also fairly sure if there was a 'pick up', which was what I thought was going to happen, that it would happen in the car park. If they were handing over a package of drugs they would be far more noticeable inside and people would be much more likely to remember them. People chatting in the car park would be easily forgettable; people didn't really look around them as they hurried from their cars to the inside. The petrol station had CCTV so I had also ruled that out as a possible location. I decided to stay where I was. I could miss something but I was far more likely to see whatever was happening out here. I stayed put behind the hire car.

My other problem was that I had no idea who I was looking out for, nor what it was they were going to 'pick up'. I assumed that if there was some kind of exchange happening that I would notice a person, or persons, from one car approaching someone from another car. I decided that was the behaviour I would have to look out for. I knew the time of the meet was 2pm and I wondered if either party might arrive early so I was also keeping my eye open for anyone arriving into the car park and just waiting. It seemed that quite a few people took a while to get out of their cars.

222

Perhaps they were putting sat navs out of sight, making sure they had their wallets or handbags, unbuckling their children or something. Down in the middle of the car park a man was sitting in his car for what seemed like ages. I started to get excited, scanning to the entrance, then back to him again. But then he got out, locked his car remotely and marched off into the services.

I looked at the time on my phone, it was ten minutes to two. I started watching with more interest. A couple of cars pulled in together. They made for opposite ends of the car park. The doors of one car opened and a family got out, a surly teenager, a small child and a screaming toddler. The mother dragged the screaming toddler along, eventually scooping him up and carrying him. The other car had a couple inside. They walked arm in arm into the services.

Another car had entered the car park. This one had a white, lady driver. She parked as close to the entrance as she could and ran into the services. Probably desperate for the loo, I thought. I returned to the entrance. A black car was just pulling in, and I could see behind the wheel a black face but it was obscured by the dull light from the clouds reflecting on the windscreen. I quickly reached for my binoculars and my heart leapt, beating faster and faster. My legs buckled beneath me and I pressed onto the roof of the car with my elbows to stop myself falling over. All my instincts were screaming at me to get out, go back to the services and hide, that I was in over my head and I should leave all this to the experts. I steadied myself and stood firm. *Shit, shit, shit. This is it, Verity. Keep your wits about you.* Without a shadow of a doubt, the man who was just pulling into the car park in a black A Class Mercedes was Champion Obote. Then it dawned on me. The text; '*Got it. C*'. C for Champion. He was a few minutes early and he came through the car park towards me. I peered through the binoculars and it felt as if he was looking directly at me. He seemed so close. I scribbled down his number plate and watched intently.

32

It was only a couple of minutes and a few cars later that he stepped out of his car. I was trying to keep an eye on everything, looking backwards and forwards between Obote and the entrance. It was not an easy task. A grey BMW 5 Series had just pulled into the car park and parked a couple of lanes away from him. I'd noted down the number plate as it had entered the car park, as I had with the other cars that had entered in the last few minutes. Champion Obote got out of his car and answered a call on his phone. He was so tall it seemed as if he was unfolding as he got out of the car, like a beach umbrella being pushed up to full height. He looked round; clearly on the phone to whoever he was due to meet. A slim white man got out of the BMW and headed towards him, also on the phone, and Obote dropped the call, going over to meet him. I quickly scribbled out all the other number plates I'd written down so that I would know I had the right ones, Obote's and the slim man's.

The two men met in the middle of the car park and shook hands. The white man gently held Obote's elbow as they shook hands. A gesture of familiarity. They looked for all the world like a couple of friends, or business partners exchanging greetings. They stepped to one side next to an old red Ford Fiesta as another car pulled past them. Obote dwarfed the slim man, although I guessed he must have been about 6' tall. He was dressed in what looked like a smart suit. I scanned them from head to foot through the binoculars. Obote clearly worked out; he had the build of a boxer with his big arms and trim waist and his long hair tied back at the nape of his enormous neck. The man he was meeting looked like a squirrel in comparison. He was slim and appeared to be in his mid-30s, maybe early 40s. He wasn't a very good looking man; he was facing my way and he had a puffy, swollen, face despite being quite slim, with big bags under each eye as if, over the years, he'd had too much to drink. Or too many drugs. His lips were thick and sat above a small, round chin. He seemed to have an air of superiority about him, despite being several inches shorter than Obote, and I got the impression that, whatever they were in together, he was higher up the chain.

I watched through my binoculars as they exchanged words. Their hand gestures and smiles implied that they were exchanging friendly greetings. There didn't appear to be any disagreement or argument going on. After a couple of minutes, the

226

white man returned to his BMW and opened the back door. My heart thumped so loudly I was surprised they didn't turn to look at me. It was pounding against the side of the car with every beat. What was he going to get? Perhaps he was reaching in for a packet of drugs. Maybe I should take photos on my iPad camera, but I didn't feel I had time to get it out of the rucksack and I wanted to carry on watching to see what it was the man got out of the car.

I was expecting the man to reach into the back of the car, but he stood and held the door open. I didn't know what I was expecting to see, but it hadn't been this. Two young boys, or they might have been girls, it was difficult to tell, climbed out of the back seats. They both appeared small and thin, but I guessed they were about fourteen. They had short hair which made them look like boys, but their faces were soft and childlike and gave no clues. They were both white and they stood nervously near to the car. They were wearing jeans and long-sleeved hooded tops and clutching something in front of them. Bags maybe, or another top. They looked lost, and neither man spoke to them. The white man merely gestured towards Obote, and the boys, or possibly girls, followed him.

The whole group went back to the Mercedes and the boys got in the back. Obote locked the car, with the children inside, whilst he exchanged a few more words with the puffy-eyed guy. This exchange had a less friendly feel than the initial conversation they had had. The white man was holding up a hand, and Obote was nodding and raising his eyebrows as if to say 'yeah, I know' and the white man made an emphatic, palms down gesture with both hands. Obote nodded again, raising his hands and shrugging his shoulders. They stood there talking for a little while longer and then they shook hands again. The white man went back to his BMW, and Obote watched him until he had driven away. He unlocked the car and folded himself back inside, closed the door then began to drive off.

I quickly ran around the car, threw the binoculars onto the passenger seat, along with the number plates I'd scribbled down. I watched Obote pull out and then I followed behind him. I repeated his number plate over and over so that it was indelibly stamped on my brain. I followed him towards the exit of the car park, staying a little way back so as not to look too suspicious. And then, just as I was passing the petrol station, an elderly woman driving a Nissan Micra pulled out in front of me, obscuring my view. At first, I thought that was not so bad because it would hide me from Obote and make it less likely that I would be spotted in his rear-view mirror, but then the woman drove painfully slowly towards the exit.

Obote sped up and pulled into the traffic on the M1 but the Nissan Micra held back. I was getting anxious but there was no way to get past; the exit slip was only made for one car at a time. The traffic on the motorway sped past and the Micra pootled along nervously looking for a gap to pull into. I was jittering in my seat, willing it to pull out, or at least pull far enough along the slip road that I could move past. Cars were passing by in their dozens and I was feeling a sense of despair. After what felt like hours, the Micra eventually reached the part of the slip road that opened out slightly. I didn't care what the driver thought of me or my driving skills, I put my foot down, sped around the side of her, and shot onto the motorway to a blaze of a horn from the lorry that I had just cut up.

-33-

I got up to full speed as fast as I could. I wasn't sure how long I had been waiting or how many minutes Obote had on me. Neither could I remember how far it was to the next exit, and I needed to catch up with him before then or I wouldn't be sure if he had turned off or not. I put my foot down and pulled into the outside lane, overtaking about four cars. I continued to repeat Obote's number plate over and over like a mantra as I sped along trying to catch up with him. I prayed that he wasn't driving really quickly; I imagined his Mercedes was capable of much greater speeds than my Vauxhall and he could have got away from me. I spotted what I thought was a black Mercedes up ahead, but it was some other model and I hurtled on past.

I was nervous and almost in despair. I couldn't believe that I had let him pull away from me before even the first hurdle. I was a rookie at this and I was kicking myself that I hadn't waited until we were on the motorway before putting some distance between us. *Stupid woman.* Then, I spotted him. He was driving along on the inside lane. I slowed a little and checked the number plate, not that I needed to; I could see the outline of his long hair and his big body behind the wheel, but I wanted to be sure. I pulled into the inside lane, leaving a couple of cars between us. I was surprised that Obote was driving along at around 70 miles an hour, signalling clearly each time he overtook or pulled back in. But then, of course, if he was travelling with two young people who had been trafficked I guessed he really wouldn't want to be pulled over by the police. He was doing everything perfectly legally and was driving so as not to draw any attention to himself.

I settled in behind him. Sometimes letting a couple of cars come between us and sometimes just one. I didn't want him to notice me. There were other cars about that had been driving along leapfrogging each other for a few miles too, so I didn't think he would have any cause to suspect that he was being followed. Even if he noticed a car behind he would just assume, as I did, that it was merely someone heading in the same direction as him.

We continued up the motorway for about sixty miles before we turned off at junction 21a just past Leicester. I managed to follow him and stay a few cars behind. Luckily it was quite an easy junction so it wasn't too hard. I was thankful that there wasn't a large junction or traffic lights to negotiate after my last debacle. We were now heading up the A46; back up to Lincoln, I thought. It seemed feasible that whatever was going on was going on in Lincoln so I wasn't surprised to be heading back that way. We kept on along the A46 for miles, driving impeccably. It was a hugely boring drive but at least there was the odd roundabout to break up the monotony. It was getting hard to concentrate and I had to keep reminding myself, every time we came to a junction, to keep focused. Obote could turn off at any moment and I would need to be prepared to follow.

But he didn't turn off. We followed the A46 all the way to Lincoln. As we drove along the dual carriageway from Newark, I felt suddenly alert and interested, the boredom of the journey falling away. We had to be nearing our destination, so I'd have to keep my wits about me. I'd come all this way and I couldn't afford to lose him now. I overtook a couple of the cars I had kept between us and pulled in with just one car separating us. I sat up in my seat and really concentrated. We turned up the bypass, past Whisby Nature Park, the magnificent cathedral looming into view. It looked massive from this distance, dominating the city from the top of the hill with the houses tumbling down below it. On the second stretch of dual carriageway, Obote pulled into the right-hand lane and I followed, pulling in right behind him. I wasn't going to make the mistake I'd made in the service station and have someone hesitate in front of me. If the need arose I was prepared to jump a red light to keep up with him.

We turned off the bypass and drove into the city past the old racecourse. We negotiated the lights at the end of the road, turned left, then right, along past the Council Offices and through the city centre. As we approached the pedestrian crossing I revved up my engine; people were about to run across between us and I sped up, narrowing the gap, not wanting to risk losing sight of the car when the road spread out into three lanes a little way further on. Some of the pedestrians no doubt thought I was being a bit reckless but I could live with that—I hadn't knocked anybody over. At the end of the road, Obote got into the middle lane ready to go straight across and into Monks Road. The lights were red so I hung back a little, swung the sun visor down as far as it would go and pulled my hat down almost to my eyes. If Obote looked in his mirror he wouldn't be able to get a clear view of my face.

The lights turned green and we carried on past the college. I didn't give my place of employment a glance. We drove on past the arboretum and then, a little further along the road, Obote indicated to turn right. I slowed down a little. I wasn't going to risk being too obvious. He drove about halfway down the road and parked on the left-hand side. This was one of the streets where you could park on both sides and there were one or two spaces on either side of the road. I let a couple of cars go past me in the opposite direction and then pulled into the road and parked on the right.

Obote got out of the Mercedes and opened the back door. The two young boys got out, and he ushered them towards one of the houses, pushing them roughly along the pavement and grabbing one of their arms as they got close. The houses were mostly terraced, with groups of five or six to a terrace and then a gap between the terraces. Obote took the boys down the side of the house at the end of the first set of terraces. The house had a slightly bigger garden than the other houses and a wall along the front. To the far side of the wall, at the front of the house, there was a gap that led to a path which ran along the side of the house and, presumably, to the back door. Obote took the boys down this path and disappeared from view.

-34-

I got out of the car, but didn't lock it. I figured that if I needed to get in it quickly and drive away I didn't want to be fumbling for the key. I walked along the road and passed the house, peering down the gap between this one and the next. Obote and the children had disappeared, presumably inside. There would have been enough room to pull a car into the gap, but perhaps it belonged to next door. The wall that surrounded the house Obote had gone behind encompassed a path of about three feet that went around the side and to the back. There was no garage.

I thought about going round and having a look but I didn't want Obote to see me. I returned to my car and waited. I was feeling quite hungry now, my tummy letting out deep rumbling noises every few minutes. I hadn't eaten anything since the service station sandwich and that was about three hours ago now. I couldn't risk going to buy something to eat, though, so I sat and waited. It wouldn't be long before it got dark and I hoped Obote wouldn't be too long. Hopefully he would be hungry too and want to get home and eat something.

A car further up the street pulled out and I parked in the empty space. I could get a good look at the house from there. I looked around, trying to take in every detail. Most of the houses had front doors which were next to each other, alternately on the left and right of the house as you looked at them. I assumed that each house would be a mirror image of the other. This house was at the end of the terrace and the door was on the left of the house; as it was the end house it had no partner door like most of the others. It looked as if it might be slightly bigger than the others. There was a bay window in the front room to the right of the door and also on the bedroom above. The window directly over the front door was smaller and the windowsill was falling away in places. The whole house looked in desperate need of renovation. The paint was peeling off the window frames and many of the bricks were worn away. A piece of guttering hung from the corner of the roof and missed the top of the drainpipe so I imagined when it rained, the water would pour directly off the gutter and down the side of the house. Every window at the front had the curtains closed, and those in the front room were hanging off the rail in several places. I glanced around at the other houses in the street. Many of them were in a poor condition and this one didn't really stand out particularly. I didn't think anyone would notice that it looked neglected.

My tummy rumbled as I sat in the car and waited. It was also getting colder as night was beginning to fall. I didn't want to start the engine just yet as I didn't want to attract any attention. So I sat there, shivering, waiting and looking.

Eventually, Obote emerged from around the side of the house. He didn't turn his head to look up the street; he just ran across the road and jumped into his car. I waited. I didn't want to make him suspicious. He drove to the end of the road and indicated to the left. As he pulled away I turned on the engine and then waited until he had disappeared around the corner before pulling out and following. I was just in time to see him disappear left again up the street which ran parallel to the one we had just been on. I followed, hanging back a little and watched him turn right back onto Monks Road. Once he was out of view I quickly followed. As I pulled on to the road I saw him turn left again a few hundred yards further along. I knew those roads led nowhere so I followed slowly.

The road went steeply up hill. It had a wall at the end with trees and waste ground beyond. There were terraced houses on both sides and everyone had their wheelie bins outside. Each house had a small yard at the front. Many had a wall along the edge of the yard with a gap leading six or seven feet up to the front door. Most of the walls were much deeper at the bottom end than the top as the road hard such a sharp incline. Some people had rendered and painted the walls, others had knocked them down all together. Some of the gaps in the walls had had gates put across them of varying designs. Almost all of the houses looked fairly well cared for, with plants in their front yards, or trees and shrubs. There was the odd For Sale sign. It was a pleasant residential street.

Obote drove about three quarters of the way up the hill, parked his car and got out. He opened the boot and removed an overnight bag, or a sports bag, before locking the car with the remote control and disappearing into one of the houses on the right-hand side, close to the top of the hill. Once he was in the house, the lights at the front came on, leading me to presume that no one else was in the house. I made an assumption that this was where Obote lived. I parked at the top of the road and walked back down to have a look. The wall around his house was a bit deeper than some of the others and it had a gate to the left which was open and pushed against the dividing wall with next door's. There were no plants in the yard, apart from the odd weed coming up through the concrete. The hallway light shone through the glass above the front door, but the front room was now in darkness. If Obote had any sense he would be in the kitchen getting himself some food.

There wasn't much to see so I got back in the hire car and went back to the house Obote had taken the boys to. I had only been gone half an hour at the most, but the road had filled up a little with cars and I had to park just around the corner. I grabbed my rucksack and put it on my back. I pulled my hat down over my hair and walked towards the house, thankful that my dark clothes would hide me a little. It was quite dark now and many of the houses had lights on.

Quite a few had drawn the curtains but as I walked along the street towards the house, I caught a glimpse of several couples and families, watching television or playing on video games, living normal lives. I felt intensely envious; I wanted to go to my own house only a short distance from here and watch something boringly normal like The X Factor Results. I'd never watched The X Factor before John had died, but since his death I had become quite obsessed with it and followed it every week. I never voted, although I got really cross when the public voted off the decent singers over the good looking ones. I'm not sure what John would have thought, he had an inherent loathing of all reality TV. I pushed that thought to the back of my brain; I couldn't afford to drop my guard and I certainly couldn't afford to be getting maudlin for home.

35

I got to the house and stood in front of it. It was all in darkness. I toyed with the idea of calling Charlton and letting him know where I was, but I couldn't think of how to phrase it without sounding like I was in a heapload of shit. I was, after all, definitely in a heapload of shit and was getting more nervous by the minute. I was fairly sure that he would tell me not to get involved any further, but I really didn't want anyone to talk me out of things now. I had a confusion of emotions swirling around inside me, anxiety and fear but predominantly curiosity and a need to see this through. If I had any chance of helping the children Obote had taken inside I couldn't hang about waiting for the cavalry to arrive.

I walked up the short path and tried the front door, probably unnecessarily pulling my sleeve over my hand just in case anyone came dusting for fingerprints later. What I hadn't noticed before, when looking from a distance, was that the front door had several locks keeping it firmly closed, at least three or four. It was well and truly shut and there was no way of getting in. I walked past the bay window and tried to peer through it and into the front room. The curtains had a small gap in the middle, where they had come away from the curtain rail and didn't meet up properly but I couldn't see much; the room was in complete darkness. I carried on round the side of the house and into the back garden, which was completely overgrown, although it was hard to see properly in the dark. It wasn't large; it was about 12 feet to the fence at the end, and the lawn was about a foot high. The fence that separated the garden from the one next door was broken and falling down in places. There were a few shrubs and trees at the end of the garden and several bags of rubbish strewn about.

Everything was dark. I had expected there to be a light on somewhere in the house; I assumed the two boys that Obote had brought here were still inside, but the house was utterly black. I tried the back door. Again, as with the front door, several locks kept it firmly shut. It was a solid wood door, so I went over to the window and peered in through that. The curtains at the window, unlike those at the front, had not been closed so I got out my torch and turned it on. I held it flat against the glass so that the light would shine through. The kitchen was almost empty. The remnants of a fitted kitchen— cupboards and drawers—clung to the walls but there didn't appear to be any appliances. Paint was peeling off the walls, and the different shades of fading indicated where the fridge, washing machine, or maybe a cooker had once been. The worktops were empty and some of the cupboard doors hung open. Bare electrical wires stuck out of the walls. A serving hatch above the cupboards led through to the next room. It was closed and, although I couldn't see it clearly because of the angle, appeared to have a grill of some sort over it. I could see an open door in the corner that belonged to what looked like a walk-in larder, but the shelves were bare. On the floor in the middle of the kitchen was a broom and a shovel, and lying in front of one of the cupboards, a dustpan and brush and what looked like bits for an electric drill. The door at the far side of the kitchen, which presumably led through to the hallway was closed and across the top, middle and bottom were industrial strength bolts with locks that were keeping it that way. *Jesus, what is going on here?*

I moved on to the next window. This one was close to the fence of the next-door house so I turned the torch off until it was pressed against the window. I guessed that this room was supposed to be a dining room, but it looked as if it hadn't been used for ages. A table was folded up and shoved into one corner of the room. There was a step ladder in the middle of the room and in the corner what looked like tins of paint, or varnish or something. The door through to the hallway was, once again, bolted shut with three massive locking bolts. I thought about the logistics of achieving this; someone must have put the bolts on this side of the door, then climbed through the serving hatch and into the kitchen, then put the grill over the serving hatch. I took a step back and let out a deep sigh, unease filling my body as I fought to prevent panic overtaking me. What on earth were they doing? Why bolt *children* into an unattended house.

The sound of voices jolted my attention away from the house. *Shit.* Voices that were getting closer, coming down the side of the house. I turned off the torch and ran to hide behind the shrubs in the corner of the garden. It was in complete blackness and, thanks to my dark clothes, no one would be able to see me. There were two deep voices, and they sounded as if they were in a heated argument.

"Don't be stupid, there's no way you can do it, no way," said one of the voices and, as the men rounded the corner and approached the back door I saw that this one belonged to Champion Obote.

Following Obote round the corner was a much smaller man who I recognised immediately from his photos as Adrian Darnold, and between the two of them was a young black girl. She looked about fifteen, but could have been younger, it was hard to tell with so little light. Obote fiddled with the locks on the door, undoing at least three, I lost count, before opening the door. The kitchen light went on, and I moved forward a little. A bare bulb, one of those old-fashioned, high-energy types, hung from the ceiling. I had a perfect view inside the kitchen and I was sure they wouldn't be able to see me out in amongst the darkness of the garden. The girl was small and had long hair braided really closely to her head. She had a pretty, petite face but had an impassive look, almost a blank stare. She stood with her hands in the pockets of her trousers and made no effort to move or speak. Obote locked all the locks on the back door behind him and then gave Darnold a glare. He grabbed the girl by her upper arm, unlocked and undid the bolts on the door to the hall and then disappeared with the girl. Darnold pulled the bolts again once the girl and Obote had gone through the door. He paced around the kitchen with a thunderous look on his face. No lights came on further inside the house. Apart from the kitchen, the place was in darkness. I crept forward a little more, crouching behind a low shrub.

A few minutes later, a loud knock sounded from inside the house. Darnold unbolted the door and let Obote through, who then bolted and locked it behind him. Obote looked angry, his brows furrowed deeply across his forehead and his lips curled back revealing his teeth. The two men turned to face each other. They were shouting but I still couldn't quite hear what they were saying, and I strained to catch the gist of the conversation. They were gesticulating wildly with their hands and their faces contorted as they argued. It was clear that they were both furious. They were both raising their hands, pointing, shaking their fists and their heads as they moved in a slow circle around the room.

Obote was screaming, "…can't just walk away…not as simple…" but each time he turned his head slightly I lost a few words.

Darnold was bright red and spitting as he spoke, "…not his gofer…too big for his own…just ring me up…bring his kids back…"

I couldn't really follow what they were saying, but as the conversation got more heated their voices got louder. Obote looked even bigger as he pulled himself up and stood to his full height. Darnold was a good six inches shorter but he was shouting just as loudly. Their words were coming clearly through the glass now.

Obote snapped round to face in Darnold's direction. "You're in too deep already, you can't get out now."

"I don't care," Darnold spat the words out.

"You'll be ruined, you know he will see to that."

Darnold was so red I thought he was going to catch fire on the spot.

"Listen to me," he shouted. "I don't care. I've had enough. Covering a few things up, that's one thing, but these kids! They're *ill* for God's sake." He threw his hands up in the air in a gesture of despair. Whatever it was they were doing, he clearly didn't want any further part in it. He was getting louder, "I'm sick of him, thinking he can tell me what to do, expecting me to jump whenever he says."

"He *can* tell you what to do," Obote shouted back. "He's the one paying you to do it."

"Not anymore. I'm not doing it anymore. I won't make trouble for him. I'll resign from the force; I'll come up with a story. I won't implicate any of you sick bastards. Don't fret about that." Darnold made to go to the back door.

With one stretch of his massive arms, Obote caught him by his collar and dragged him back into the room. He said something to Darnold, but his voice had quietened down and I couldn't hear him.

Darnold span round on his heels so that he faced Obote, jabbing his finger towards Obote, and shouting at full volume, "I'm out. I don't care if I lose my job. I don't care if I lose the money. This"—he gestured around him at the house—"is not worth it." And once again he made for the door.

"Get back here," Obote barked at him.

"No," Darnold shouted. "Tell Townsley from me, I'm out."

Darnold fumbled at the locks on the back door but he wasn't quick enough. Obote grabbed him and pulled him back into the room. Darnold tried his best to punch Obote in the face, but it had minimal impact. He pulled his arm back to punch him again, but Obote saw it coming and danced to one side, grabbing Darnold's arm as it swung past his face. He twisted the arm sharply as Darnold cried out in pain and pulled it up behind Darnold's back. Obote pushed him forward across the room, smashing his face into the corner of one of the work surfaces. He pulled him back up to standing, blood pouring out of a gash just above Darnold's eye. Obote crashed Darnold's face into the worktop again, and this time when he pulled him up his nose was twisted sideways and his face was covered in blood.

Obote let him go, moved away and circled round. He looked like a boxer preparing to strike. Darnold shook his head, trying to reorient himself ready for the next attempt, but he was being too eager,

246

like a yappy little dog facing up to a Rottweiler. He kicked Obote in the shin, and it looked as if this might have worked. Obote seemed to lose his focus momentarily, and Darnold took advantage by punching him again, this time in the shoulder. Obote, however, quickly regained his control and charged at Darnold with his shoulder, pushing him back against the cupboard. Darnold appeared to be completely winded—he struggled to breathe and his hand went up to his chest. He staggered onto his feet and stepped forward a couple of paces but Obote had been quick. He'd bent down and picked up the shovel. As Darnold approached, Obote took his arms back as far as they would go and swung the shovel with all his massive force against Darnold's head, which twisted horribly on his shoulders. An arc of blood spurted out from somewhere, his ear or the side of his head, and he dropped to the ground like a felled tree. I lost sight of him as he fell but Obote went over to him and swung the shovel once more at his head. I thought that this was probably an unnecessary precaution given the angle that his head had twisted round to with the first blow. I shocked myself at the coldness of my thoughts but I felt disconnected, almost as if I had been watching a movie. As the reality of what I had just witnessed kicked in, bile rose in my throat and I had to fight to keep concentrating and not give in to the urge to vomit. Obote stood up, looked as if he kicked Darnold on the floor, and then threw the shovel to one side. He wiped his hands on his jeans, undid the locks on the back door, switched off the light and then calmly left, locking the back door, before walking quickly down the side of the house.

36

I waited a moment to check that Obote had gone. I listened to the sound of a car engine start up and pull away, and then I gave it a couple of minutes to make sure that he wasn't coming back. I crept up to the house, lifted the torch up against the window and scanned the floor of the kitchen. Darnold was lying there, his feet hidden beneath the window but his body clearly visible. His head was twisted round in the most unusual way. My stomach churned when I saw it. I took a moment to catch my breath, moving away from the window and leaning my hands on my knees. I looked back into the kitchen. Darnold was staring lifelessly to one side, a pool of blood collecting beneath his head. There was no doubting that he was dead; not that I could have got in the house to do anything about it if he hadn't been. I went to the back door and tried it, but there was no way of opening it with all the locks and bolts it had. I peered once more through the window and Darnold was still lying there, staring off at nothing with his head at a bizarre angle.

I stood back and scanned the building. The house was quiet with no sounds coming from inside. I shone my torch up at the upstairs but there was no light and no signs of any life at all. I was more confused than ever. I knew there were people inside but there was no sign of anyone. What on earth could be going on? I knew that the only way to find out was to get inside, but there was no way I could get in without the keys. Even if I smashed a window, I wouldn't be able to get through the door into the hall. I presumed all the downstairs doors would be the same. *God, I hope there isn't a fire.* I had to get the keys and to do that I had to get at Obote. I sighed at the thought and leaned against the outside of the back door. He was a foot taller than me and probably about 100lbs heavier. I would have to plan, and I would have to be careful. The thought of ending up in a pool of blood like Darnold made me shiver with fear.

I sat on the back step and thought about what to do. I needed to make sure that I knew what Obote was doing. Would he come and try to clean up? It was dark and that would give him cover but maybe he would figure that there was little chance of anyone finding the body during the night. Desperate as I was for a rest, I didn't think I could take the chance. Reluctantly I got up and walked to my car. I slung the rucksack into the passenger seat and drove off back towards the city parking in one of the small car parks. It was Sunday, and after 6pm, so there was no need to pay. I walked to Tesco Express and bought a few supplies – a take-away coffee, some sandwiches, crisps, sweets, some fruit, a couple of small bottles of no-calorie lemonade and a couple of snickers bars. I looked in my basket; having never staked anywhere out overnight before I wasn't sure what I would need. I thought about it and put the lemonade back. I wouldn't have access to a loo for a long time and I thought dehydration seemed preferable to wetting the seat of the hire car. It felt oddly surreal to be here in this shop, where I had been many times, and see people carrying about their business as if nothing had happened. It seemed as if I was living a life that was oddly disjointed from theirs; it bore no relation to theirs and the reality of what I had just witnessed made me feel heavy and depressed. Someone laughed and I looked at them as if there were two different dimensions which had collided in the same place, like I was observing what was happening without being a part of it.

After paying for my things, I walked over to the pub opposite and sneakily used their toilets. I grabbed a couple of handfuls of loo roll, just in case I needed to find a bush somewhere during the night, and stuffed them in my pockets. Then I walked back to my car and drove back to Obote's road. I drove at crawling pace past his house. The light was on in the front room and Obote was sitting there alone. He looked like he was watching television; the flickering light reflected around the room. He had a can of beer in his hand which he was swigging as he watched. I drove on, turning round at the end of the road so that I was

251

facing down the hill. I parked as close to the top of the hill as I could and sat and watched. I was outside a house which was for sale and looked empty. Nothing happened. I sat even longer. Still nothing happened. I guessed that Obote was now in his house for the night and I was in for a long and very boring, not to mention cold, night.

I started to think about what had happened at the other house. My memory of Darnold and Obote's argument had been dimmed a bit by the events that had followed, but I tried to recall as much as I could. Thoughts of Darnold's head twisted round on his shoulders, and his staring eyes, came unbidden into my brain. I shook my head as if it might make the image fall out of my ears or something, but it didn't work. Each time the image reappeared I closed my eyes and breathed, concentrating on what they had been arguing about and trying to piece it all together. Darnold had wanted out. But out of what? He'd clearly been telling Obote to pass the message on to someone; someone who was too big for their boots. And the name he had mentioned was Townsley. Townsley was the person who had signed Dr Neasden's death certificate. I had thought that he was perhaps in on a cover-up of something, but maybe he was the leader? And what were the children doing in a locked and bolted house? Darnold had said 'they're ill'; had he meant the children? Or had he meant the people keeping them there. He'd gestured round at the house when he had said he'd wanted to be out of 'all this'; was what was going on centred on the house? Could they be using the children for prostitution? It was a horrible thought

252

but I knew from my research that that was a common—in fact the most common—reason that young people were trafficked into the country. Was that what was going on? Had the police been covering up a child sexual exploitation ring and Darnold had had enough? Would they be earning enough money from it to make it worth their while to kill Darnold to keep it from getting out? Probably, more to the point, it would be very damaging. Townsley was a world-renowned and well-respected professor, researching treatments for cancer—if he were the head of something like that then his career would be ruined if it came out. Not to mention the lengthy prison sentence that would be likely to be meted out.

But something was not right. Obote had said that Townsley had been paying Darnold; paying him to cover up I assumed. Clearly he'd helped to cover up Dr Neasden's death but something had pushed him too far. Something, worse than covering up a death, had made him want to get out. What could be worse than that?

By ten o'clock I had eaten the sandwiches and most of the fruit. I had also started on the crisps. I was cold and bored but I didn't want to risk turning on the engine to warm myself up in case I attracted attention. So I continued sitting and watching. A man came out of a house further down with a small white dog. He led the dog up the hill and let it go on the wasteland behind the wall at the top. The man stood smoking a cigarette whilst the dog ran off for a last wee and a quick run around and then they returned to their home. That was the most exciting thing that had happened for the last three hours.

Whilst my attention had been diverted away by the man with the dog, the light in Obote's front room had gone off. It was gone 11pm and I guessed he was going to bed. Lucky him. An upstairs light was on, probably on the landing and then the front bedroom light came on. Obote appeared briefly in the window, closing the curtains, and then after about fifteen minutes the light went out and the house was in darkness. I settled in for a long night, staring out into the darkness. A few drunken revellers walked past the end of the road, presumably on their way home. They looked like students, shouting and not caring that most of the people would be asleep. Their voices carried up the hill and one of the girls let out a shriek of laughter.

There was little going on down Obote's street. Lights started going off in houses on either side. Occasionally a light would come on upstairs in one house or another. Presumably someone going to the bathroom, or possibly waking up to feed a baby. I wanted to turn the radio on to relieve the boredom but I didn't dare make any noise. I slunk down in my seat and closed my eyes, just for a moment. Just to rest them from staring into the darkness.

MONDAY

37

I'm lying on the grass on a warm summer day, with my eyes closed. I've just finished a picnic with someone, although strangely I'm not clear exactly who. There's a lot of noise and I open my eyes to find a massive wasp in front of my face. I shout out and flail my arms but it gets louder and bigger and more menacing.

I woke with a jolt, not knowing where I was. It took me a moment to reorient myself and there was a blissful second where I was unaware of what had happened the night before. I thumped back into the present, hearing a noise outside the car but I couldn't place it. I struggled to wake up properly; I must have fallen into a deep sleep. I wasn't very good at staking out overnight. It was still dark and I glanced at the clock. It was 4.30am. The noise came again, like a scraping. I peered around me and then suddenly, a man loomed out at me under the orange glow of the streetlight, standing behind the car, staring at me through the back window.

I was instantly wide awake. My heart, and the rest of my body, seemed to flip around. I stared back at the man. He was bending right down and peering through the back window. I recognised him straight away. He was the man who had peered at me in the shoe shop on Steep Hill, the man who had been following me after I had left my ransacked home. I wondered if it had been him who had done the ransacking. He took a step away and the baseball bat he was holding came into view. I watched him, blood rushing in my ears making me feel light-headed and strange. He grinned at me. Everything seemed to have slowed down and he drew the baseball bat back in slow motion. I sat, transfixed. He brought the bat down on the back window with a dull thud. The glass was safety glass so although the window shattered it stayed in the frame. He hit it again, and then again at the top of the window so that the glass came away from the frame and bent precariously into the car. It still didn't shatter and I was amazed, and pleased, at its resilience protecting me for a while. He stood away, as if admiring his work and then he approached the car again. I was terrified, and momentarily paralysed. I just sat and watched him, not knowing what to do.

He swung the bat again, hitting the rear lights and then the boot. Thank goodness for the extra insurance I'd taken out. He came round the side and grinned in at me through the side window of the back door. He had a horrible smile; his teeth were mostly missing and those that were there were black and worn away. He leaned away and then brought the bat down again on the side window at the back. This one was not safety glass and the window exploded into the car, sending glass flying all over the back seat and the floor. I jumped, almost hitting my head on the roof of the car. As the man stepped away again, and my mind became capable of sane thought, I realised that I would need to do something. I fumbled in my rucksack and located one of the bottles of my home-made pepper spray. I took one of the small knives and put it in my pocket, and held the pepper spray in my right hand, partly hidden up my sleeve. The man came further round the car towards the driver's door. He tried to open it but it was locked.

I barely had time to dodge out of the way, turning my back to the door, as the man hit the glass on the driver's door. The glass shattered into fragments, not shards; they weren't sharp but they went everywhere. They rained down on my head and down the inside of my jacket. They cascaded down my neck and back and even in my shoes. As I sat upright again, the man leant through the door and opened it up. He was still smiling his horrible, toothless smile. I tried to twist round to aim my pepper spray at him but he grabbed my arm and dragged me out of the car and onto the road. I gripped the pepper spray tight in my hand and my knuckles scraped across the tarmac. He held me by the back of my jacket, pulling the neck into my throat as he lifted my head and chest off the ground.

"Back off," he hissed in my ear and then threw me onto the ground again.

I scrambled to sit up and as I turned he took a swing with the baseball bat. I managed to roll out of the way so that it came down on the road and not my head.

Once again, he hissed through his barely-there teeth, "If you don't want to end up like the last person who interfered then take it from me. Back. Off." His voice was menacing, and the fact that he was so calm was frightening. I took it that he was referring to Dr Neasden and I wondered if it had been he that had fired the fatal shot. I looked at his scruffy jogging bottoms and remembered the man who had pushed past me when I'd been on my way to the doctor's house, unaware of the carnage that would greet me. They could easily have belonged to the man who'd run past me down the hill but I couldn't be sure.

I turned and sat up; he was swinging the bat again, ready to strike, and I was now up against the car so I had nowhere to escape to. I put the pepper spray in my left hand and reached in my pocket for the knife. As he lifted the bat I pulled the knife back and sank it hard into his leg, just to one side of his shin bone. He dropped the bat and cried out, clutching at his leg. I took the opportunity and scrambled to a standing position, grabbing the bat as I did. He looked at me, enraged. He wasn't very tall, just a few inches taller than me so his face was not too far from mine. He snarled and came towards me, as if he were going to push me back against the car. I let him come as close as I dare, and then I held up the pepper spray and pumped it into his eyes. He didn't have a chance to grab the bottle off me before the spray took effect. The little pump action bottle I had bought did a sterling job. It wasn't as efficient as an aerosol, clearly, but it pumped the spray all over his face and coated his eyes. As he cried out, I pumped more of the spray into his mouth.

He fell to the floor, clutching at his face. He was drooling from the heat of the spray and clawing at his eyes. I grabbed my rucksack, and the book that I had taped into the carrier bag and carried them up to the top of the road. I jumped up over the wall and into the waste ground that stretched uphill beyond. I looked back. The man was still writhing on the floor; my pepper spray seemed to have worked well. In the dull light of the streetlamp, I could just make out the outline of the knife sticking out of his leg, but he was distracted by the more immediate pain in his face. I needed to hide; I was convinced the police would arrive soon. In fact, thinking about it, I was surprised that they hadn't already shown up. Perhaps no one had heard anything. There was a reasonably strong wind that would have carried the sound away from most of the houses, and the one I was parked outside was empty. The car alarm hadn't gone off because I'd been inside and I'd just locked my door manually, not with the remote. It didn't look as if disturbances were a usual occurrence around here. But then, I supposed if you heard some glass breaking in the middle of the night, you might just assume it was bottles or something. If I were asleep in bed, would I be bothered to get up to have a look and check it out? Maybe not.

-38-

I glanced back at Obote's house. It was still in darkness. Had it been him who had realised I was outside? I thought I'd been really discreet, but perhaps sitting outside in a car all night was too much of a giveaway. Not for the first time I felt out of my depth and unsure how to progress. It was almost sunrise by this point. I stood behind a tree and tried to think about what to do next. Every muscle in my body was telling me to get further away but I needed to track Obote. I needed the keys to the house and he was the only link I had; I had to wait for him to leave and then lay a trap for his return. I couldn't see another way. He was a massive man who had killed someone with one swing of a shovel and I had to get the upper hand if I had any hope at all of getting the keys off him. I leaned against the tree and sighed. I really didn't want to be in the middle of all this. But what else could I do? I couldn't go back to my house until this was all sorted out or the chances were even greater that I'd go the same way as Neasden and Darnold.

I searched for a new vantage point. I could circle through this bit of ground, go back down the hill further along and watch the end of the road until I saw Obote leave. I thought about this. The advantage would be that I would be able to see what direction he went in. But my main focus had to be, actually, when he came back. No, I would wait where I was. Here I could watch the door discreetly. I could make sure that he had gone and I could stay well hidden. The danger if I went to the bottom of the road would be that either he would see me, or someone else would see me loitering around; there was nowhere to hide down there and if the police did arrive, they'd see me. Here, I could hide behind a tree and I didn't think Obote would come up and look for me. He'd make the assumption that his goon had frightened me away, or that I'd run off or something. And even if he did come up this way, the trees and the thick undergrowth would hide me. Unless he actually came determined to look in every corner I would be well hidden, and I really didn't think that he would.

I sat on my rucksack behind the tree and fished out the bits of glass from inside my clothes and shoes. I watched as the light came up from behind me, gradually illuminating the street below. My knuckles throbbed where they had been ripped against the road. I wished I had thought to buy bandages and painkillers on my shopping expedition. I wrapped my scarf around my hand and tried to ignore it. At some point the man who had smashed up the car hobbled off down the hill. I wondered if he would call in at Obote's house, but he didn't. He didn't even give a sideways glance as he hopped past. I couldn't tell if the knife was still in his leg or not, but he was limping quite badly. He didn't look back up the hill to where I was standing. I wondered if he was connected to Obote and the mess they were involved in in any way, if he knew that Obote lived here, or whether he was just a hired thug who had been asked to batter a woman in a Vauxhall Insignia.

As the light came up, the street came gradually to life; curtains were thrown back, lights came on and then off again, more people were getting up and leaving their homes. It was Monday morning and people were going to work. Some left quite early; I assumed to either catch the train or start a shift somewhere depending on the way they were dressed. Some carried small children and put them in cars or buggies and took them off to childcare. I felt sad for a moment that this would be something I would never experience. Then one of the toddlers started screaming and refusing to get in the car, the mother running her hand through her tousled hair, and I felt more relieved than sad. A postman came up the hill and then down again calling in at several of the houses along the way, sometimes causing a dog to bark from within the house. Obote got no mail that day. People didn't seem to notice the broken and battered car. Maybe it was because it was parked near the top of the hill so most of them didn't actually go past it. Maybe people thought it was none of their business. Maybe it wasn't an unusual sight. Although I was pleased that no one seemed to care about it, or think it was anything to do with them, I thought it was a sad reflection of society that I could have ended up with more than bloodied knuckles and nobody would have done anything about it.

After the initial flurry of activity, the street quietened down a little. The sounds of a school nearby filtered over, children running and shrieking in the playground; then a bell and quiet once more. I sat and watched Obote's house in the near silence, hidden behind the tree. I looked at my hand; it wasn't too bad really. I desperately needed a shower but I certainly couldn't afford to move. I needed to get the keys to the house, and I needed to figure out what was going on, and for both of those things I needed Obote. I still wasn't quite sure how I thought I was going to overpower him, but I pushed that thought to one side. I had no alternative. Whilst I waited, I tried to come up with a plan, it wasn't a particularly well-formulated plan as there were a number of unknowns to contend with, but it was the best I could do.

39

It was about 11am when Obote's front door opened and he emerged. He was wearing jeans and a sweatshirt and a light, zip-up jacket. He locked the front door behind him, making me even more convinced that he had been in there alone. He got as far as the gate and then felt all his pockets. He'd forgotten something. He went back into the house, leaving the front door opened before re-emerging a few seconds later. He locked the door again and headed back out of the gate. He didn't go to his car, and he didn't look at my battered hire car either. I watched him walk down the hill, crossing the road halfway down and then he turned right at the end. He was heading in the direction of the house with the young people; the house with Adrian Darnold's twisted body on the kitchen floor. I waited about fifteen minutes so that I could be sure he wasn't about to return for another forgotten item and then I came out from my hiding spot behind the tree.

I looked around. The street was pretty much deserted. Everyone seemed to have gone to work, or school, or be inside their house. I carried my things down to Obote's house and crouched down behind the garden wall. It was about four foot high at its deepest so it was a good cover. Plonking myself down on the ground, I started to get my things ready. I put the book that I had Sellotaped into the carrier bag on the ground next to gate. I got out the full bottle of pepper spray and put that down next to the book along with one of the knives with a 6" blade and one of the pairs of handcuffs I'd bought in Ann Summers. I took out the gun, which had no bullets in it, and tucked it into the top of my trousers, sticking over the waist band, a bit like Clint Eastwood might do.

Then I studied the gate; it was open and resting against the wall between Obote's and the house next door. It had quite sturdy hinges which were attached to a post that ran up the inside of the gap in the wall. They looked in reasonable repair. On the opposite side of the gap there was another metal post which was attached to the brickwork and which housed the closure mechanism. I fished out my clear curtain wire and stretched it across the gap. I hesitated a while about attaching it to the gate posts. I was worried that someone would see it. But then, when you walked to your door along the same path every day, did you always look down? I thought about it. I decided, on balance, that it would be worth it. I guessed that, if Obote saw it, I would at least have a warning that he was here and I could try to get him with a knife to the calf like the toothless thug from last night. I crawled over towards the gate without putting my head above the level of the wall.

I attached the wire quite easily around the post that supported the gate. There was a gap of about half an inch and it was easy to thread the wire through and wrap it round the post a couple of times. I tied and retied the knot and positioned it so that it was behind the post to make sure it wouldn't be visible from the road. It took me a lot longer to attach the wire to the other side of the gate. There was hardly any gap at all between the wall and the gate post and I had to painstakingly thread the wire through. There was a fastening about six inches above the ground and I pushed the wire through the gap just above this, pushing it a little at a time until it was past the post and then pulling it hard to tighten it. When I had wrapped the wire a couple of times around the post I pulled it as tight as I could make it and then tied it off and hid the knot, just like the other side.

I crawled away to the far side of the yard and looked back at the gate. I could see the wire, but only just, and I knew that it was there. I looked at the distance between the front gate and the front door. It was probably about 5 feet. If Obote fell flat on his face, he would actually hit the front door as he was so tall, but I didn't think he would fall completely on the ground, so I would have to move really quickly. Thankfully, I would have the element of surprise. I certainly didn't think he would be expecting me to be waiting with my makeshift armoury, especially if he was behind the attack on me and my car last night. My knuckles were swollen and raw, the skin hanging off several of them. I hoped I would be able to do this without wounding them any further. I stuffed my bloodied scarf into my rucksack – I didn't want to have anything around me that Obote might be able to use to hurt me.

I sat down on the ground behind Obote's wall. I kept surveying my weapons – a book, some homemade pepper spray, a gun with no bullets and a knife. I sighed. I hoped it was enough. I fished out one of the other knives and tucked it into my sock just in case I needed something extra. I touched everything, making sure that my hands knew exactly where everything was. I couldn't afford to make a mistake. Obote was huge and not afraid to kill. If I gave him a chance he'd have the upper hand in no time and I didn't want to risk Townsley having the chance to sign off my death as natural causes.

The noise of footsteps drifted up from further down the road. I held my breath but then realised that the footsteps were accompanied by the sound of wheels rolling along the pavement. A buggy I assumed. The footsteps stopped before the house, and then a series of sounds – a mother talking to the child in the buggy, the cooing of an infant, a door opening and closing, then the stillness returned. It was irritating that I couldn't risk putting my head over the wall; not only because Obote might see me, but also because I didn't want anyone else to see that I was here. This was, thankfully, a quiet road, but people might get suspicious if they saw me peeping out from behind the wall.

I waited patiently for over three hours, my bottom gradually going numb with sitting on the cold ground. I was bored beyond description, sitting there staring at the front of the house; but I couldn't risk getting my iPad out to amuse myself because I couldn't afford to be distracted. I had to stay alert. I knew that my only chance of getting the better of Obote was to be ready to pounce the minute he arrived. I needed to surprise him. So I sat and counted the bricks in the wall, and the blades of grass in the yard to try to maintain my alertness. I had heard a few sounds over the wall but I had resisted the urge to look. Then, after all the waiting—footsteps. I knew immediately it was Obote. I could tell that the footsteps belonged to someone with a long stride and they were walking purposefully up the hill. I took hold of the carrier bag and waited, holding my breath and sitting perfectly still.

40

Time slowed down. I seemed to be sitting in a vacuum, the air rushing past me, the leaves blowing across the yard in slow motion. The footsteps were heavy and slow. They were loud, and getting louder. It was all that I could hear. *Thud, thud, thud.* Like a giant from a fairy tale stepping up the hill. There was no other noise. Silence apart from the footsteps. What probably took seconds – from the time I'd heard the footsteps to the time I saw Obote's toe through the gap in the wall – seemed to take minutes. I felt like I had been holding my breath for way too long. Then, all of a sudden, things changed. Everything whooshed into sharp focus as the adrenaline my body was producing hit my brain. The world was still operating in slow motion, but every detail was crystal clear.

The toe of Obote's right shoe appeared in the gap in the wall. It was a dark brown leather toe.

Expensive shoes; beyond the budget of a young people's advocate. These were the shoes of someone being paid off. The full shoe and the bottom of Obote's jeans came into view and then his shin caught on the wire and Obote fell forward. His massive body fell heavily through the gap and onto the path. He fell onto his left knee, his leg buckling underneath him as his natural momentum was disturbed by the wire. His right leg folded and his arms went out in front of his chest to stop his fall. He was unaware of what was happening, tumbling to the ground.

I jumped up. Before he even had a chance to turn his head, I sprang over to him. I swung the carrier bag at the side of his head and it twisted to the left as the heavy book made contact with the right hand side of his face. He was dazed and I swung again, this time hitting him on the back of the head as hard as I could. He fell forward, trying to turn around, trying to see what was happening and who was behind him, clearly a little stunned from the two blows. I snatched up the pepper spray and as he moved his head towards me, I pumped the spray action of the little bottle as fast as I could into his eyes and nose and mouth. He choked and spat, shaking his head.

I picked up the handcuffs whilst he was trying to rid his facial orifices of the pepper spray. I tried to grab his wrist to attach to one end of the handcuffs, but even with the distraction of the pepper spray and some harsh blows to the head he was strong. I hadn't incapacitated him as much as I had hoped. He yanked his arm away from me and, though he couldn't open his eyes, he scrambled for my knee and pulled it sharply

272

from under me. I fell, hard, on the concrete floor, cracking my shoulder against the wall. I reached for the pepper spray again, but it rolled away from me. I fumbled to reach the bag with the book but he was dragging me by my leg and it slipped out of reach. I clawed at the ground, desperately trying to hold onto something but there was nothing within reach. All I managed was to clutch hold of the gun in my waistband. A gun with no bullets; great.

As he pulled me closer to him by my leg, I managed to twist round. He was still struggling to open his eyes, drool pouring down his chin from the spray. I drew my other leg up and, with as much force as I could muster, I brought the heel of my sturdy boots down straight onto his knee cap. He let out a sharp cry and released my leg. Whilst he bent over and took hold of his knee, I hit him again with the butt of the gun. He gave another yelp and turned his head upwards, furiously blinking as if he were trying to diminish the pain in his eyes. I wanted to tell him to be quiet, or someone would start taking notice and call the police, but instead I raised the gun. He was clutching at his knee with his right hand and leaning on the floor with his left, he hadn't noticed the gun yet. I lifted my foot up again and this time I stamped it down on his left hand. There was a crunching sound that made my stomach churn, I'd definitely broken something. I scrambled far enough away from him to make sure that he couldn't reach out for me again and, maintaining a crouching position behind the wall, I pointed the gun at his head. There was a trickle of blood coming from his forehead; I'd caught him just above the eye with the handle of the gun. I'd hoped to knock him out, but he was a massive man and it would clearly take more than a couple of blows to the head. As he struggled to open his eyes, he looked at me through what must have been very blurred vision.

I had to bluff. I had to hone my newly discovered talent to lie and I prayed that he didn't spring for me. I hoped my tough-girl act would wash. I continued holding the gun at his head as steadily as I could and reached for the pepper spray with my other hand. I was about four feet away from him; just too far for him to try to reach and grab the gun. I held it up and, as he caught sight of it, he flinched. A flicker of something, fear perhaps, crossed his face. His eyes were regaining some ability to focus, but he was still struggling to keep them open for more than a few seconds. I had to take my chance.

"What's going on, Obote?"

His eyebrows lifted and his mouth opened as if he were surprised that I was calling him by his name. He shook his head, but said nothing. I had to bluff as much as I could. And that meant faking a little bluster and bravado.

"What is Townsley up to?"

He shook his head again, but I'd surprised him again by mentioning Townsley's name. He wiped his chin with the back of his good hand, and then cradled his bad hand in his arm.

"What is going on with the children in the house?" I got up onto my knees and knelt on the floor. I put the pepper spray down and held the gun with both hands outstretched in front of me. "Look at me!"

He moved his head in my direction and tried to focus.

I held the gun so that it was pointing at his kneecap, the one I hadn't just broken. "Obote, tell me about the children."

"Who are you?" he rasped, barely able to speak.

"Who am I? I'm a fucking interested bystander that's who I am. Now, tell me about the children." I surprised myself with how confident I was sounding. I was feeling anything but.

He tried to focus on the gun. "They're ill," he said, his voice like sandpaper. I guessed the pepper spray must have burnt his throat a bit.

"Ill? How so?"

"I'm not telling you anything, you're not my boss, you're not paying me." He struggled to get the words past his throat.

"Well, if you hadn't noticed I am currently pointing a gun at you, so perhaps it might be better to worry about that later." There was a slight crack in my voice and I hoped I sounded suitably convincing. "How is Townsley involved?"

He looked up and blinked into the light, still struggling to open his eyes, which were red and swollen and weeping down his cheeks. He wiped his nose with his sleeve. His whole face was blotchy and swollen. I indicated the pepper spray. He understood.

"Townsley is treating them. It's his research," he said, and then added sarcastically, "He's going to cure the fucking world."

"Cure the world? What's he researching?"

"Cancer."

Townsley the cancer specialist. Of course. His biography said he was leading some research. But it still didn't add up.

"Why are you keeping them in the house?"

He shook his head. He spat out onto the yard and wiped his mouth again, with the sleeve of his jacket.

"They're not supposed to be here are they?" I offered.

He shook his head again, more to say no than to refuse to answer this time.

"Is someone trafficking children here? Children with cancer? And then Townsley is treating them?"

"Townsley. He arranges it all. He has contacts. They bring him the kids."

Contacts. Of course; I remembered the man in the car park.

Obote coughed and spat again.

"And he treats them?" I asked.

He nodded.

"Hasn't anybody noticed?"

"Why would they? He sees people all day long."

The well-respected Professor. Why would anyone take any notice of him treating patients?

I changed course a little. "What kind of cancer?"

"I don't know."

I pushed the gun a little closer, and he said it again, louder, "I don't know."

Jesus. Townsley was treating young people, who were here illegally, as part of his research. *Bloody*

276

hell. And if he found a treatment that worked effectively, he could make a fortune. Drugs were worth millions.

"Why are they locked up?"

He shrugged. "They need the treatment."

"But why lock them up?"

"To make sure they take the treatment, and get to appointments."

Is that what Darnold was doing when he took the young girl to the house? Was he bringing her back from an appointment? I almost said something, but then I thought that now was probably not the time to let Obote know I had seen him kill Darnold so I didn't ask that question.

"You don't want them to get away?"

He shook his head again. Through the mess of his swollen face he looked sad. He was supposed to be an advocate for young people. I remembered the children smiling up at him in the photo. I could imagine that he had been tempted by the money he'd been offered to get involved but had then got into something beyond his depth.

I whispered almost, "But what if there's a fire?"

He glanced up at me. The light in his eyes obviously hurt and he immediately looked away again. I don't think he had thought about that before. He slumped a bit. He seemed resigned; he blinked up again at the gun.

"Where does Townsley see them?"

"Fuck off and leave me alone and stop asking questions."

That irritated me. Before he could open his swollen eyes, I lifted up one of my legs and brought my heel down onto his already broken hand. It crunched again and he winced in pain. I picked up the pepper spray and prepared to pump it into his eyes again.

"Where does he see them?" I hissed between clenched teeth. Luckily my anger was compensating for my fear and keeping any self-doubt out of my voice.

Silence.

"Don't make me use the pepper spray again, Obote."

He whispered, "He sees them at the hospital."

"Where? Does he have a clinic? A surgery?"

He shook his head. "No, he sees them later, in the evenings. When it's quiet."

"Where?"

"In the outpatient's unit."

"Outpatients?"

"Yes, they finish in there by the end of the afternoon. He has some rooms there." He made a half-laughing sound. He was grimacing and rolling his red and puffy eyes. "He can do what he wants," he said with a note of bitterness ringing through his words. He spat again, perhaps to get rid of the remains of the pepper spray, perhaps in contempt of Townsley. "He could ask for the moon and they'd give it to him. He boasts about it; he thinks it shows how important he is. They think he's God. His research brings them big money. They need to keep him happy." He clearly had no respect for him at all.

I got the impression that Obote would be glad if Townsley was exposed and this whole thing could shudder to a halt. He was now guilty of murder, maybe he realised it had all gone too far.

"Every evening?"

"Most. He sees them one at a time."

That would make sense, I supposed, in terms of them not being able to run away or compare notes. If they were isolated they were less likely to be able to find safety in numbers.

I gathered my thoughts. Townsley was seeing the children in the evenings when the hospital was quiet and the research was happening without anyone knowing. At least without anyone knowing who the subjects were. If he could lie about other stuff like the cause of Dr Neasden's death then what was to stop him lying about who he was treating? I doubted that using illegally trafficked children as part of a research study would be viewed particularly well by the ethics committee. It would completely discredit him. I also wondered about the children's families; had they paid for their children to be sent to the UK in the hopes that they would be cured? Had they struggled to find the money? Or got into debt to do so?

"What's the treatment? The research? Is it working?"

"He says he hasn't got it quite right yet."

"So the children aren't getting better?"

"Not all, no."

I struggled to focus. I needed to keep the gun pointed firmly at Obote but I felt like sinking to the ground. He sounded weary now, as if he'd had enough too. But I really needed to do something, and quickly. I toughened up.

"Give me the keys to the house."

"No." He hung his head down so that he could keep his eyes open a bit more.

I moved closer and pointed the gun directly at his good knee cap. "Obote, give me the keys. Don't make me shoot your other knee cap."

He sighed. He seemed resigned, as if he had thought that things would be found out eventually. I put the gun closer to his knee. His eyes flicked up to meet mine. My heart flipped. I thought he was going to dare me, but he looked down and fished into his pocket. I glared at him, as if I shot people in the kneecap on a regular basis. Or at least, that was the look I was aiming for.

He handed me a bunch of keys. "My house keys are on there," he said.

"I don't think you'll need them for a while." I reached down, all the while maintaining my stare into his eyes, and with the gun pointing at his knee. I picked up the handcuffs. "Give me your wrist."

Once more he shook his head. I pointed the gun back at his head.

"Oh, Obote, don't play silly buggers, come on for crying out loud." I aimed the gun back at his knee. It seemed like a more realistic menace.

He shrugged his shoulders and held out his hand. I didn't think he really thought I was going to shoot him in the head, but he seemed to be taking my threat on his knee a little more seriously. I put the handcuffs round his wrist with one hand. I surprised myself at how steady I could keep my hand. I was still crouching and I had the gun close to him. I quickly put the other end of the handcuffs around the gate and locked them and then I backed away, wanting to get well out of reach in case he tried to kick the gun out of my hand and disarm me. If he found out it had no bullets in it heaven knew how he would react. He rattled the handcuff against the gate and they sounded surprisingly secure.

"Now, give me your phone."

"What?"

"I don't want you ringing anyone the minute I leave you here."

He looked down and said nothing.

"Obote, for fuck's sake just give me your sodding phone."

He carried on looking at the ground.

I hissed at him through clenched teeth. "Obote, if I have to fucking kill you I will and then I will have to rummage through your pockets for your phone. One way or another I will get it so give it to me now."

I had handcuffed his good hand up, and his other hand wouldn't work properly. I wasn't sure if he had broken a finger or two, or some bones in the main part of his hand but he clearly couldn't use it. That was good, it would hold him up for longer.

"Tell me which pocket it is in."

With his head he indicated his jacket pocket so, being sure to keep the gun pointed firmly at his head, and keeping my crouching position, I moved round and felt in his pocket. I pulled out a Samsung smartphone, which I put in my pocket. I looked at the key ring, it had about a dozen keys on it.

"Does this have all the keys for the house?"

He nodded.

"Including the inside bolts?"

He looked surprised, raising his eyebrows high, but nodded again. I thought he was about to say something, ask me how I knew maybe, but he stayed silent.

I kept the gun held up and felt in his other pockets, patting the pockets of his jeans and rummaging through his jacket. I found a wallet in his jacket, which I threw over to my rucksack, but nothing else. No other keys. I guessed he was telling me the truth. I backed away and when I was right across the yard, too far for him to reach, I began to gather up my things and put them back in my rucksack. I stuffed his keys and wallet in my pocket next to the phone. Finally, I lowered the gun and placed it in the rucksack with everything else.

I found my phone and got it out ready and then I zipped up the rucksack, picked up the carrier bag which had the book inside, jumped over the wall and, without a backwards glance at Obote, I left. I hoped it would take him a long time to alert someone's attention and to get free. I figured he wouldn't be in a hurry to call the police, although I obviously wasn't sure if Darnold was the only bent policeman around, and Obote could have other contacts.

I had no time to lose. I knew there was little choice but to deal with this on my own. I couldn't call the police because I had no way of knowing how many of them were involved. Dr Neasden had uncovered some, but who knew if there were others? His cryptic coding showed how fearful he had been of these people. And that had been confirmed by my experiences over the last week. Plus, I knew at least one policeman from Nottinghamshire was involved so I couldn't even trust neighbouring authorities. I just didn't know what else to do. Charlton was at least a couple of hours away, and what good would it do to call him? If he alerted the local police out of fear for my safety we were back round to the issue of not knowing if they were involved or not. There was just no two ways about it, I needed to do this my way.

I had to get to the house as quickly as I could. I had to make sure I had the children out before Obote could get free and alert someone. He might just recover his resolve and want revenge when he was free. I wouldn't want to come across him when he was angry. I'd seen what he'd done to Darnold. I had only got the better of him because I'd waited for him and surprised him. I got a move on.

41

After I had leaped over Obote's wall, I started running down the hill. I ran as fast as I could go, crossing the street and heading towards the house where the children were. I dumped the carrier bag with the book inside in a bin at the side of the road. I got out my phone and paused briefly whilst I found Collette's number and punched 'call' as quickly as I could. *Pick up. Pick up.*

She picked up after a few rings, clearly not recognising the number that had called her. I couldn't even remember if I was ringing her on my newest phone, or the first one I'd bought. I began running again and shouted in the phone.

"Collette, it's me. I need you to do something. It's urgent—"

She interrupted me, "Vee? What are you on about? Where are you—?"

This time I cut her off. "I don't have time to explain. You have to trust me. Honestly, Collette, this is the most important thing that I have ever asked you to do." I stopped running and stood still. "Collette, I need you, really badly. I need you to help me. No questions. I don't have time to explain, okay?"

She sounded unsure. "Okay?" I had stunned her into silence.

"Listen, Collette, I need you to get hold of Robert and Keith. I need you to meet me at a house." I gave her the address. "And, Collette, I need you all to get there as soon as you can. Tell Robert and Keith to come in separate cars. Have you got that?"

She repeated the address. "Separate cars? What if they are at work?"

"Collette, they have to come. This is really urgent. If they're at work, tell them to leave." I quietened down. I didn't want her to think I was being over-dramatic but at the same time I wanted her to get a sense of the urgency. I couldn't afford for her to not believe me. She had to come to the house, and she had to get the guys there too.

"Collete, it could be life or death, please."

"Verity? What? What did you just say?"

"Just do it. Now. I can't waste any more time. Honestly, it is really, really important. Do it. Collette, please." And I put the phone down. I didn't have time, and it certainly wasn't the place to feel guilty about being so abrupt with her. I just hoped she'd come through for me.

I started running again. I ran along the road, ignoring all the stares and I turned into the road the house was on. I was pleased the whole trip was downhill, but even so, I was seriously out of breath by the time I reached the house. *Maybe I should use my gym membership to do some actual exercise rather than sitting in the sauna.* I ran around the back and, before I attempted to open the door, I looked through the kitchen window. There was no sign of Darnold's body. Obote must have been round and done something with him this morning. Unless someone else had been called to come during the night to get rid of him. The kitchen looked clean; whoever had come round had washed all the blood away too. There was nothing to suggest that there had been a fight here, let alone a death, the night before.

I fumbled with the locks, no longer concerned about leaving finger prints, I just wanted to get inside. There were about a dozen keys on the key ring and I had to try each of them in four different locks. I kept forgetting which keys I'd tried and it seemed to take me ages to get the right ones for the right locks. Eventually I had all four locks open and I cautiously opened the door. The kitchen stank of a potent mixture of cleaners. I guessed I had to be grateful that someone had been and cleaned up, otherwise I would have had the stench of death and a dead body to contend with. It would also have made things very difficult to explain when, or if, Collette and the others turned up. They might have taken a negative view of leaving a dead body lying in a kitchen and not reporting it to the police. I glanced around the kitchen—there was nothing much to see that I hadn't been able to see from the outside. There was a sink below the kitchen window, with units beneath it that had no doors. A sponge and a pair of rubber gloves lay on one of the shelves and several half-empty large sized containers of what looked like industrial strength cleaners, but nothing else.

I moved across the kitchen to the door which led through to the hallway. I found the key for the bolts reasonably quickly and, luckily, the same key fitted them all. I turned the three bolts and opened up the door. Instantly, a strong smell of faeces and urine stung my eyes, making them water. I brushed away the tears with the back of my hand. I walked through the hallway. I knew the door immediately to my left led to the dining room and I also knew it was bolted from the other side. The kitchen and dining room doors were close together at this end of the hall, and the hall then stretched away towards the front door. To my right was a door which led to an under-the-stairs cupboard. The door was open, but the only thing inside was an old iron bed frame. Along the hallway there was a door on the left just before the front door. This had to be the front room. I tried the door but it was locked. Probably bolted from the other side again. I imagined someone attaching the bolts and then what? They had to have climbed out of the bay window and shut the windows somehow from the other side.

I turned towards the stairs, took hold of the banister and slowly began to climb. There was no carpet but the wood was painted white at the edges, as if the carpet that had been there before hadn't quite reached the edges. The stairs creaked and cracked as I climbed them and I wondered what the children were thinking. I assumed they were still here. Oh my God, I hadn't thought of that; my stomach lurched. What if they weren't here anymore? What if Obote was sending me on a wild goose chase?

"Hello!" I shouted out, but there was no reply, just silence. I carried on climbing. The stairs turned sharply at the top at a 90 degree angle and led to a long landing which ran along the length of the house with two doors off to either side. I pushed the first door to the left, which was open. It was a bathroom, but clearly hadn't been used for ages. The smell of shit was not coming from there. The window was covered with what looked like a grill, similar to the one that was in the serving hatch between the kitchen and the dining room.

I looked down the landing. The other three doors were all bolted from the outside. "Hello," I shouted again, but again there was no response. I paused and listened, but I couldn't hear a thing, not a single sound. I tried the door opposite the bathroom, the first door to my right. The bolts were closed and locked so I found the keys and used the bolt key to unlock them. This was the room that was above the front door. Gingerly I opened the door but there was nothing in there; the room was completely empty. This was a small room, little more than a box room. Then I noticed the windows. There were bars on the inside of the windows. *Bars for heaven's sake.*

I carried on down the landing. I undid the bolts on the next door on the right and cautiously entered.

Again it was empty. I glanced around; it did look as if there had been someone here at some point, but I wasn't sure how recently. There was a soiled mattress on the floor and some filthy bed linen slung over to one side. But there was no one in here now. I was in despair. Obote must have let me come here, knowing that the children weren't here. Where could they be? He had said Townsley saw them in the evening, but perhaps he had been telling me a pack of lies to throw me off the scent. I turned to the last door. This one was next to the bathroom and would overlook the back garden. I unlocked the bolts, slid them across the door and slowly opened it. I stopped, open mouthed. *Oh. My. God.*

-42-

What I saw made little sense, I scanned the room to try to comprehend what was in front of me. The smell was overwhelming. I gagged, trying not to throw up. The smell of ammonia from urine stung my eyes, and tears began to flow, unbidden, down my cheeks. The smell of faeces overpowered the smell of urine and together they formed a fowl, rancid odour that invaded every part of me. In the room, by the far wall, a double bed mattress had been flung on the floor. It had no sheet or cover, and was hideously dirty. A couple of overflowing potties, which were the obvious source of the stench, sat in the corner and next to them a bin with used toilet paper spilling out onto the floor. And there, sitting on the mattress, huddled together and blinking at me with wild, open eyes, were five young people. There were the two boys, or girls, I still couldn't quite tell, I had seen Obote pick up in the

Toddington services car park yesterday afternoon, the black girl I had seen brought round by Darnold the previous evening, a young white boy who looked about twelve and an Asian girl, perhaps from Vietnam or Cambodia or somewhere similar. She had a tiny frame but appeared a bit older than the others, maybe sixteen or seventeen. They all stared at me with their questioning, terrified expressions and I instantly knew that they had all suffered horrors I couldn't even imagine. The scars were writ large across their faces.

This room, like the other bedrooms, had bars on the windows; these kids had no chance of escape. There was an old television in the corner of the room playing some daytime drivel. It had a coat hanger for an aerial and the signal was really poor. There was nothing else in this room to keep these children amused; no books, no games, no cards, nothing. There was no light bulb in the fitting and there was a makeshift shutter behind the bars of the window meaning that the only light was coming from the flickering television. Presumably the shutter had been put there to prevent anyone from seeing any light that the television might throw. I ran across the landing and opened the opposite door to give a little more light. I ran back and glanced around the room. Scattered about the floor were a number of empty pill bottles. I picked one up; it had a name on it that I couldn't pronounce and the name of a drug which I didn't recognise. There were more bottles lining the windowsill, only these were full of pills. I looked back at the frightened children. I had to get them out of here fast.

"I've come to help," I said, directing it at no one in particular, and wiping the tears off my cheeks.

I was rewarded with blank, scared, stares.

"I'm here to help you," I said it slower this time.

Still the blank stares.

"Do any of you speak English?" I asked.

The children shuffled about. One or two had understood that. I asked them again and then, one of the young people that Obote had picked up sat up.

"A little," he said with a heavy Eastern European accent.

I crouched down so that my face was closer to his and asked him what his name was.

"My name Andrei."

Definitely a boy then. "I want to help. I want to take you away from here." I indicated the house with my arm.

The boy opened his eyes wide, his forehead deeply furrowed. He looked terrified. *Of course he was terrified.*

"Can you talk to the others?"

"No speak." He gestured at the two girls. One was Asian, one African, no wonder they didn't speak. He turned to the boy who had been with him in the car with Obote. "Radu, he Romanian." And then the young white boy. "Stefan. Romanian too."

"I'm going to take you away."

"No." He shook his head violently, tears welling up in his eyes. The terror returning to his face.

"What is it? Why are you so scared?"

He shrank away as if I were about to hit him. He stared at me and said nothing.

"I'm not here to hurt you," I said gently. "I want to help you. What is it that is scaring you so much?"

"Stefan had friend. Friend try." He struggled to find the right English words. "Run…he try…they lock him. In prison. Policeman lock him."

I thought of the young lad that Dr Neasden had been helping, the one who had been arrested for burglary by Sanderson. Could it have been him?

"Where was the friend from?"

He turned to Stefan and spoke to him in what I took to be Romanian and then turned back to me. "Rwanda," he said.

That was it, that was it. Was that what they had done? Could they have been punishing him for trying to run away? By staging an arrest and getting him convicted. I couldn't comprehend this. Then I remembered; Neasden had been helping him access medical treatment as part of his support. *Oh shit, this is getting worse.*

"He was ill?"

"Yes, he very ill. He die."

"He died?"

"Stefan say he die soon." He looked back at the floor. His utter helplessness overwhelmed me.

I knew he had only been here, in this house, for a night but who knew what had happened before that. He clearly felt that he had nowhere to go, no one to turn to, nobody who could help him. He looked desperately alone. The others looked as if they had been here for some time. They looked completely resigned to the fact that they had no control over what was happening to them; that their lives, literally, were in someone else's hands. I wondered if the dying child had access to medication now, and prayed that he was hopefully in a hospital somewhere. If Neasden had been helping him access treatment, had Townsley stopped treating him because he had tried to run away? As well as being locked up, he had been denied further treatment. No wonder these kids were scared. *Bloody hell.*

"I'm not one of them. Do you understand?" I had to try to get them to trust me, but I was fighting a losing battle. Why would these children trust any adult?

He looked blank again. His staring, vacant, black eyes suggested he was completely world weary. He couldn't have been more than thirteen or fourteen; I felt achingly desperate.

"I'm going to help you."

"Help?" It was as if he had just recognised the word. He turned to his companion and said something in Romanian.

I gestured to the pills on the windowsill. "You're ill?"

"No," he said, pointing to himself. "Not ill."

"You're sick? The pills are for you because you are ill."

"No. Not sick." He pointed at the small Romanian boy. "He sick." Then at one of the girls. "She sick."

"But." I tried to phrase it in as easy language as I could. "I thought you came here, to England, because you are sick?"

"Not sick." He pointed at his companion. "Radu not sick"

"What are you saying? You and Radu are not sick?"

He nodded.

"But the others are?"

He nodded again.

"Stefan not sick"

"You said he was sick?"

"He sick now."

"He is sick?" My head was spinning, I was confused. I thought these children had been sent here illegally for treatment because they were ill.

"He come here. He see doctor. Now he sick."

I shook my head "What? What, what are you saying? Are you saying that Stefan was well, not sick, when he arrived in England but after he saw the doctor, then he became sick?"

Andrei looked up at me with those desperately sad eyes and just nodded.

The realisation hit me like a physical blow; like someone had punched me in the chest. I fell back onto the floor, on my bottom. All the blood rushed out of my head and I thought I was going to faint. There was a loud rushing in my ears and the room went black. I struggled to regain my composure. I breathed heavily, putting my hands down to steady myself. I stood up again and gazed at these displaced young people.

Townsley wasn't trafficking children here who were ill to take part in his research. He was trafficking healthy children here and *making* them ill. He was giving these young people cancer and then experimenting with treatment. *Fuck, fuck, fuck.* No wonder he didn't want anyone finding out. *Oh shit.* I pushed the thought of Townsley out of my head. I had to get these children out of here. I had to get them out. I had to persuade them that I wasn't going to hurt them.

I reached over and touched Andrei on the arm. "I won't let the doctor make you sick."

He looked up at me, his eyes full of disbelief in what I had said. I hoped I could come through on my promise.

"Get the others to come with me," I said, standing up and gesturing that they should follow me.

They all seemed reluctant. I stood near the door and indicated that they should follow me. I looked directly at Andrei.

"Get them to come. I'm going to help you. I'm going to get you out." I wanted to scream at them to hurry up, to get a move on before Obote broke free and came and hit me over the head with a shovel, but I couldn't. I just hoped they would trust me. I implored Andrei with my face, and he slowly stood up, grabbing his companion Radu by the arm and dragging him to his feet. The other boy and the two girls slowly, timidly, followed suit.

A loud knocking pierced through the stillness of the rancid room, and then a shout from downstairs. It was Collette. A rush of relief flooded over my body. *Thank God, Collette.*

"Collette," I called out, trying to maintain my composure. "Hang on, my darling, I'll be down in a minute. Just wait in the kitchen."

"Okay." The reply drifted up the stairs with a distinct note of uncertainty.

I tried to indicate with my gestures to the children that they needed to hurry.

"Quick," I said to Andrei. "Hurry." And I indicated running with my arms.

I thought he might be about to smile at my mime, a flicker passed over his lips and he hurried the others along, speaking in Romanian to those who could understand him. I led them down the stairs and into the kitchen. My three friends were standing there, looking bemused, and I instantly indicated to them with a finger across my neck and then against my lips, that they should stay quiet. I wanted to run over and throw myself at them, I wanted to hug them and bury my face in their necks and breathe in their clean, familiar smell. Instead I ushered the children forward.

"Guys, thank you, thank you so much, I've no time to explain. You need to take these children, now, away from here."

Now it was my friends' turn to stare blankly.

Robert said, "Vee, what are you doing? Where are these children from?" Then he blinked and paused and said, "And more to the point, darling, what *have* you done to your hair?"

Just like Robert, in the middle of a crisis to focus on my new hairstyle. But I had forgotten. I had got so used to it, it hadn't occurred to me that my appearance might be a bit of a shock to my friends.

Thank goodness the cut had healed on my lip and the red mark had gone from my neck. And at least they couldn't see my aching shoulder where Obote had pulled me into the wall earlier.

"Rob, darling, I can't explain right now, except that these children need our help. They need to get away from this house as quickly as they can. Someone might turn up any minute and catch us. They are hurting the children, making them ill. Please?"

He swallowed, he looked at my face, beseeching him for help. He looked at the children, huddled together in a bewildered group. He shook his head, after all it was completely out of character for me to be behaving like this. He must have seen the look of desperation in my face, because he looked again at the children and suddenly switched to 'efficient' mode.

"What do you need us to do?"

"You need to take the children. You need to look after them, just for a short while. We can't phone social services right now."

Keith raised a sceptical eyebrow.

"I'm sorry, you'll have to trust me, we can't phone them just yet."

Collette looked at me as if I had just utterly taken leave of my senses. I ran over and hugged her.

"Collette, you are my dearest, dearest friend. Please, you have to trust me."

"Why not social services?" She moved away.

I wanted to snap at her, but now was not the time. I tried again. "Not yet, we can call them soon, but not yet. You have to trust me. I will explain but I need to make sure that these children are safe and I need to make sure that the person who is hurting them is brought to justice."

Silence.

"Please, please. There is a really good reason we can't call social services or the police just yet. We will. I promise, but you have to believe me for now."

Collette was wavering. She knew what had happened to Dr Neasden. She looked across the room at me.

"The notebook," she whispered.

"These kids have been trafficked here, they are here illegally." I was begging now. "Some of them are very sick. We have to get them out of here. We'll deal with the rest of it later. Please."

I was met with another silence. I appealed to Collette's maternal side. "Collette, I know you think I'm mad, but these children are in real danger. Imagine if they were yours, you'd want someone to help, wouldn't you? If your kids found themselves at real risk, you'd want a random stranger to help out."

"Vee, are you sure we are not doing anything illegal?" Robert asked, and I wanted to weep. I wasn't at all sure that this wasn't illegal but I didn't have the time to debate the law with him. I took a deep breath, reminding myself that this was all very new to my friends; they hadn't been on the journey that I had over the last few days.

I looked him in the eyes and repeated my mantra, "They are here illegally already, Rob. They've been trafficked, and they are sick. They need our help."

I could tell that my closest friends all thought I was bonkers but eventually, after a little more imploring on my part, they seemed to accept what I was saying and agreed to take the children. They also agreed to hang fire with calling social services for now.

I fought the urge to feel relief, knowing we were not out of danger yet and we had to get a move on. I took Radu by the shoulders and crouched down so I could look him straight in the eyes.

"You are going to be safe now," I said to him. He looked back and nodded slowly. He turned to the others and without saying anything he indicated with his shoulders that they should follow his lead. I gestured to them all with my hands that they should go with my friends.

The children made no effort to resist, to argue or to ask where they were going. I sensed that they were used to being taken from one place to another by people they had never met. I felt a sense of unease, that perhaps I was exploiting their vulnerability. But at least I knew that this time they were being taken somewhere nice where they would be treated well and that it would be for their benefit. I just needed to get them away from the house.

As we got out the front to the cars the children naturally divided. The three Romanian boys followed Robert and Keith and the girls latched onto Collette. I was scanning around for any sign that someone was coming down the street to prevent us leaving; I couldn't risk being interrupted now. I bundled the children into the cars, made sure everyone had their seat belts on, and bid them a hasty farewell. Time was pressing and I had a professor to get to.

It was dusk by the time the children went off in the cars. I couldn't believe it was so late; I'd spent most of the day sitting in Obote's front yard waiting for him to come back but all of a sudden the time had slipped past. I needed to get to the hospital and find the room that Townsley used for seeing the children. I needed to be in there before he turned up. The element of surprise seemed to have worked quite well with Obote, there was no way I could have overpowered him if I hadn't lain in wait, and I wanted to use that again with Townsley. I hoped that Obote hadn't worked his way free, and hadn't been able to tell anyone that I was on to them. I didn't want Townsley to be expecting a visit from me.

I didn't want to walk past Obote's road. I preferred to remain in the dark as to whether he was free or not. I figured that the only way he could have got free would be if he had alerted a neighbour and I wasn't sure he would want to do that. I supposed he wouldn't want to remain handcuffed to the gate for too long, but he couldn't ring anyone as I had his phone. He wouldn't be able to use the hand I had stamped on, and one of his knee caps was pretty well smashed up. I wondered what Charlton would make of all this. Then I thought I'd probably committed several crimes in the last few hours, including grievous bodily harm, but I pushed that thought to the back of my mind; I'd have to cross that bridge when I came to it. The important thing now was to get to Townsley as soon as possible and prevent any more children's lives being ruined in the name of his research.

The hospital wasn't too far away from the house and I walked up a small road that led up the hill and came out near the back of the site. It took me about ten minutes to get there. I walked in through the staff car park and paused a while, near the curb. I quickly got out my iPad and Googled the hospital website where I found a map of the site. This told me where the outpatient clinics were, over to the right from where I was standing. I thought or a while about what to do. I watched a couple of people come into and out of the car park and hovered around trying not to look too suspicious. Each time someone came in I watched them to see what they were doing. Most had an ID badge around their neck and they walked towards various different entrances, some disappearing off round a corner out of sight.

After watching about a dozen or so people come into the car park and walk off to work, I spotted someone I thought could help. She wasn't wearing her badge, she was carrying it on top of a bag which was spilling over with paperwork. I ran up to her, doing my best to look a bit flustered.

"Excuse me! Excuse me!"

She stopped and turned towards me.

"I'm really sorry, I seem to have got a bit lost. Can you tell me where the main entrance is please?"

She seemed happy to help and turned round, pointing in the direction I should take. I leant in close to her as if following the line of her finger with my vision and gently, slowly, and without looking, I picked up her badge and slipped it into my pocket. I thanked her and ran off in the direction in which she had been pointing. I didn't think she would realise I had taken her badge, she would probably assume that she had left it at home. There would be some procedure for getting a new one I was sure. It would be a bit of an inconvenience, but never mind. I had bigger problems to think about.

Once I was out of her sight I stopped. I turned round and headed over to the other side of the hospital, where the entrance to outpatients was. I had been here last year and knew my way; I'd had a referral for a painful swelling in my knee. It was, apparently, a problem with the ligament, which actually had gone away of its own accord in the end. But I had been here for a consultation.

The pass I had stolen identified me as Gillian Legge and I hoped no one would take too close a look at the picture; it showed a round-faced woman with shoulder-length curly hair. There was little resemblance to me, even if you had thought I'd cut and dyed my hair and been on a diet since the photo had been taken. I put the badge around my neck, making sure that photo was against my body, and walked purposefully through the corridors, hoping that no one would have cause to ask to look at it. I thought the key was to walk along with a confident air as if I was in a hurry to get somewhere, so that was what I tried to convey.

I walked along the corridors, following the signs for the outpatient unit, passing nurses who were bustling along, pushing people in wheelchairs, or carrying drips, or notes. They all looked incredibly busy and didn't give me a second glance. There were a few patients, wearing night clothes and dressing gowns, sitting on chairs in the corridor or outside wards and a lot of what I took to be relatives walking towards the wards. It had to be visiting time soon, I thought. I went past a café area that was closed and eventually found myself in the outpatient unit. I had to access it with my card and I paused and took a deep breath before entering. *Come on Verity, you've found a new talent for acting as well as lying. You can do this.* I pushed the door open and went in.

The unit was not very busy; there was one person hanging about in a waiting room, the last of the day's clients I imagined, or a relative waiting for someone else to emerge from a clinic. The reception desk was deserted and several of the lights further down the corridor had gone out. I imagined that they were the kind of lights that came on when there was movement. There had clearly been no movement along there for some time. I walked along, following the signs for the clinics, numbered from 1-8. Some had a sign on the door with the name of the consultant who was seeing patients that day, some had a slot for a name but the name had been removed. I guessed those clinics had finished for the day, although looking through some of the open doors there was nobody about. I strode past all of the doors, looking as if I knew what I was doing. I passed two nurses whispering in a corner. They glanced over at me but turned away again to continue their conversation. I was amazed at how I could get by unnoticed because I had a name badge around my neck, especially as I was dressed as if I was about to go on a hike. I'd been lost in hospitals before and had only got a couple of yards before someone had asked me what I was doing.

Then I saw the name. It was on the door of consulting room 5. Professor Kenneth Townsley. Obote was right; Townsley had a consulting suite in the outpatient department. I wondered how much money his research brought the hospital; probably a lot. Obote had said they thought he was God. I'd known consultants before who acted as if they owned hospitals and no one ever questioned them because they were so powerful. They ruled the hospital. Townsley was probably even more powerful; he was a professor, a well-renowned professor who was bringing lucrative research to the hospital.

Nobody was around this part of the corridor and I opened the door and slipped inside. I turned the light on briefly, to get a sense of where things were. It was a typical hospital consulting room with an examining table that had a curtain you could pull round, a sink, a desk with a chair either side, another chair further into the room and some cupboards on wheels with all sorts of medical equipment spilling out of them. There was a connecting door to another room and I peeped in there. This had a desk and a chair, some lockable cabinets, some shelves that were filled with books and another chair off to one side.

I hadn't a clue what to do. I really needed to get myself a bit more prepared for these occasions. I had been so keen to actually get here before Townsley that I hadn't given a thought to what I was actually going to do, or say to him when he arrived. I took my rucksack off my back then fished out a knife and a pair of handcuffs, hanging the handcuffs from the waistband of my trousers. I put the rucksack on my back again; I didn't want to trip over it in the dark and I certainly didn't want to leave it anywhere if I had to go in a hurry; it had everything in it, most importantly all my notes and figuring outs. I turned off the light and sat on the bed and thought, holding the knife in my hand and feeling incredibly nervous.

-44-

I wasn't allowed the luxury of being able to think for very long, because about ten minutes later the opening snick of the door in the next room, alerted me to someone's arrival. Just when I could have done with some waiting time, he had turned up before I had expected him. I assumed it was Townsley. I didn't know what he looked like; I hadn't been able to find a decent photo, so I would have to guess. I held my breath and sat there in the dark, listening to the movements next door. There was a scraping of a chair—he was sitting down at his desk. A drawer opening—looking at a file? Maybe he was studying the file of a person he was expecting to see tonight. Unless he had other children in another house somewhere, he thankfully wouldn't be seeing anyone this evening. And unless Obote had worked his way free, and felt inclined to hobble up here with his gammy leg, Townsley would still be expecting them.

I could feel myself getting tenser. I clenched my jaw and gripped the edge of the examining table. The chair in the next room scraped again. He was standing up. Footsteps, and then the door handle rattling. The door opened and the light went on. Townsley looked around him and took a step back when he saw me sitting on the bed. He was a tall and thin man, probably about mid-50s. He had a full head of grey hair swept to one side, a wrinkled face with hooded eyes and a bulbous nose. There was an air of self-importance about him as he strode into the room. He was wearing a tweed jacket and a pair of tan coloured trousers, with an open necked shirt.

"Good evening, Professor Townsley. I've a few questions I would like to ask you."

He opened and closed his mouth a few times before taking a step back. He was clearly shocked to see me, although he quickly recovered his composure, spreading his shoulders and lifting his chin before he spoke. Obote had obviously not been able to warn him. Or maybe hadn't felt the inclination to tell him.

"What the hell do you think you're doing in here? How did you get in?"

I held the knife up in front of me so that he could see it and he took a step back.

"I'd like to ask you about the children you've been using for your 'research'." I made the internationally accepted sign for inverted commas with both hands.

"Get out of here. I'm not talking to you or anyone else. Get out of here, go on." He pointed to the door as if to reinforce his point.

I sat tight and said nothing.

"Get out of my room. You have no idea what you are talking about. Believe me, you should just go now." He wasn't shouting; he was calm and measured. That made him all the scarier. He just looked at me directly in the eyes and spoke with a slow, cold tone. I could see how he managed to frighten people into doing what he wanted. But I had no intention of going anywhere.

"I know what you are doing, Townsley."

He started to move towards me but stuttered when I held up the knife again. I had the upper hand, he didn't really know what to say and I wasn't about to leave voluntarily. I was inwardly congratulating myself on getting the better of him. I was about to tell him that I had taken the children somewhere safe but my thoughts were suddenly disturbed by the sound of a commotion outside in the corridor.

A woman was shouting from in the corridor. "Stop! You can't go in there."

And a man's voice replying, "I will go anywhere the fuck I like."

The woman again, "I'm calling security."

And with that a man burst through Townsley's door followed by a flustered middle-aged woman in a nurse's uniform.

"I'm so sorry, Professor," she stammered. "I tried to stop him. I'll get security."

"No!" Townsley replied as quickly as he could whilst still maintaining an air of calmness. "No, no need for security. You go home. I can handle this."

The nurse looked dubious. She glanced from Townsley to the intruder and back again. She didn't even appear to notice me sitting on the bed with a knife in my hand. I was partly obscured by the curtain at the end of the bed and she wouldn't have been looking for anyone else.

"It's okay," Townsley reassured her. He put a hand on her shoulder and ushered her to the door.

She shook her head doubtfully and glanced over her shoulder but Townsley reiterated, "It's okay. You go home. I'll be done here soon." He shot a glance at the intruder.

The nurse disappeared through the door and Townsley closed it behind her.

He turned to the man, ignoring me for the time being, and hissed at him, "Sanderson, what the fuck do you think you are doing here?" He then turned and gestured at me. "What is going on tonight?"

Sanderson. The last of the acronyms. I'd found them all now. Sanderson was a tall, slim man who appeared to be in his early forties. He was wearing a sharp suit with an open neck. He was a good looking man with a shaved head and a dark five o'clock shadow.

Sanderson glanced at me but immediately shifted his gaze. It was as if he was so incensed that he didn't care who or what else was in the room. He kept his voice low.

"Darnold is dead. That's what the fuck I am doing here. You've gone too far this time."

"He deserved it, the little prick." Townsley snarled at Sanderson and paced further into the room, but Sanderson was just getting warmed up.

"I'm going to report you. I'm going to ruin you. Murdering a police officer. That's too much. I'm going to have your veneer of respectability in tatters before I'm finished."

"Don't be stupid, Sanderson. No one is going to believe you. He was a bent police officer anyway, I'll discredit him as fast as you can blink." Townsley continued pacing around the room, puffing himself up with importance. He had moved away from Sanderson and closer to me but he carried on pacing backwards and forwards.

"Bent because of you! You're the one who corrupted him."

"Like you. Ha! You're all the same," Townsley curled his lip and spat the words out the corner of his mouth. "So easy to buy off. Who on earth will believe you over me?"

"You're not infallible, Townsley. I have evidence that even you can't get changed or fabricated. Your reputation will come tumbling down round your ears when people realise what you are really up to."

And then, catching me completely unawares, Townsley turned towards me. I didn't have time to react. Before I could think about stabbing him, he grabbed my knife and poked it towards me. He yanked me off the bed by my arm and turned me round, holding me by my neck and putting the knife to my throat.

"You think Darnold's murder was too much? What about this bitch? I can slit her throat easily."

"You can't keep covering up one death after another."

"Ah, well that's where you're wrong. The benefit of working in a hospital is that I get to sign the death certificates. I can do what the hell I want. They need me here. What do you think she will die of? A disease? Pneumonia perhaps? Trauma? From a car crash maybe?"

45

I couldn't move. The knife was pressed hard against my neck, the blade digging into my skin. He was gripping my neck with his arm, and I grabbed it with my hands, trying to pull it away. I could barely touch the ground with my toes and my weight was adding pressure onto my neck. It had only just recovered from being strangled in my hotel room a few days earlier.

Sanderson looked shocked but he was still quite cocky. He still obviously thought that knowing about Darnold's death was enough to bring Townsley down. He spread his arms. "Townsley. You've got to realise. It's gone too far."

"No, no… It hasn't. We're back on track now. Or we will be when we've got rid of this interfering cow. Everything was going okay, Sanderson. It was all going smoothly. It still would be now if you hadn't let

314

that stupid, snooping Neasden poke his nose in where nobody wanted him. Everything was going fine until then." He was getting emotional and he gripped my throat even tighter.

I thought about kicking him with my walking boots, but I didn't want to risk him stabbing me in the neck. I was helpless.

"You'd cut that lad off." Sanderson was getting louder now. "He was dying and you'd cut him off. Getting him locked up is one thing but he had to get treatment. You just left him to die."

"He was going to die anyway. Why bother?"

"You were supposed to be treating him."

"He tried to run away." Townsley took a few steps back, dragging me with him. "I," he said, gesticulating towards himself with the knife as if to emphasise his own importance. "I was making him better and he tried to run away, the little fuck. He didn't deserve my help."

Sanderson seemed taken aback at Townsley's arrogance. He paused, took in an audible breath and frowned. His voice took on a higher tone, "What about the others? Will you cut them off too?"

"They should be grateful. I'm making them better. They're getting the best care available." He shouted, "They should be falling at my feet."

I couldn't stand it. I tried to shout out, "They're not ill!" but it came out more like, "hmm hmm hmm."

But Townsley knew what I was trying to say. He squeezed my neck tighter in an effort to stop me speaking, and pushed the knife against my neck a little more. I let out a sharp squeal through my nose; my mouth was pretty much covered by Townsley's arm. Sanderson could tell that Townsley was trying to silence me and he moved a little closer.

"What did she say?" He looked at me and then at Townsley, his expression worsening with the fear of what he had got himself into. "What did you say?"

I forced my mouth above Townsley's arm and shouted out. "They're not ill." But before I could say anything else, Townsley jabbed the knife back into my neck. An intense, sharp pain took over all other thought, and it would have knocked me off my feet, had Townsley not been holding me up. Then the feeling of the point digging into the skin and a trickle of blood running down my neck. It was all I could do not to start panicking but it felt as if I was getting Sanderson on side. He came towards us, a look of incomprehension playing across his face.

"What do you mean?" he asked. He scrunched his eyebrows together in a knot and looked at me. "What does she mean, not ill?" He looked back at Townsley. Then he shouted at the top of his voice, his face contorting, "What does she mean?"

Townsley tried to back away, still gripping me by the neck. Sanderson lurched towards him and pulled at the arm he had around my neck. Townsley tightened his grip but Sanderson managed to pull his arm away from my mouth enough so that I could shout out.

"They're not ill when they come here. They're healthy kids. He makes them ill so that he can use them in his research."

But Townsley was strong and he pulled his arm back over my mouth again and dragged me away from Sanderson.

Sanderson was enraged. He paced around the room. He walked to the far wall, turned suddenly then pointed a finger at Townsley.

"Townsley! You lied to me. You lied to everyone. Is this why Darnold wanted out? You told us the kids were ill. You told us their parents had paid for them to come here to get treatment. You made us think it was all for the good."

"A white lie," Townsley said. His calm and calculated demeanour contrasting with Sanderson's fury. He pulled me back a few paces, towards his desk. I scrabbled for purchase with my feet, trying to maintain contact with the floor. "You wouldn't have helped otherwise. It was for the greater good. Think of the lives we'll save. Think of the money we'll make." Townsley took the knife away from my neck.

I didn't understand what was happening or why he had done that. He moved his arm, although I couldn't see why and the knife ended up beneath the examining table. He must have thrown it away. I was confused. What was he doing? He still had his other arm tightly round my neck and I couldn't turn round to see what was going on.

"Well it's gone too far," Sanderson shouted back at him. "You have to stop. You have to be stopped."

"No! I'm too close."

"You can't keep on just killing people."

"I can!"

Sanderson didn't seem to have noticed but Townsley had reached down to his desk. As he bent down and twisted me round, I had a clear view of what he was up to; he was putting his hand out towards the desk. Sanderson was so incensed he wasn't paying attention.

"You arrogant bastard—" he started to say, but he was cut off in mid-sentence, stunned into silence when he realised that Townsley had opened a drawer in his desk and pulled out a gun.

He held it up with his right hand, still gripping me round my neck with his left arm. It was a black handgun with a long thin round barrel, very different to the one I had in my rucksack. It had something attached to the end but I wasn't sure what it was, it looked like an extension of the barrel.

Sanderson tried to reach for the door handle, whilst still staring at Townsley. The look on Sanderson's face was of sheer horror. Although I couldn't see Townsley's face, I could tell by the way Sanderson was looking at him that his intent was writ large all over it. Sanderson opened his mouth to speak and he lifted his hand a tiny way upwards as if to make a gesture. He managed to do neither. There was a 'pop' from behind me and Sanderson's head exploded onto the wall behind him. He was thrown against the wall by the force of the shot and then he slowly slumped down onto the floor, his body leaning against the wall. A trail of blood followed as he slid down the wall. As Townsley had pulled the trigger, his grip on my neck had loosened and I pulled his arm away from me and ran to the far side of the room, still behind the desk but

318

away from Townsley. The noise the gun had made had not been loud and I realised then that the extension on the barrel must have been a silencer. It had worked. Although it was far from silent, if there had still been anyone around they wouldn't have heard anything that would have alarmed them.

I couldn't take my eyes off Sanderson. The look of horror was still etched on his face. He had a hole in the front of his forehead, above his left eye and slightly down towards his ear. That was quite a neat hole, but the back of his head had completely disappeared. There were bits of it all over the wall; little bits of skull with hair still attached stuck to the wall behind him. There was blood; loads of blood in a massive swoosh, as if someone had thrown a bucket of red paint onto the wall. And there were bits of other stuff. I wasn't even going to start thinking about what they were.

46

I gasped and I could hear myself breathing heavily, as if the breaths were coming from someone else. The smells that whipped around the room were almost overwhelming. The stench of excrement where Sanderson's body had emptied itself, together with the smell of blood and brain. Into this mix swirled the tart smell of a recently discharged gun and I heaved as I tried not to throw up. I tore my eyes away from the remains of Sanderson and looked at Townsley, my mouth open in astonishment. He was still holding the gun in front of him. He turned to me.

"You should have left that meddling Doctor Neasden in his poky little house and got out."

He knows who I am. Of course, the man in the night with the baseball bat. Townsley had been on to me.

I tried not to let that thought show in my voice. "And let you carry on getting away with what you're doing?"

"I'm curing people! I'm doing good! It's my mission to save lives!" he shouted, spit pouring from his mouth in an arc, landing on the desk and the floor.

I shouted back, feeling the rage inside me, shaking my finger at him, "No, it's your mission to be a hero. You want everyone to see you as a saviour, as some kind of god."

"I am," he roared. "I'm going to cure the world."

I leant forward and pointed, gesticulating with my whole arm. "You can't cure people by killing other people. Those children haven't asked to be part of your grand plan."

"They're doing good too. They're doing good for the world."

I quietened down. "They're children. You bring them over here, telling them I don't know what stories to get them here and then you use them for your own ends."

"No. Not my own ends. For the greater good. You've got to look at this from the perspective of all those people I will save."

"But doctors don't kill."

He glanced over at Sanderson, still propped against the wall, still with that look of horror on his face.

He looked back at me. "In the future I will go down as a hero. No one will care how I did it. The ends will justify the means." He puffed himself up grandly.

"Making children ill? Making them die?"

"But it's only a few." He had calmed down now. "And their families don't care. They're prepared to send them over here. No one will miss them." He sat on the desk and spoke quietly, "We have to continue studying how the cancers grow and how they hide in our bodies so that we can find an effective treatment." He paused, glancing over at Sanderson again, and I thought I saw a look of recognition, of shock, pass over his face. Then it was gone. "Treatments only help once the cancer has grown but if we can understand how they grow, make that less unpredictable to us, we can attack the cancer at the earliest stage. Maybe even before that if we can understand *why* they develop."

He looked up at me. "Do you know how many people a year die across the world because of cancer? What these children are doing, they are doing for the good of the world."

"You're a doctor and you don't care about them. The boy in prison, you just discarded him." I was horrified by what he was doing but I had to keep a check on my emotions.

He became agitated again. "He was dying anyway."

"Because of you!" I couldn't believe the arrogance of this man. If he hadn't had a gun in his hand I would have stomped up and smacked him in the face.

"My research will save thousands of lives!"

"But you can't do it like this. You can't make some people ill, let them die, to save others. You just can't do it like that."

Townsley looked at the gun in his hand. He lifted it up and aimed it directly at me. I couldn't think straight, I couldn't even breathe. I leant against the wall, gripping it behind me with both hands to stop myself from falling. I had never been more frightened in my life. I stared at the gun. *This is it.* This is it. Maybe those were John's last thoughts too as the lorry hurtled towards him. This is it. My mouth had become so dry I could barely speak. But I had to try something.

"What about the oath?" I tried to keep my voice as level as I could.

"Oath?"

"The oath you take as a doctor."

"The Hippocratic oath?"

"Yes. Doesn't it say something in there about saving lives, not taking them?"

He sighed and looked at me as if I was being particularly stupid. This wasn't going well. He spoke slowly and calmly, "The end will justify the means. We will be saving lives."

"You're ruined, Townsley." I indicated towards Sanderson. "Killing me won't help. You're ruined anyway."

"I think killing you will help me greatly," he said. He lifted the gun up and aimed it at my forehead. "All you meddlers will be out of the way then and I can carry on with my research in peace."

"And who will you get to cover up for you the next time?"

"I don't need anyone else. I'll take care of everything. Everyone else just gets in the shit anyway. I'm better off operating on my own."

"I moved the kids out of the house," I said, my voice wavering; having a gun pointing at my head was scarier than I could ever have imagined. I hoped he hadn't noticed.

He looked genuinely surprised at this, his mouth twitching before he forced it into an unnatural smile. He exhaled sharply and took a step backwards, lowering the gun. He opened his mouth as if to speak but said nothing.

"They're safe. You won't find them. And the Human Trafficking Unit is on to you too."

He looked at Sanderson again. That flutter of something passed over his face once again. Perhaps a recognition of what he had become; something as far removed from a doctor as you could get. He looked back at me and this time his eyes were filled with sadness and horror.

"I've got an iPhone in my pocket, Townsley, I've had a call in to DI Sam Charlton from the Unit. It's been on since before you arrived. All this has been going through to him. He's probably recorded it. Townsley, killing me will make no difference at all. Either way, you're finished."

"You're lying."

"You're through."

Townsley looked up at me again, the fire back in his eyes. "No, I'm going to carry on. I'm going to finish my work. The world needs me."

324

"The world doesn't need you to be killing people who have no one to turn to. Or"—I indicated Sanderson—"people who have been covering up for you but got fed up with your megalomaniac tendencies. I don't think the world wants to be saved by someone like you."

He looked at Sanderson again, then at the gun, then at me.

"You're a doctor, Townsley, you're supposed to save people not kill them. No end justifies that method. That was the argument the Nazis used; it didn't wash with the world then and it won't wash now."

"I want to go down in history," he said quietly. "I want the world to remember me."

He lifted the gun up and for a moment I thought he was going to aim it at his own head. I held my breath. I had seen enough death over the last few days, and braced myself for another. But then a phone beeped in his pocket and he took it out and looked at it. A smile spread slowly across his face.

He pointed the gun back at me.

"We'll see who's finished. Come with me." He nodded towards the door into the next room.

I was confused; what was he doing? Where was he taking me? I checked my rucksack was firmly on my back and made towards the door to the adjoining room. Although the thought made me feel queasy, there was no way I could get out of the door without trampling all over Sanderson's blood. I looked at his body still slumped against the wall; his face a vision of horror and everything else splattered across the room.

The blood had pooled around him and spread out covering the area near the door. Shiny hospital floors were not designed to stop the flow. I pitied the poor person who would stumble across this scene in the morning.

Townsley followed closely behind me as I left the room, pushing the muzzle of the gun into my side so that I knew not to try anything. I wasn't about to try anything; I had seen what this man was capable of and now was certainly not the time to make a move. *Pick your moment, Verity.*

47

We walked through to the adjacent room in silence but as I approached the door to the corridor, he grabbed my arm and stopped me.

"Don't try anything stupid. Just walk. I'm going to cover the gun with my coat. If we see anyone just keep walking. You know I am not afraid to use it." He grabbed a coat that had been hanging on the back of the door and put it over the gun. He positioned himself so that it looked as if we were walking closely, perhaps father and daughter visiting a relative, and hid the gun between us. The muzzle was sticking into my side.

I didn't take this as an idle threat so I walked as calmly as I could through the, now deserted, outpatients department and through the corridors of the hospital until Townsley pushed me towards a side entrance. We passed a few people but they didn't give us a sideways glance, so there was no way I could even try to attract their attention with my expression. Townsley pushed me roughly through the door, closed it behind him and pushed me down the path towards one of the staff car parks. He kept his coat over the gun and continued to stick close behind me so there was no chance of getting away. I looked round to see if there were any bushes or buildings I could run to and hide behind but I knew that I would only get a couple of yards and he would have pulled the trigger. The gun had a silencer and there was no one around; he could easily kill me and then drive away without anyone noticing. If I was going to make a move I had to do it at the right time.

The car park was almost deserted; there were a few cars dotted around but I guessed that this car park was generally used by people who worked during the day. At the front of the car park in one of the bays marked 'consultants parking only' there was a dark grey jaguar. I noticed the missing apostrophe and thought what a stupid thing that was to notice in a moment like this. Townsley had some keys in his hands, he must have fished them out of his pocket whilst we were walking, and he blipped the car open. He led me to the passenger side and told me to get in and then slide over to the driver's side. I wondered why he didn't just tell me to go round to the other side but then I realised that by doing it this way he could keep the gun aimed at me the whole time. I wondered if he had done this before.

Once I was in the driver's seat he got in beside me. I hoped he wasn't expecting me to drive; my legs were making jelly look fairly solid. The rucksack was digging painfully into my back as I sat in the driver's seat but I ignored it. I wasn't letting go of it under any circumstances. It had my remaining armoury inside it and I was clinging to it like a security blanket in the hope that I might, just, get a chance to break free at some point.

He passed me the keys. "Here, drive to the house."

"House? Which house?"

"The one where you reckon you've stolen my patients from."

I put the key in the ignition and tried to concentrate on getting the car going. It was a huge car. I had never driven anything like it and I didn't want to scratch it; I didn't want to do anything to antagonise the man pointing a gun at my chest. I also didn't really want to make any sudden or jerky manoeuvres in case it caused him to accidentally press the trigger. I tried to forget that there was a gun pointing at me, instead focusing on getting some feeling in my legs to pull away smoothly.

"You've probably condemned them to death, you know?"

I was silent. I couldn't hold a conversation *and* drive with a gun pointing at me.

"They need their medication and treatment. I hope you don't mind having that on your conscience."

I wasn't going to get into an argument in the car, so I let that pass and ignored the irony of his statement. Hopefully, if I ended up shot and dumped in the boot, my friends would make sure those children were looked after.

I drove carefully out of the car park and along the roads to the house. It was dark outside and there weren't many cars on the streets. Those that were wouldn't have noticed anything particularly distinctive about the jaguar passing the other way. How would anyone know that I was driving along with a gun against my ribs? I wondered if I could wind down the window and shout for help, but there were no pedestrians at all. So I concentrated hard on getting there as smoothly as I could. When I turned into the road, my heart sank; the street was full of cars and there was nowhere easy to park. I hated parking at the best of times. I often used to get out and let John parallel park; he could get into the tightest spot. It was one of our more frequent arguments – he would tell me you could get a bus into a space that was actually the size of a Smart car and then get cross when I overlooked it for something larger.

I found a space right at the end of the street, near the corner. The car was partly on the double yellow lines but I thought I would let Townsley worry about the parking ticket. He held the gun at me whilst he got out of the car and then made me slide over and out the passenger side. He pointed in the direction of the house and without saying anything poked the gun in my side and pushed me forwards. Reluctantly I walked towards the house, a feeling of dread creeping over me. Why was he bringing me here? I thought of all the locks and the bars on the window. Things were not looking good.

We walked around to the back of the house. The kitchen light was on. Someone was in there. Townsley pushed me up the steps and into the kitchen and there, standing in the middle of the kitchen was Champion Obote.

48

Champion Obote was nursing his broken hand, which was now heavily bandaged, and he had a look of intense fury on his face. As I walked into the kitchen, he looked me directly in the eye and held up his hand. He didn't say anything. He didn't need to, the look said all that was necessary; payback time.

"Look what I found," exclaimed Townsley.

I moved into the room. I had to do something. If I was going to end my days here in this gloomy depressing house then I would go down fighting. I thought about John. I didn't feel ready to join him yet; I wanted to go on living. But my last knives and leftover pepper spray were in my rucksack, and I didn't have time to take it off my back and rummage through it; I'd be dead before I had even moved. Then the thought of the knives made me remember something – I'd tucked a knife into my sock, hadn't I? Earlier that day when I'd been waiting for Obote in his yard; I had tucked a spare knife into my sock in case I had needed it. I surreptitiously felt one ankle with the other. Yes, it was definitely still there. Perhaps this was my chance.

I slowly walked further into the kitchen and closer to Obote. Obote moved forwards a little; he was limping heavily from where I had smashed his kneecap. I glanced round, looking as if I was really nervous, to try to get a sense of where Townsley was. I whimpered a little and tried to look as if I were about to cry. I got as close to Obote as I could, but far enough away that he couldn't easily grab me. I positioned myself directly between Obote and the barrel of the gun. I hoped that Townsley wouldn't want to accidentally kill Obote, although I could be sure of nothing under the circumstances. I kept up the whimpering, hoping that this would make them both relax their guard. Obote was smiling a dreadful, sickening, smile as I moved towards him and a wave of nausea passed through me. He clearly hadn't relished being overpowered by a woman. I positioned myself as well as I could, gave another little whimper and then dipped down really quickly, grabbing the knife from my sock and standing up in one smooth movement. As I stood up, I caught Townsley by surprise and punched at his hand from below, sending the gun flying up in the air and across the kitchen.

I had caught them unawares. I stabbed the knife at Townsley, getting him deep on the thigh. He screamed out in pain. Obote was behind me, but the sound of shuffling feet alerted me that he was about to make a move. I yanked the knife out of Townsley's leg, keeping hold of it, and spun round, slashing Obote across the arm. I wrenched the handcuffs off my belt and rushed towards Townsley, pushing him to the floor. But Obote was too quick, even with a smashed kneecap; he was tall and it only took him two paces to stride across the room. He struck me from behind and pushed me to the ground. The knife fell out of my hand. He snatched at my shoulder and turned me round, slapping me hard across the face with his good hand. He pulled the handcuffs from my hands and dragged me by my wrist towards the sink. I managed to reach the knife, which had fallen near the sink, picking it up and stabbing wildly behind me but I merely grazed his leg. He pulled me under the sink where he attached my wrist to the water pipe. I was trapped. I pulled on the handcuffs but there was no way it was going to come loose. *Fuck, fuck, fuck.* What the hell was I going to do now?

Townsley was hobbling across the room for the gun. Obote grabbed him and pulled him away, kicking the gun out of his reach.

"I'm going to kill that fucking bitch," Townsley spat. But he was so much smaller and shorter than Obote that he couldn't fight him off.

"Leave her," Obote snapped at him. "There's been too much killing already. We'll fit her up for something. Sanderson can have her put away for years. Give her twenty years in a high-security prison and she'll soon wish you had shot her." He glared in my direction, and I imagined myself in a prison somewhere, charged and convicted of some crime I hadn't committed.

But Townsley was determined. He tried to make another run for the gun. Obote grabbed him and threw him on the floor. Townsley skidded like a bowling ball across the floor and landed in the pile of leftover cleaning products. I thought for a moment that he had been knocked unconscious but he suddenly leapt up. He had a plastic container in his hand.

"Sanderson's dead," he shouted at Obote and then he threw the contents of the container into Obote's face and over his clothes.

Obote screamed and fell to his knees, and Townsley dropped the container onto the floor near his feet. Obote was scratching at his face; the pain in his eyes must have been agonising, they had to have still been tender from the pepper spray earlier. He writhed on the floor, trying to peer up at Townsley and summon the energy to charge at him another time.

Townsley stood up. He calmly took a cigarette out of his pocket and lit it. He looked down at Obote crawling on the floor, clutching his face. Obote looked up as Townsley lit the cigarette and took a couple of drags on it, standing there as if he didn't have a care in the world. Obote's eyes opened wide, despite the pain he must have been in. He knew what was coming and so did I. He scrambled across the floor in an attempt to get through the kitchen door and into the hall. I clutched desperately at my back, trying to reach into the rucksack for the last set of handcuffs, so that I could use the keys from them to undo myself. Townsley looked at Obote and then me; suddenly the calm demeanour left him and a manic grin spread across his face. Slowly and deliberately he threw the cigarette at Obote as he struggled for the door. The vapours of the cleaning product caught fire and flames engulfed Obote. He thrashed about and threw himself into the hallway, madly trying to beat his body against the walls, screaming for help. But the vapours also led back to the container which Townsley had dropped at his feet. The floor in front of him and to the side of him lit up in a sheet of flame, trapping him in the corner of the room.

The flames quickly spread as the liquid left in the container caught fire and flames began to lick at Townsley's legs. He was beating himself frenetically with his arms but I ignored his agonised calls while I tried to get the opening of the rucksack within reach. It wasn't easy with one arm attached to a pipe and I had to contort myself right round so that I could reach the zip. I held the material in my teeth whilst I pulled the zip open and then I twisted my body as far as I could and fumbled blindly into the depths of the rucksack with my loose arm. I struggled to pull the handcuffs free from the bag and I could feel my lungs beginning to fill with noxious fumes. The room was thick with dark, acrid smoke. I looked round. Townsley was trapped in the far corner of the room behind a wall of flame and smoke; his legs were well ablaze. He was still frantically wafting his arms at his legs, in a futile attempt to stop the flames from climbing further upwards. Although he appeared to be fanning the fire in the process. He was screaming and there was a look of sheer horror and agony on his face. The pile of discarded and half-filled cleaning containers whooshed up into a raging fire. The curtains were taking hold and the whole room was searingly hot.

I grappled with the spare handcuffs, releasing the keys and struggling to unlock the pair around my wrist. I dropped the keys twice before I managed to unlock them. I yanked my hand free and tried to cover my mouth with my arm, desperately trying to stop the fumes from getting into my lungs. I pulled myself up by grabbing onto the sink and I turned the tap on, hoping to soak Townsley in water but nothing came out. The water had been cut off. Of course, that would be why the children were using a potty and not the toilet. Townsley was trapped, unable to move through sheer terror, the flames licking higher up his legs, he was screaming for help. Obote was crashing about in the hallway trying to do something. He had stopped screaming now which somehow seemed much more sinister.

I choked and spluttered, the fumes going to my head. Everything was becoming fuzzy. I got back down on the floor and crawled to the back door. I hit the knife with my knee as I crawled along and I picked it up, stuffing it back into my sock where it had been for most of the day. I reached up for the door handle and tried to open the door. The handle was slippery and I struggled to grip. Eventually I managed to get a firm hold and yanked at the door, all the time trying not to breath in the thick air. There was a rush and a breeze as I pulled the door open and it felt as if the air from the garden was being sucked from the outside and into the house. The sudden increase in oxygen fuelled the fire, raising the temperature levels, and the leftover chemicals exploded into a ball of intense heat. The flames leapt instantly to the ceiling, brighter and hotter than before. I didn't glance back at Townsley. I knew there was no hope. I didn't want to see what had become of him. There was no noise from the house at all, save the crackling of the fire. I wrenched open the door and staggered into the open air, gulping the air into my lungs. I coughed and choked as my body readjusted to the clean air.

I was about to reach for my phone to call the emergency services but as I did so, the sound of approaching sirens pierced through the air. Someone had obviously called them already. The fire must have taken a stronger hold of the front of the house than I had realised. I stumbled to the back of the garden and climbed through a hole in the fence. I threw myself onto the lawn of whoever's garden this was and took a minute to regain my composure. I didn't want to be seen anywhere near this place so I quickly gathered myself together and headed through the back gardens of the neighbouring houses until I found a passageway through to the adjacent road.

I walked through there as calmly as I could and I headed into the night.

I slowed down to a stroll. I didn't want to do anything that would draw attention to me. There were a few people milling about, coming out to see what emergency the sirens were signalling, or attracted by the flames to watch the horror unfolding before them the way we humans like to do. A story to tell at dinner tomorrow. I walked slowly through the streets heading slightly away from the centre; I aimed to go more or less straight downhill towards the river. When I reached the river, I was about half a mile from the city centre opposite a small business park made from a group of disused warehouses. A bridge crossed the river at this point, a very high-arched bridge; it was likely built that way to let taller boats sail underneath it. I walked onto the bridge and stopped halfway across. It was quite dark and there was no one about. It wasn't the nicest area of town and people didn't really even walk their dogs there at that time of the night, not along this stretch of water. I fished out the gun from my bag and wiped it all over with one of my tops. Then, double checking that there was no one watching, I dropped it into the middle of the river. I zipped up my rucksack, put it over my shoulder and hurried on across the bridge.

As I walked along, I fished out my phone and called Charlton.

"Verity, how are things?" he asked calmly.

On hearing his voice, a rush of emotions overwhelmed me and I collapsed in a heap on the far side of the bridge, near the car park of the business park.

"Tense," I mumbled, trying hard to maintain control. "A little tense." I slumped down onto the tarmac and leant against the wall of the nearest building. Charlton was gentle, asking just a few questions. There would be time for that later. I described briefly what had happened, giving a less than graphic description of what had happened to Sanderson, so as to spare myself from reliving that scenario. Then I attempted to tell him what had happened when we'd got to the house. I had to stop mid-sentence.

"I'm sorry," I said, breathing heavily, just about managing to fight back the tears. "I can see him beating the flames, flapping uselessly. And the screams." I stopped again, trying to erase the howls that were on repeat in my head.

Charlton made all the right sympathetic noises down the phone, but really, what can you say to help in that situation?

"What do you think I should do?" I asked Charlton. "Should I call the police now?"

"No." He was emphatic.

"But…"

"No buts. Go and check into a hotel. I'll come and find you. I've been meeting an old colleague in Stevenage so I'm already near the A1. I'll be there in a couple of hours."

I ignored the first part of this advice. "But, what…?"

"No buts. Listen, does anyone know you were at the house?"

"No."

"Is there anything of yours at the house?"

"There'll be my fingerprints from earlier, when I went for the children."

"It sounds like there won't be much left of the house, anyway."

A vision of Townsley flapping and twizzling and screaming came back into my head and I stifled a sob.

"There's nothing specific that will point to you being there just now?"

"No. I don't know why I thought I might need it, but I took my knife with me."

"Instinct," he laughed.

I laughed too. It was a bit of light hysteria I think.

He insisted on driving up to Lincoln that evening. I couldn't persuade him not to. Having said that, I found myself looking forward to seeing him. We agreed that he would drive straight up. I would go and check into the Royal Hotel and get cleaned up and he would let me know when he had arrived and checked in himself. I put the phone down and stayed alone on the car park tarmac for some time. Was it finally over? Was that it? I had got the children to safety and Townsley, by his own stupid actions had ensured that he would never harm another young person. I felt a wave of relief that it was over, quickly followed by a wave of nausea; I thought the memories of the last couple of hours would stay with me for a long time to come. But overwhelmingly I felt liberated, free from the tension of the last week. I stood up and headed into town, suddenly light-hearted and giddy from the reprieve.

I looked at my phone, it was gone 10pm. I put the phone in my back pocket and walked all the way into the city centre along the south side of the river and then I crossed the main road via the footbridge and headed towards the train station where I knew I would be able to climb into a taxi and head to the hotel.

-50-

I was almost at the taxi rank when my thoughts were interrupted.

"Hey!"

And again, "Hey!"

I turned round, beyond surprised to see Stephen Ibbetson running after me. I stopped and let him catch me up.

"Ibbetson," My voice coming out slightly higher than I'd intended. "What are you doing here?"

"Same as you, I guess." He smiled. "I've been figuring this all out a few paces behind you, it seems. I got to the house and it was ablaze. It looked like quite a fire."

I was so relieved to see someone I knew, and with a familiar face in front of me, I felt some of my tension dying down and my shoulders drooped.

I let out a great sigh. "I thought I was going to die in there."

"Was there anybody still in there?"

"Townsley and Obote. Do you know who they are?"

"The organ grinder and one of his monkeys, yes. Thank God you're all right, though. I've been really worried about you. I couldn't drop it, after your phone call. I felt really bad about what had happened and I had to try and find out what was going on." He put a sympathetic hand on my arm.

I looked at him and smiled a weak smile.

"Are you okay?"

"I'm fine, thanks," I lied, not really feeling fine but desperate to get into a hot bath.

"What else has been going on? It looks as if you've had a tough time."

"Have you been up to the hospital?" I asked cautiously.

"No, should I?"

"I wouldn't. When did you get here?"

"A couple of hours ago. I finally realised exactly what was happening, and I headed straight for the house."

"Well, welcome to the madness."

"What about Charlton?"

"He's on his way up, actually. He's been a great help. Thanks." I smiled at him, surprised at how nice it felt to see a familiar face. "We're meeting up at the Royal Hotel when he gets here." I suddenly felt overcome with emotion again and staggered forwards a step. Ibbetson took my arm and steadied me.

"Let me give you a lift," he offered. He indicated a car park a street away and we walked over to his car together.

I took off my rucksack and threw it in the back of the car, relieved that I would no longer be in need of the makeshift armoury, and I jumped gratefully into the passenger seat.

"I am so looking forward to a long, hot bath," I said, stretching out my arms and feeling my body start to relax from the strains of the last few days.

Ibbetson pulled out of the car park and started heading down the High Street. He seemed to know where he was going so I didn't offer directions. I guessed he must have been up here before as part of his work with Dr Neasden.

"How did you know where to find me?" I asked.

"I saw you leave the house."

"But I left out of the back of the house, through the garden."

"Yeah." He glanced over and smiled. "That's where I saw you."

That seemed a bit strange. "You were following me?"

"I followed you from there for a minute or two, I saw you heading along the river and I thought you might need a moment to yourself. So I drove up here and headed back towards you."

"And how did you figure out who was involved and what it was all about?"

"Same way as you I guess, information and a bit of digging. I've got contacts."

"Have you been keeping in touch with Charlton?"

"Charlton," he mused. "Yes, Charlton has been keeping me informed."

I sighed and relaxed into the seat.

"You did well, figuring this all out." He sounded impressed.

"Yeah, well Townsley won't be hurting any more children, although the outcome for him was a little bleak."

"And the police you were so untrusting of?"

"Did Charlton not tell you?"

"No. I haven't spoken to him for a while."

"At least two of them. They're both dead too." I thought of the mess in Townsley's room at the hospital and wondered if anyone had found it yet. The thought made me sick.

We sat in silence for a minute, staring out at the dark.

Ibbetson glanced over at me. "Townsley must have been paying someone a lot of money to bring him those children."

I closed my eyes. "Well, that's unfortunate for them. But good for the children and any potential future children."

"Have you any idea who that was?"

"No, and I will leave that for someone else to work out. All I want now is a long soak in a hot, bubbly bath."

"Where are the children now?"

I opened my eyes and looked at him. He smiled his rugged smile.

I smiled back. "They're safe, with some friends."

"Which friends?" He sounded inquisitive.

"Some old friends, that I can trust. You won't know them."

"In Lincoln?"

"In Lincoln, yes, why?"

"I'm just curious as to how you got to the heart of what was going on so quickly."

"They're safe, Ibbetson."

"Thank God," he said. "I'm just concerned, that's all."

"You've really got into all this haven't you?" He seemed to have genuinely figured it all out.

"I'm interested."

I said nothing, just looked out of the window.

"And what did you do with the notebook?"

The hairs on my neck prickled and I shivered involuntarily. "You knew about the notebook?" My stomach sank and I began to feel queasy.

"Of course."

I looked out of the window. "Ibbetson, this isn't the way to the Royal Hotel. You've turned the wrong way."

"I haven't," he said.

"You have." I turned towards him.

"You should have left that notebook well alone."

"Ibbetson, what are you doing?"

He pulled the car to a stop at the side of the road. I grabbed at the door handle but the car was locked. Panic rose inside me.

I looked over at him. The smile was still there, but it was no longer rugged, it was a smile of hatred. His face contorted. I rattled the door handle in a vain attempt to get out of the car. And then I saw him draw back his fist.

And then nothing. Just blackness.

51

As I came to, a searing pain pierced the front of my forehead. It felt as if someone was driving an ice pick into my head. I didn't want to open my eyes. I hadn't a clue how long I had been out cold or where I was. I moved my head and then immediately wished I hadn't.

I noticed then that I also had pain in my arms and legs and I tried to move. My hands seemed to be tied behind my back and my legs were squashed up underneath me. I couldn't move and when I opened my eyes I couldn't see anything either. I was in complete darkness. There was movement, though, and a rumbling noise. It felt as if I was in something that was moving. A car. I was in the boot of a car. *Oh fuck.*

I tried to remember what had been happening. Ibbetson. *The prick.* What the fuck was he doing? How was he involved in all this? One minute I had been as close to a bath as I'd been in a long time and the next I was tied up in the boot of a car as far from a bath as I'd ever been. I thought about the sequence of events. Ibbetson had been there, near the station when I'd gone to get a taxi. I had been surprised, but it had seemed feasible that he had figured things out too, and had come up to Lincoln where his old work colleague had lived. But then he had asked about the notebook, hadn't he? And the children. Where was he taking me?

Once again, a wave of nausea came over me. I was in deep shit. I had no idea where I was being taken, or why. And who would know where I was? I suddenly thought of the phone in my back pocket. My hands were tied behind my back but maybe if I manipulated them a little I would be able to pull it out. I shifted around in the boot and tried to free my arms from any weight. It was a difficult manoeuvre as my body was all cramped up and I didn't have room to move my legs. I pushed my hands towards my back pocket and carefully removed the phone. I tried to press the buttons that I knew by memory would unlock it but I dropped the phone. *Shit.* I scrambled around in the dark with my tied-together hands and located the phone. Now I didn't know if it was locked or unlocked, but I held it tight and started pressing the buttons again. I saw in the darkness of the boot that a light was shining from behind me so I assumed I had unlocked the phone. I pressed what I hoped was the call button a couple of times and hoped for the best. Suddenly I heard Charlton's voice emanating through the darkness of the boot. I shouted at the top of my voice.

"Help!"

I just kept repeating over and over, "Charlton, help! Help!" I hoped that he could hear me, I hoped that he might be able to do something. I wasn't sure what. Then I heard him shouting as loudly as me into the darkness and over the noise of the car.

"Verity! Shut up! Shut up and listen."

"Okay," I said quietly, hoping he could hear me.

His disembodied voice came back at me. "Where are you? What's happened?"

"I don't know," I shouted back. "I'm in the boot of a car. I think it's Ibbetson's car."

"Verity, whatever happens keep your phone on. Okay? Keep this call open."

"I'm scared."

"Keep the phone on. Okay?"

And then I remembered the knife in my sock. I lay the phone on the floor of the car boot, touching my thigh so I could feel exactly where it was, hoping that I didn't accidentally turn it off. I pushed my ankles as close to my hands as I could and tried to retrieve the knife. I had to hold onto it without dropping it. I inched it out of my sock and held it tightly. I tried sawing with the knife against the rope tying my hands together. I couldn't get much purchase and I couldn't move it very far or very fast but I could feel the strands of rope begin to give a little. My hands didn't feel so tightly bound. I felt one of the pieces of rope break and I started sawing at one of the others.

Charlton's voice echoed into the boot, "Verity, are you okay?"

I was just about to answer when the car stopped. The jerking movement of the brake made the knife fall out of my hand. I cursed under my breath. I felt around but my hands were still tied and I couldn't locate it. The sound of the car door being opened and then slammed shut brought the panic back into my chest, and I realised that I didn't have time to hunt for it. Instead, I grabbed the phone from next to my leg and stuffed it as quickly as I could up the back of my top and slipped it inside my sports bra. I thought it was less likely to get turned off there than back in my pocket. I had just managed to secure the phone in my bra when the boot was yanked open. Ibbetson grabbed my arm and dragged me roughly from the car. I couldn't move my legs fast enough as they had been curled up beneath me and they wouldn't straighten so I fell head first over the edge of the boot. Ibbetson kicked me and yelled at me to get up, pulling once again at my arm and dragging me to my feet.

I looked around. I seemed to be in some kind of garage. As Ibbetson held my arms, the car backed out. I saw it stop just outside and the lights went off and the engine died. A thickset man jumped out and locked the car, then came inside and shut the garage door. He lurked in the shadows where I couldn't really see him. The garage was large and looked like it was used as some sort of workshop. There were shelves with tools, batteries, wrenches and random tins. There were hooks with jacks hanging from them and some with ladders and other items. I had no idea where I was or what was going to happen.

Ibbetson pushed me roughly away from him and, as my hands were still tied behind my back, I fell onto the floor on my knees. With no means of breaking the fall my knees hit the ground with a thump, sending a jarring pain up through my body. Ibbetson kicked me and shouted for me to stand up. I struggled without free hands and he grabbed my arm and dragged me to my feet. He walked round in front of me and leaned into me.

"Where are those children?" He screamed into my face, his friendly smile firmly replaced with a grimace. He was bearing his teeth.

"Why do you want to know? Ibbetson? What are you doing?"

He laughed, "What am I doing? I'm trying to recover my property is all."

"The children?"

"Yes, the fucking children," he screamed at me. "Have you any idea how much those kids are worth to me?"

"But some of them are ill." I was dumbfounded. I couldn't believe Ibbetson was involved in this.

"Ha! They'll bloody stay that way now that you've killed off their doctor."

"They're safe now. Out of harm's way."

He screamed at the top of his voice, "They're mine. I want them back."

"You've known all along?" I could barely speak, I was so stunned.

"Yes, I've known. Of course I've known. How do you think Townsley got the kids in the first place?"

"You? You were getting him the children? But the paper…"

He laughed again. "The stupid, meddling, interfering *Doctor* Neasden. If he had kept his nose out, everything would have turned out alright. And *you.* You're as bad. Why didn't you just give up? Charlton was supposed to get you back here. You just couldn't keep from snooping could you?"

Charlton. I gulped. He was on the phone. I didn't know how much of this he could hear and I started to worry that keeping the phone line open might not have been a good idea. *Shit. Not Charlton too.* I yanked at my hands, the knife had done some work and they weren't as tightly bound but I still couldn't free them. I pulled and pulled at the rope in an attempt to loosen it some more.

"Charlton?" I asked.

He threw his arms wide. "The great Samuel Charlton," he laughed. "I should never have introduced you to him, he's too clean for his own good. He was supposed to just call the police up here, get you out the way before you knew anything. But you just wouldn't give up and he actually wanted to help you. Idiot."

Ibbetson calmed down. He took a step back. The thickset man stepped forward out of the shadows and I instantly recognised him as Kevin Lambert, the flabby man from my hotel room. He grinned at me and rubbed his hands together.

Ibbetson nodded towards me. "Lambert, get her to tell me where *my* children are."

Lambert moved towards me, and I backed away, trying to keep him in my vision, but I stumbled over a paint pot and fell heavily onto my bottom. I struggled to stand up. Lambert waited for me.

He grinned again. "Got to be an equal fight," he said and threw a punch which hit me on the shoulder, causing me to spin round and hit my head on the corner of one of the shelves. I shook my head. A bright light had exploded over my eye and the pain seared through my forehead. I turned to Lambert.

He indicated with his hands, *come on, fight.*

"I have no arms free," I shouted. "How can that be equal?"

He laughed. "Well, almost equal." And he threw another punch.

This time I saw it coming and I span out of the way, his fist piercing the air near my ear. He took a step forward to steady himself and I kicked out my foot to try to trip him over. I caught his ankle but he only stumbled a little. It was only as he recovered that I noticed he was holding a wrench in his hand. I ran across the garage, but Ibbetson grabbed hold of me and pushed me back towards Lambert.

"Tell me where my children are," he screamed as he pushed me away, and Lambert swung with the wrench.

I managed to move my head out of the way quickly enough but the wrench hit me on the shoulder and I shouted out in pain and fell to my knees.

I stumbled back onto my feet and moved away from Lambert, closer to the wall, stretching my arms behind me and scrabbling against the wall with my hands. I grabbed something that felt like a jack that had been leaning against the wall and held it behind me as I moved closer to Lambert. He was still holding the wrench and he swung it round above his head. As he tried to bring it down, I ran out of the line of fire and swinging round as fast as I could behind him, I brought the jack round and into his back. Because I was holding it behind me I couldn't hit with as much strength as I wanted but the force of it, coupled with the momentum from him swinging the wrench made him fall forwards. I ran up to him and kicked him as hard as I could on the back of his legs, so that he fell face first onto the garage floor.

"Lambert, you girl," shouted Ibbetson from the side lines, and then he ran over and pushed me away so that Lambert could get up.

As he pushed me, I dropped the jack and I would have stumbled over but he yanked my arms back and dragged me to the other side of the garage. As Ibbetson held my arms behind me, I tried to pull away and the extra tension was enough to finally snap the last piece of rope. I felt my hands come free and, even though the rope was still wrapped around each wrist I finally had my arms back. I pulled my leg forward and smashed it behind me as hard as I could into Ibbetson, thankful that I had bought the new walking boots. I didn't know where I hit him but he shouted out. He gripped my arms even tighter and so I hit backwards with my leg once again, harder than the first time. I connected my heel with his shin and this time he let me go so I span round as quickly as I could and kicked him hard in the balls.

Lambert came up behind me and swung another time with the wrench, and I just managed to move out of the way, although he glanced a blow at my elbow which hurt so much I temporarily couldn't feel the whole of the bottom of my arm. I felt sick with the pain but I had to stay focused. I scrambled about along the wall of the garage and took hold of the nearest thing to my hand, which turned out to be a wooden mallet. Lambert was coming at me again with the wrench; Ibbetson was writhing on the floor still, clutching his balls, so I circled around Lambert tempting him to lash out. As he lifted up the wrench one more time, I swung high with the mallet, knocking the wrench out of his hand and probably breaking a couple of his fingers in the process. He shouted out as the wrench clattered across the garage floor and he rushed forward but I swung the mallet again, moving slightly to the right as I did so, and hit him squarely on the back of the head. He sank instantly to the floor, out cold for the second time that week.

I snatched at the door, still clutching the mallet, desperate to get out of that place. I couldn't figure out how the door opened, and Ibbetson was coming after me. I knelt down on the floor to try to lift the door but Ibbetson grabbed at my feet and pulled me. I found a handle in the middle of the door and twisted it round, heaving the door up an inch, but he was dragging me away. I got hold of the mallet and tried to swing it round. I barely caught him at all. As he dodged back, I turned and lifted the door another inch. Ibbetson gripped my ankles tighter. I clutched at the floor, clawing myself back towards the door, kicking out with my boots to stop him being able to hold on to my feet. I managed to push the door up another inch or two and I took a strong hold on it, this time leaving the mallet and pulling with both hands. I pulled myself slowly under the open door, scrabbling to get away, aware that he had picked up the mallet and was preparing to bring it down on me. I rolled as quickly as I could, feeling the mallet coming down on my foot, feeling the intense pain but glad that my boots must have deflected the worst of it, scrabbling under the door, feeling the phone at my back shatter and break, groping, clutching at the door, rolling out the other side of it, escaping, grasping.

And then I felt a pair of hands helping me, pulling me away from the door, lifting me up and out into the night.

I was lifted up and into the arms of Detective Inspector Sam Charlton. I looked around and saw that there were about half a dozen police cars lined up outside the garage. I wasn't sure how long they had been there; I didn't ask and I didn't care. Finally, I felt that I might be safe.

As Charlton pulled me away, several police officers rushed into the garage. Someone was checking Lambert and calling for an ambulance; someone was grabbing Ibbetson and handcuffing his hands behind his back. There was a flurry of activity going on around me but it fell into the background. Charlton took me further away, taking me by the hand and suddenly noticing the rope still tied around my wrists. He fished into the pocket of his jacket and pulled out a pen knife.

358

He took first my right hand and then my left and gently cut the rope away. He examined the scars where the rope had rubbed the skin away. There were deep red marks all the way around my wrists; they would be sore later on.

He let my hands drop by my sides, put his hands onto my shoulders and looked me in the eye. "You okay?"

I nodded. And then I rested my head on his chest and he held me to him.

TUESDAY

52

It was the early hours of the morning before we finally made it to the hotel. I had given a brief statement to the police, and I was exhausted. I knew I would have to talk to them more formally but they seemed happy for me do that at a later date. For now they were happy to know the bare bones of what had happened. They had wanted to know where the children were, and I was anxious that the powers that be would make sure that they were alright. They assured me that they would make arrangements with social services to ensure they were safe and well cared for. Charlton wanted to take me to be checked over at the hospital, but I managed to persuade him that I really didn't want to go back there right at that minute. I agreed to go in the morning if anything appeared more than just bruising. I had retrieved my rucksack from Ibbetson's car and been glad to get away. Lambert had been taken to hospital under a police guard and Ibbetson had been carted off to the police station, hopefully to be locked away for a very long time.

The receptionist at the hotel appeared a little shocked at my rather dishevelled appearance, especially as I had asked for a top-of-the-range room, but other than look me up and down she kept quiet about it. I was so shattered I didn't care anyway.

My room was on the ground floor, down a long corridor, and Charlton walked me to the door. We agreed to meet up and chat over breakfast. There was nothing to say that wouldn't wait until then. When we got to my room, I turned to him to say goodnight. He looked down at me and took my elbow in his hand. I glanced up at his face and for a fleeting moment I saw something in his eyes that I really wasn't ready for and I lowered my gaze quickly. As I caught his eye again, whatever it was that I had read in his face had gone. I gave him a peck on the cheek and rushed into my room.

I breathed a huge sigh of relief when I got inside and closed the door behind me. I flopped onto the bed and marvelled that I wasn't shaking or crying; I was just thankful that I would be able to go home safely, hopefully, very soon. I'd have to let the guys and Collette know that I was safe but that could wait for another half an hour, they were probably all in bed anyway. What I really needed right there and then was to get clean.

I walked into the bathroom and realised that it had been worth paying for a top-of-the-range room. There was an enormous bath, with expensive toiletries and a fluffy white bathrobe with slippers. I turned on the taps and ran a hot bath filled with bubbles.

The bath was a long one and I could lay stretched out so I periodically dunked my head under the water and breathed out through the water. I lay there relaxing and allowing my muscles to free up after all the tension of the last few days. I stayed where I was, with my eyes closed, until the water had gone cold.

When I got out of the bath, I examined the damage I'd incurred all over my body, twisting to see some of the bruises in the mirror. My foot hurt the most where Ibbetson had hit it with the mallet, but it didn't appear to be anything more than bruising. I had bruises on my legs and arms and up my back and a big mark on my shoulder. I had a cut on the right side of my throat where Townsley had held the knife against it. I had a big red mark on my face where Obote had slapped me and a massive bruise on my elbow where the wrench had caught me. It was all superficial and would heal within the next few days. The images of Obote and Townsley in flames, and of Sanderson with the permanent look of horror etched on his dead face, would take longer to leave me. I wrapped myself in the oversized bath robe, put on the slippers and made myself a cup of tea.

Once I was in my pyjamas, I fished out my spare phone. I wrote out a message and sent it first to Collette and then to Robert. I knew it was late, but I needed to let them know I was okay.

All ok. I'm safe! Hope the kids are doing ok? Police may be in touch about them. Everything will be sorted tomorrow, latest. I will be back at home soon! Will talk in the morning. Thanks for all your help. Lots love V xx

Then I climbed into the king-size bed, curled up under the duvet and fell into an instant and deep sleep.

53

Charlton was already tucking into a full English when I arrived for breakfast in the morning. I ordered coffee and porridge and we chatted until all the other diners had left and the waiting staff had set up all the tables for lunch and abandoned us.

I spoke more than he did, telling him all that had happened over the last two days; how I had followed Obote up the motorway and found the house where the children were being kept; how I had seen Darnold being killed through the kitchen window and how I'd lain in wait for Obote and overpowered him with my home-made weapons. I wasn't sure if Charlton was more impressed with my ingenuity or cross that I had put myself in such danger, but he let me carry on. I told him how I had figured everything out from a combination of the information in the notebook, what he had told me and what I had managed to get from Obote after I'd sprayed him with pepper spray. Then I filled him in on the events at the hospital and how I was concerned about the grisly mess that must have been discovered this morning by cleaner or a nurse.

"Ah, that wouldn't have happened," Charlton said. "I rang the local police on my way up." He clearly saw my anxious look. "Don't worry," he interjected quickly. "The scene needed to be secured quickly. There was no way I was going to let someone stumble across that. I've made sure the powers that be know about this, it will be all above board. No more cover ups."

Charlton had also spoken to the emergency services and discovered that it had taken several fire engines quite some time to put out the fire. Townsley had been found dead in the kitchen and Obote had been taken to hospital. He was alive, barely, but was covered in third-degree burns. His prognosis was not good. If he survived, which was looking unlikely, he would be in severe pain for the rest of his life and would need months of intensive treatment.

We sat in silence for a minute, thinking.

He looked up. "What about Ibbetson, then? I didn't think he was capable of that."

"Absolutely. I thought he did all sorts of work to *help* children."

"He did," Charlton pondered, "but I guess it must be easy for someone in that position to fall prey to the lure of 'easy' money. He passed those children around at several thousand pounds a time."

I said nothing, just sighed.

"And he was in such a good position to cover up what he was doing. He was a weak man and they can be the most dangerous."

I was deep in thought. "I'll need to sort things out with my friends." I wasn't sure where to begin with that one and, lost in my memories, I pursed my lips and looked off to one side. I hoped those poor children got the medical attention they needed. I sighed, shifting my thoughts onto other matters.

"And what about me?"

"What about you?" He smiled and raised an eyebrow as if he was amused by my concern for myself.

"Well, I think I may have committed a few crimes over the last few days and probably been an accessory or witness to several others."

"I can't see Lambert or Ibbetson putting in a complaint to the police. Obote isn't going to survive and even if he did it would be easy to connect him to the murder of Darnold without there being a need for a witness. Ibbetson is in so deep with the trafficking offences he'll be put away for some time."

"And Lambert?"

"He is a hired small-time criminal and thug, well-known as a serial offender; in and out of prison like you and I go on holiday. I think he was brought in for the job."

"The job of beating me up." I smiled. I had still failed to tell Charlton about Lambert's gun.

"Once he has recovered from the blow to his head I think they will have a small string of offences they'd like to do him for."

I said nothing.

"There is one thing you might be needed for, though."

"Oh?" I started to get worried.

"Well, they will probably be re-opening and investigating the case of Dr Neasden's murder. Apparently, Nash had complained to his superiors about Darnold getting involved but had been turned away. I think the corruption went further than him; but how much others knew will obviously need to be investigated. And there will be a proper inquest into Neasden's death I imagine, it'll be referred to the coroner anyway."

I nodded.

"Hey," he said. "You'll come out well in all this."

54

After leaving the hotel, Charlton and I drove up to my house in Charlton's car. It felt surreal, walking up the path to my front door. It seemed like years had passed since I'd walked in, a week before, to find it ransacked. I put the code into the key box and retrieved a new front door key and then cautiously opened the door. I couldn't believe it; the place was spotless. I walked into the front room and all the books were back on the shelves and the ornaments carefully placed around the room. All the photos that had been lying in broken frames had been picked up and now stood in pride of place on the shelves with new frames; frames that went together but didn't match, just the way I liked it. There was a vase of fresh flowers on the table and another empty vase on the bookshelf. When I looked a second time, I realised that this one was John's heirloom vase which had been carefully, professionally, glued back together. I knew it would be worthless now but I didn't care about that.

In the kitchen, everything had been restored to normality, and in the bedroom all the clothes had been put back in the wardrobes and drawers, and the bed had been made up with what looked like new bedding. Whoever Robert had hired to clean up had done a fantastic job, but I suspected his hand in this as well. Not everything was in the right place but that would be a small task to sort out and, actually, I thought it might be the right time to jumble things around a bit.

I left Charlton in the kitchen whilst I had a shower and got changed. I looked in the rucksack; everything was still there – the almost used-up pepper spray, the knife, the handcuffs, it was all there. I wasn't really sure what to do with it all now. I left it in the corner of the room whilst I showered. I put on a short skirt and some thick black tights and pulled a tight fitting jumper over my head. I paired that with some knee-high boots that had a small heel and applied a bit of make-up. It was nice to be back in normal clothes and not in the outdoor gear I had been wearing for the last week. I brushed through my short, blonde hair and looked at myself in the mirror before going downstairs to get Charlton.

We walked the familiar route down the hill to the city centre. I pointed out the castle and the cathedral as we passed, and also the road where Dr Neasden had lived. I wondered if his house had been cleared up too. I showed Charlton the place where I had picked up the notebook and took him into the coffee shop where I had met Collette that morning. I went and sat down whilst he ordered and paid for coffee and cake and I watched him at the counter. He was a good man and I was grateful for the help he had offered, especially in getting the police to the hospital and keeping my name out of it all, well out of most of it. I didn't know what he had said to them and I wasn't about to ask. He never offered an explanation and I thought it was best to leave it unsaid. As he turned away from the counter and walked towards me I thought that, out of all this mayhem, there had come something good. I'd met Sam Charlton, and I knew that he wouldn't be leaving my life with the closing of this, rather tempestuous, chapter.

Later, as we left the café, I said good-bye to Charlton promising to keep in touch, and I headed towards the High Street. I bumped into lots of people I knew, although many didn't recognise me with my short hair. I told everyone that I had just fancied a change and they all looked sympathetic, held my arm or hand and said that they understood. They didn't really understand, but I smiled and nodded. It was nice to see so many familiar faces and feel the rush of normality coming back into my life. I walked down the steps from the High Street to the river and dodged down behind the stairs. I worked the brick lose where I had hidden the notebook. It was still there, wrapped in several sandwich bags, and I retrieved it and replaced the brick. When I got home, I stood in my living room and assessed the repaired vase. It would never hold water again, and if I am honest it had never been my favourite ornament. But I held it fondly and remembered John's affection for it; or maybe he hadn't liked it either but had just thought that it was worth some money.

I put the vase back down on the bookshelf and I took the notebook out of my pocket, flipping through its pages and remembering how, what seemed like a lifetime ago, I had sat in the kitchen puzzling over what it had all meant. Of course, I understood it all now and I realised why Dr Neasden had wanted to expose the vile goings on in Townsley's clinics. I wondered whether he had had any inkling that Ibbetson was involved. His notes were a bit haphazard and it had taken some research to figure out what was going on, but I'd got there. I'd exposed Townsley, and I'd saved those five children, at least. I knew that was a tiny drop in the ocean, but it was a start. I had helped and that was the main thing.

I held the notebook in my hand and then said aloud to the empty room, "Dr Neasden, I hope you can rest in peace now, knowing that your notebook led me where it needed to. And, John, my darling, I hope you are up there somewhere, showing him the ropes in the hereafter." And with that I put the notebook into the vase, the symbols of the closing of my old life and the beginning of my new one together in one place.

-Epilogue-

Two weeks later, I was sitting at the dining table with my closest friends. There was loud chatter as several conversations were going on at the same time, and laughter drifting across the room. I had spent the day preparing dinner and I had really enjoyed it. It was the first dinner party I had hosted since John had died and I looked around the room. It wasn't a big gathering, just those closest to me. Collette and her husband Marcus were there, having drafted in Marcus' mum as a babysitter, as well as Robert and Keith. I was eternally grateful for having such good friends; I couldn't have got where I was without them.

They had taken the young people off and looked after them without question. Marcus had arrived home that night to find Collette entertaining two young girls who could speak no English. They had been sitting on the sofa with Charlotte and Sophie and playing a video game. They could all understand this and there was no need to be able to communicate with actual words. Collette had little understanding of what had gone on except to tell him that I had rung her out of the blue and insisted that she come and help with some young people. She'd later told me that he had been sceptical to start with, considering I had disappeared for a week without any explanation and then, equally as suddenly, had reappeared and demanded help. He'd thought I'd had had some kind of breakdown and completely taken leave of my senses. But Collette must have done a reasonable job of convincing him not to call either the police or social services on the spot because he had resisted picking up the phone.

It turned out that finding foster homes for the children wasn't as easy as I'd thought. I had just assumed there were people out there, waiting, but the social workers who'd become involved had found it difficult to find places for them to go. They'd hastily done checks on Robert, Keith, Collette and Marcus who had all agreed to hold onto them for a few days. After a couple of days, the girls had gone off to a foster family in Market Rasen; they'd seemed happy to go together. The boys had left Robert and Keith's separately over the following few days and I think the guys had actually been quite sad to see them go. They had bought them games and books and new bedding which they'd insisted they took with them. The children who had needed medical treatment, I'd been assured, would get good care and would be allowed to stay in the country until their treatment was completed.

All the children would be assured foster placements and a school place until they were adults and then their future would be decided through the normal legal channels. At least they would get the decent education they had been promised. I hoped that they felt able to stay where they were and weren't frightened into leaving like so many of the children I'd read about in the research.

And so, there I sat, amazed at the goodness of my friends and how they had given their time and energy willingly to help me out. It was lovely to be here, watching them laughing and chatting and having a good time. I thought that I had changed almost beyond recognition in the last few days, but I slipped easily into this company and had no problems sharing their jokes and small talk. I thought that, for the first time since John's death, I actually felt happy; really happy. A momentary waft of guilt threaded its way through my body but I glanced over to a photo of John, one of my favourites, where he was dressed in his dinner jacket and bow tie; he was holding up a glass to the camera and saying cheers. He was smiling broadly at me, at my position hidden behind the camera. He wouldn't want me to feel guilty for being happy. He would want me to feel happy. I held up my glass to the picture and said, "Cheers!"

Everyone turned round and shouted, "Cheers!" in return, and I laughed.

"Here's to not going back to work." I clinked glasses with everyone around the table.

"Not going back to work?" Collette asked and raised her eyebrow.

"I've made a decision," I said emphatically. "I am not going to go back to the college, but I think I will be working."

"What are you going to do?"

"Oh, I don't know for sure, but I think after all this, jobs will somehow find me."

From the author

Thank you so much for reading No Deadly Medicine, I hope that you enjoyed it. As an independent author, without the marketing budget of a big publishing house, I rely heavily on reviews of my book and word of mouth. If you liked it, it would make me really happy if you could find the time to write a review, and tell all your friends. I read all the reviews. Verity will be making another appearance soon in the book A Hallway of Gallows, so if you are interested in finding out more about her next adventure you can follow me on Amazon. I am also active on Twitter and try to respond to all tweets and messages.

@ladyermintrude

Yours
Trudey

References:

The Children's Society (2013): *Still at Risk: A review of support for trafficked children.*
https://www.refugeecouncil.org.uk/wp-content/uploads/2019/03/Still_at_Risk-Report-final.pdf

The United Nations (2009): *Global Report on Trafficking in Persons*
https://www.unodc.org/documents/Global_Report_on_TIP.pdf

Andrew Boff (2013): *Shadow City: Exposing human trafficking in everyday London*
https://www.west-info.eu/human-trafficking-modern-slavery-children/shadow-city-exposing-human-trafficking/

HM Government (2013): *Second report of the Inter-Departmental Ministerial Group on Human Trafficking.*
https://assets.publishing.service.gov.uk/government/uploads/system/uploads/attachment_data/file/251487/9794-TSO-HMG_Human_Trafficking.pdf

Acknowledgements

Firstly, my heartfelt thanks to Sarah Smeaton for her editing and for helping the story flow. Thanks also to all my friends who read initial drafts and gave constructive comments. And to the various professionals who read the manuscript and gave such helpful technical advice. And, lastly, to my longsuffering husband, who endured several weekends of inattention as I finalised the book ready for publication.

Printed in Great Britain
by Amazon